CRIMEUCOPIA

Chicka-Chicka Boomba!

A Murderous Ink Press Anthology

****

Murderous Ink Press

CRIMEUCOPIA

Chicka-Chicka Boomba!

First published by Murderous Ink Press
Crowland, LINCOLNSHIRE, England
www.murderousinkpress.co.uk

Acknowledgements

To those writers and artists who helped make this anthology what it
is, I can only say a heartfelt Thank You!

And to Den, as always.

Contents

* First published in *After Dinner Conversation* (Vol. 4 #5, May 2023)
** First published in *The Whitworth Mysteries* (Clarendon House 2021)

The Lipstick On His Collar Still Doesn't Match Mine
(An Editorial of Sorts)

It would be hard to pinpoint exactly when Crimeucopia moved from being a 'scratch project title' and became a masthead—but it seemed to match our idea of presenting as wide a spectrum of Crime fiction genres as we could.

From there it was probably Fate which brought together the Aly Fell base artwork, and the 16 contributors who went on to become the initial *Countesses of Crime* and appeared in *The Lady Thrillers*.

Since then, there have been a further 22 Crimeucopias, including this one—but that's about as much 'statistical analysis' as we're prepared to bore you with. We couldn't tell you exactly how many submissions we've received over the last 4 years. We couldn't tell you how many of those came from established writers, some successful in other genres, who decided to take a chance on us. Nor could we tell you how many of those submissions were from writers who came to make their very first sale to us—and hopefully went on to bigger and better things. Because when it comes to submissions then everyone is equal, regardless.

But the one thing we *can* tell you is that, looking back over all 23 anthologies, we know we would not have changed a thing. Which is why, 4 years down the proverbial publishing line, we felt it was time to celebrate the anniversary with another all-women anthology—and let these 19 Countesses of Crime—

Nina Mansfield, Vera Brook, donalee Moulton, Jill Hand,
Stormy White, N. M. Cedeño, Maroula Blades, Mary Jo Rabe,
Denise Johnson, Christine Hoag, Marie Anderson, Heather C. Morris,
Wendy Harrison, Ruth Morgan, Diane Arrelle, Issy Jinarmo,
Lyn Fraser, Kimberly Scott, and Carol Goodman Kaufman

— tell it like it is, was, or could have been….

Because, in the eclectic, off-centred spirit of our *Murderous Ink Press* motto: *You never know what you like until you read it.*

The Tao of Murder
Nina Mansfield

Celia's usual mantras had stopped working to quiet her mind.

She had read all the books. She meditated. She practiced yoga daily. She knew to embrace life like any breath might be her final one.

That last bit was causing her some angst. Because in the past month, Celia had become convinced someone was going to kill her.

It was just a thought, she told herself. She was not her thoughts, and her thoughts were not real. She'd read that in a book. Heard, actually. Celia didn't read physical books. As a young attorney some years ago, she'd realized she didn't have time for un-billed page turning. But her commute to the law firm was exactly twenty-six minutes, and she certainly wasn't going to subject herself to the morons on talk radio. Music made her anxious, and she didn't see the point of fiction.

So, instead, Celia had decided on a course of self-improvement during her commute. First, she attempted to learn Japanese, but quickly realized she didn't care for communicating with anyone in their native tongue. Next, she switched to historical lectures. Those kept her attention for a while. Discovering humans had been equally flawed for thousands of years was reassuring.

Then one day she'd spotted the meme: "He who conquers others is great. He who conquers himself is mighty." It claimed to be from the Tao Te Ching, and whether or not the attribution was accurate, the idea appealed to Celia. Initially, she thought some spiritual rah-rah, feel-good nonsense might be wildly entertaining. But then something struck her. Something about being the silent observer of her thoughts. Something about her not being her actions. Not that she had ever felt particular remorse for her chosen path in life—but this was comforting nonetheless.

She confided her new awareness to her friend Rochelle, who promptly dragged Celia to yoga class.

And that is how Celia found her breath. That is how she found peace. Peace on the turnpike when someone cut her off. Peace at Starbucks when the barista screwed up her order. Peace in the courtroom when a judge ruled against her too many times. She could stay focused on her breath through any and all of life's hardships, whether she was flashing the finger at another driver, getting that barista fired, or digging into the judge's past to find a jilted mistress who could bring down his career. She could inhale, exhale, breath it all away.

So why was she not able to breathe away this hunch about her impending violent demise? Why did it keep creeping its way into her consciousness? Was the universe trying to warn her? Did the cosmos want her to be prepared?

And who? That was what bothered her the most. If someone was going to do away with her earthly presence, who was it? Someone with a closed heart, no doubt. The truly enlightened aren't great company for those with closed hearts.

But her open heart wasn't going to point out her future killer.

Now that Celia had found inner peace, she wanted to live. And so, she scheduled lunch with her longtime spiritual advisor.

*****

Helga had discovered yoga in her early 30s after a life-shredding divorce. She'd trained as a chemist at Stockholm University, and had scored a prestigious position with a biochemical company in the States. She had given that up to raise a family, only to be reduced to every other weekend and alternating holidays with her own children. It was unusual for the woman not to gain custody of the kids. But he was the breadwinner, his attorney had argued. He could provide. Plus, what if she kidnapped the children and took them to Sweden. The faulty logic of the situation had maddened Helga, filled her with negative energy. Yoga, meditation, "These things saved me," she often said. As did her elite list of private clients.

Helga took a slow sip of ginger tea, infused with ashwagandha to tackle anxiety, and lion's mane for clarity. Her own concoction. She peered at Celia over the rim of her handcrafted mug. They sat in the incense-infused, tattered-pillow-strewn vegan cafe adjacent to Helga's yoga studio.

"Have you meditated?" Helga asked.

"Yes, and the thought still won't pass."

"Hmmm." Helga took another sip of tea.

"Look, Helga, I think it's more than stuck negative energy," Celia insisted.

Helga had never seen her client look so distraught. If anything, she'd always thought Celia's path to enlightenment had been too easy. The woman usually had no problem letting go of unwanted thoughts.

"It does seem extreme. Murder," Helga said.

"Just because I'm at peace—just because I have found the middle way—doesn't mean—"

"Remember to breathe." Helga proceeded to lead Celia through a series of cleansing breaths.

After her lungs had been filled and emptied, Celia began again. "I've done some thinking."

Helga raised a cautious finger. "Those who know do not speak. Those who speak do not know," she said, quoting The Tao.

"The truth is not always beautiful, nor beautiful words the truth," said Celia, quoting The Tao back at her. "I have a few possible suspects."

"We are all one," Helga interrupted again. "We are all connected."

"I get it. I'm at peace. I have found my breath, and I would like to keep it. Especially now that my soul is untethered, and I've discovered the subtle art of not giving a ying or a yang. But following the middle way isn't going to keep some deranged former client's ex-wife from plunging a knife into my totally open heart."

"The Buddha said to live every day like it would be your last."

"Probably because he knew someone was out to get him."

For a long moment, Helga watched Celia push the micro-greens around her plate.

"So," Helga finally asked, "Who, other than your un-quiet mind, might be adding to this mental distress?"

*****

Celia pulled out a leather-bound journal. Helga had suggested she write morning pages some years ago. At first Celia had found them tedious, but with time she learned to enjoy scribbling away her negative energy each morning.

Celia flipped to the middle of the journal, and gingerly turned the pages. She found an entry where her handwriting had become almost indecipherable, which it did when she was feeling angsty.

"OK. Here it is. March 12th."

"That's six month ago."

"I know, I know. But listen."

Celia read: "The woman called again. I know it was her. I could smell her breath through the phone. Plus, I think I heard her dog yapping in the background. Note to self, don't answer blocked numbers on cell or at the office."

"Woman? What woman?" Helga asked.

"Nut-job ex-wife of one of my clients."

"Let me guess. You slept with her husband."

"Not until after the divorce. Not until he was no longer my client. I'm not unethical."

"And why would this particular woman want to kill you? You helped end many a marriage, and I image you've slept with your fair share of former clients."

"The dog. I advised her husband to sue for sole custody of the dog. Mainly so he could put it to sleep. But really as a tactic to get him out of paying alimony."

"Did it work?"

"He kept his money. She kept her dog."

"And how do you feel about all this?" Helga reached across the table, and peered into Celia's eyes.

"Feel? The Tao has taught me to feel fully."

Helga nodded in understanding. "Has this woman—if it was her—has she called you since?"

"I don't pick up blocked calls any more. After all, The Tao says 'Anticipate the difficult by managing the easy.'"

Helga could tell Celia was pleased with her knowledge of The Tao. Her client had come a long way in the six years she had been counseling her.

"OK, that's one suspect. Let's call her Dog Woman," Helga suggested. "And according to your reasoning, any ex-spouse of one of your clients could be added to the list.

"Not everyone's a nut job. Most people realize I'm just doing my job."

"Are you?"

"My job is to represent my clients to the best of my ability. That means, no holds barred."

"Is that what the law says?" Helga asked.

"The Tao says, 'Kindness and compassion are replaced with law and justice," said Celia.

"You forgot the part that says, 'Without The Tao.'"

"There is no Tao in divorce court."

Helga couldn't argue there. Still, she waved her hand. "What does your heart say?"

"My heart? My heart is so totally open, Helga. I stop. I look at the clouds. Look up. See that cloud?" Celia pointed out the window. "There. Isn't that beautiful. Six years ago, I might not have noticed that cloud. Now, I notice clouds."

"It's a storm cloud," Helga observed.

"And it's beautiful," Celia said.

"But does your heart say anything else?"

"Look, getting people out of unhappy marriages is my calling in life." Helga noticed Celia was getting defensive.

"What about about the children?" Helga asked.

"They are better off with happier parents," Celia answered.

"True, and yet, I feel the middle way—"

Celia raised her hand, palm flat. Helga recognized the gesture. She'd taught it to Celia as a way to block bad vibes. It also worked rather well to keep overly aggressive men away in bars. "Look, I didn't call you to have my career choice criticized," Celia said. "Frankly, I'm surprised to have all of this negativity leaking out of this conversation. I really need to figure out who is going to kill me."

"If your thoughts are correct. If your mind isn't tricking you."

"I have never been more sure of anything in my life."

"And if you know, then what?" Helga asked. "You think you'll be able to stop this person?"

Celia ignored Helga's question. "OK, here's someone else I'm considering." She flipped to another page in her journal.

"Another disgruntled wife?"

"No," answered Celia. "I'll just read what I wrote."

"It's weird. My car getting keyed right after the incident with Claire. I'm trying to let the thought pass. It's not like I didn't feel bad about having her fired. She openly questioned my ethics in a staff meeting. You don't threaten a partner. I was so rattled, I had to head to yoga class at lunch. I can thank the universe Helga was teaching."

Helga nodded. "I remember that day. You were quite frazzled."

"I don't enjoy firing people, especially when I'm the one who hired her. It's like an admission of my fallibility."

"Did you personally do it?" Helga asked.

"No. But she had to have known it was me," said Celia.

"And you were OK with the decision you made?"

"There was no decision. She got testy at a morning meeting. Said something about partners getting a little too cozy with former clients. She looked right at me. I met with our managing partner immediately. Told her the girl had to go. By lunch, she was clearing out her desk."

"The experience disturbed you," Helga said.

"Her threat disturbed me," Celia said.

"You could have breathed through it."

"I did breathe through it," said Celia. "I breathed as I watched her box up her things. I breathed as she walked out the door. I even suggested to Claire that she should take a cleansing breath. That she should let go and move on. A closed door simply meant the universe was opening a door somewhere else."

"Maybe she took your advice," suggested Helga.

"She keyed my Mercedes."

"You're sure it was her?"

"I don't believe in coincidences," said Celia.

"They aren't for you to believe in, or not believe in. They just are," Helga said. "More tea?"

The women sipped their drinks in silence for a moment. "I feel like you're judging me, a little," Celia finally said.

"That's not my job," Helga said.

"I…Yeah, I know," Celia said, resisting the urge to become defensive again. She resented that Helga mentioned the word 'job.' Sure, she kept Helga on retainer for the spiritual guidance she provided, but she preferred to think of Helga as a friend.

She'd had a friend once.

"There's one more," Celia said.

"One more?" Helga asked, sounding truly curious.

"Suspect," Celia answered.

"Potential, possible, future suspect," Helga corrected.

Celia gnawed her lip for a moment. "Do you remember Rochelle?" she asked.

Had a sly smile just crept onto Helga's face. No, Celia must have imagined it. Helga would never delight in her pain and suffering.

"Now, there's a name I haven't heard from you in a while," Helga said, looking down into her tea. Then, she looked up with those all-seeing, Nordic eyes. "She's your friend."

Celia started at the use of the present tense. "Was. She was my friend."

"Your yoga buddy."

"More than that. She introduced me to yoga. She introduced me to meditation. She introduced me to you. She changed my life for the better, and I…I helped her to change her life too. I was there for her when she needed someone."

"But you had a falling out," Helga said.

Of course, Helga knew. She'd discussed it with Helga around the time it had happened.

"When was this?" Helga asked.

"Oh, four years ago, or so." Celia reached into her bag for a different, older, leather bound journal. "I could explain it all, but I'll just read."

"I told Rochelle I was starting to feel enlightened. Rochelle said she was feeling pretty enlightened too. Then out of the blue, Rochelle, the same Rochelle who introduced me to yoga, the same Rochelle whose hand I held through a bad break-up and who I guided through major life events, told me I was a horrible human being, and she wanted nothing more to do with me. She said her life would be better off if I was dead."

Celia closed her journal, and flopped her manicured hands down on the table. "Sometimes, you really put yourself out for someone, and they turn on you."

"You think after all these years, she—"

"Just four years. Four years is not that long ago. She may have introduced me to all this," Celia made a sweeping gesture with her hands, as if the cafe somehow embodied a life of yogic contemplation, "but she was clearly not enlightened."

"The journey of a thousand miles begins with a simple step," Helga interjected.

Celia inhaled. "When I met Rochelle, she was fragile and lost. She'd just discovered yoga and meditation and the middle way— but her life was falling apart. You know, it was me that suggested she dump her fiancé. The guy was so clingy and blah, and always broke. I planted the seed, and eventually she got rid of the guy. It's not my fault his tech start-up took off. Let's face it, he probably would have dumped her for some model by now. And then her job situation. She had this tedious administrative job. I told her she could do better. Got her to quit. It's not my fault the job market crashed and her old company wouldn't take her back. And she was always complaining about her body. I would never have said anything about her looks if she hadn't opened the door. I just agreed with her. Yes, she was too skinny. Yes, she was nondescript. So, I introduced her to my plastic surgeon friend. Rochelle was finally starting to live up to her potential, and then she drops the person who got her so far."

Celia paused. Helga looked at her, brow furrowed. "What?" Celia asked.

"It's just hard to imagine Rochelle plotting a murder. She's such a peaceful soul."

"You say that like…" Celia had a realization. "Does she still practice with you?"

Helga took a deep, cleansing breath that answered Celia's question. "After she quit her job, she starting coming to my morning classes," said Helga.

"Look, I told her even the best plastic surgeons make mistakes. I told her she should sue the guy. Did she?" Celia asked.

"It's not for me to say."

"Her life, it's got to be so much better now than it was."

"Her life is of no concern to you."

*****

The waiter came by, cleared their plates, and presented the women with a dessert menu. Somehow, the non-dairy cheese cake and the green tea-portobello sorbet didn't sound as enticing as they normally did.

"Look, I really should get back to the office." Normally, Celia felt so much better after meeting with Helga. Today, that was not the case.

"Here. Take this," Helga pulled a bottle out of her hemp satchel.

"Essential oil?"

"Pre-made tea. It's one of my special blends," Helga said. "For a clear mind, and a restful sleep. You can warm it up, or drink it cold."

"So herbal tea is supposed to lead me to the answer?"

"Don't be silly. The tea makes you feel better without the answer. But why don't I take your journals. I'll peruse them. Look for clues."

Celia looked down at the leather bound tomes. Had she ever written anything negative about Helga in them? No, she didn't think so. She handed over the journals.

*****

That night, after an exhausting day, Celia cozied up with a cup of Helga's tea.

The flavor was unusual. Surely there was ashwagandha for anxiety. Probably some chamomile for sleep. And there was a flowery flavor she couldn't quite put her finger on. Her mind churned as she sipped the tea. And then, just like that, Celia felt her spirit lift and her heart truly open. Authentic, unfettered enlightenment. And in that flash, before she dozed off, before her open heart stopped beating, she knew she had found the answer she'd been searching for. She knew who it was that wanted to kill her.

*****

Helga rather enjoyed the smell of burning leather. She hadn't bothered to read Celia's journals. She knew Rochelle wasn't capable of murder. Rochelle was a gentle, forgiving soul. It was Helga who had counseled her to stay away from Celia. And she knew Claire hadn't keyed Celia's car.

Helga's Pomeranian barked as the fire grew.

Helga didn't know if there might be something in the journals to incriminate her. Some passing note that indicated Celia might have recognized Helga from way back when. Unlikely, but possible. After all, Helga had been plumper then, still carrying the baby weight from her third child. And it had been so long ago.

When Celia had first strolled into her yoga studio six years ago, Helga had to take more than one cleansing breath to center herself. Maybe this woman—her ex-husband's divorce lawyer—had changed. If she had learned anything from life's journey, it was that change was possible.

But despite Helga's best efforts, some people never changed.

The beverage she'd given Celia was made of green tea, ashwagandha, chamomile, and mint. There was also a generous helping of highly toxic yellow jasmine.

She'd retrieve the bottle in the morning when she and Celia had a standing appointment for their Saturday morning mediation. She'd tell the police that Celia had been experimenting with herbal remedies, and that she had recently taken up foraging for exotic plants. She, of course, had counseled her against that, but Celia wasn't a woman who easily took advice.

She was sorry to lose such a lucrative client. But The Tao said, "The world belongs to those who let go."

Helga sat back, and exhaled. She had already let go. Her mind was quiet.

A Real Basket Case
Vera Brook

Yeah, sure, you can sit here, man. I don't mind. Plenty of room in the booth. No, I'm not waiting for anyone. Just enjoying my burger before I get on the road. Heading back to the city. Yeah, I'm from New York. We were just visiting for a few days, my fiancée and I. House-sitting a farm, actually. Where's she now? Well… she left me. I… I blew it. But it wasn't my fault. The whole plan went to hell. The goddamn baskets….

Sure, I'll take a beer. Why not? Thanks, man. Normally I'd pay for myself, but a pig ate my wallet. You're laughing, but you wouldn't be laughing if you saw it. That pig was a monster. Huge and black, with hairs sharp like razors. You don't believe me? Here. See this gash in my hand? I tried to grab it by the neck. Yeah, I know it was stupid, but I wasn't thinking clearly, with the psycho neighbor pointing his rifle at me.

Oh, it was a total misunderstanding. Didi and I were farm-sitting, right? But the neighbor didn't know about us, thought we were trespassing. Thought I broke into the storage shed to steal stuff, because the shed was locked and the Millers forgot to leave us the key. Honest to God, I only picked the lock to find another rake to clean the turkey coop, because I accidentally broke the rake I had. But then I saw the baskets, each in its own storage box, and I got curious. They were handmade and very intricate, with thin strips of wood and grass woven into fancy loops and cross-patterns, but strong and sturdy too. And very old.

It wasn't the first time I saw one up close, but it was the first time I thought to myself: damn, Gordon is onto something, his plan might actually work. Before that, I just agreed to do the job because he asked. If Gordon asks you for a favor, you can't exactly refuse, you know?

Am I into raising turkeys? Are you kidding? Before this, I've never seen a turkey up close unless it was baked.

The farm sitting was Gordon's idea. Pretty damn smart, too. The town isn't exactly a tourist magnet—I mean, there's the huge antique barn, and a pub like this one, and that's about it—so the locals look at you funny, like maybe you got lost or are fixing to walk away without paying. But any time someone would get nosy, Didi and I would just smile and explain that we're watching the Millers' place while they visit the grandkids in Tennessee, and it would shut them up.

Gordon set it up on the internet, all perfectly legit. I don't know the details. Gordon took care of all that. But let me tell you, our hosts—the Millers—waited for us on the porch like a welcome committee, with fresh strawberries and a homemade lemonade. I expected a frail old couple, but except for the white hair, they were fit and energetic, bouncing around us in their matching jeans and t-shirts, and talking nonstop. The man, Bruce, gave me a speedy tour of the coop, the veggie garden, and the composter with all kinds of nasty worms inside it, while the wife, Marcia, pulled Didi into the house to show her the bedroom and explain about the hot water heater and the stove. And then they were off in their black Dodge pickup, crunching the gravel and trailing a cloud of dust behind them.

The composter freaked me out even more than the turkeys, but Didi looked so happy, I didn't want to spoil it. Plus, just before the Millers left, Didi told them we were getting married and showed them the ring I got her, the first time I heard her tell anyone, and she sounded real proud—and it was such a rush, I almost lifted her up and carried her off to bed right then. I was a lucky guy, and we were going to have an amazing time. Business and a whole lot of pleasure, you know? Didi deserved it.

Sure, it was a little risky. But it would be an adventure—something to tell our kids about.

I don't mind getting my hands dirty—when it's worth it for me. And Gordon promised it would definitely be worth it, for both me and Didi.

Hey, is this my second beer or third? Eh, who's counting, right? I'm not in a rush. You ever get the feeling like someone is looking for you and getting closer? Didi could walk in here at any moment, and I don't want to leave without her.

She was never serious about that carpenter guy, I can tell you that. I mean she wanted me to think she was, and maybe someone who didn't know her would fall for it, but not me—I could see right through her. She only drove off with him to get back at me, because she was still mad about the cats. And the ring. But the ring doesn't matter! I'll get her another one. I'll get her all the rings she wants. I mean, you don't break up with someone you love over something stupid like that. We've been through a lot together, Didi and I. We have a connection.

Damn, I wish I used that knife, though. She told me to, she was serious about it, but I just couldn't do it. Maybe if I had more time to mentally prepare. But in cold blood like that? No way. It's just not the kind of person I am, you know? I don't like violence, except in movies. If she wasn't rushing me, I could've thought of another way, but everything happened so fast, and then she was gone.

She'll be back, though, and we'll forget this whole mess ever happened. Probably leave New York for good.

Why? Why do you think, man? Because I don't want to run into Gordon again, that's why. When he warned us about the auction houses and what they do to anyone who tries to damage their reputation, I didn't believe him. I thought to myself, the art world couldn't be ruthless like that. Isn't art about beauty and compassion and bringing people together? But I had a small taste, and that was enough.

A favor is one thing. But Gordon got cocky and messed with the wrong people, and I don't want to be around when he needs a scapegoat. Why should I risk my neck for him twice? I doubt he ever planned to pay me and Didi at all. Just take the baskets and keep the money for himself. What could we do—sue him?

Oh, you want to know about the baskets? All right. I'll tell you about the baskets.

First, you've got to understand: there was supposed to be only one basket. Totally unique, no other like it in existence, the artist long dead, whoever they were. So the plan was simple. We get the basket nice and quiet—no fuss, no drama—and then we're gone, and no one is any wiser.

That's what we signed up for, Didi and I. That was the deal.

Except Gordon was wrong. His precious basket wasn't the only one.

We weren't supposed to contact Gordon at all after we got into town—no calls, no texts, nothing. But when we found the second basket, out of the blue, I couldn't resist. I had to brag about it. I called Gordon and left a voice mail. He called me five minutes later, pissed off but excited too. A new plan. Find *all* the baskets. If one basket sells for sixty grand, a collection will bring in a cool million.

Why couldn't I keep my mouth shut? The dumbest mistake I ever made. Would Gordon find out about the other baskets anyway? Yeah, probably, eventually. The man has eyes and ears everywhere. But Didi and I would've been off the hook by then.

Me and my damn big mouth.

To be honest, I still have no clue how Gordon sniffed out that first basket. I guess you can find any information online these days, if you know how to look or can afford to pay someone who does. No such thing as privacy, right?

Anyway. One day, Didi and I met up with him in a club, and he pulled out his tablet and showed us the photo. It was the digital edition of some small-town newspaper, full of ads for guns and fertilizers. The photo showed a thin woman in an ugly red dress, her lips and cheeks red to match. She held out her cupped hands to the camera, and a white kitten lay in them. The photo was so grainy, that it took me a moment to notice the gray marking on the kitten's side: a perfect heart. The caption read, *A woman rescues a stray and finds a Valentine.*

Aww, look at that cutie, Didi crooned, and I had to agree the heart-shaped marking was cute, even if cats aren't my thing. I'm allergic, you know?

Gordon touched the screen, flicked his fingers apart to zoom in on the background, and said, See that basket on the bottom shelf, filled with yarn? That basket, my friends, can pass for a one-of-a-kind, museum-grade item, worth about sixty grand, more if we can get a few serious collectors bidding on it in auction. I know a respected appraiser ready to confirm it's the real thing. The town isn't much, but you'd only stay a few days. The woman lives alone, works at the water treatment plant one town over. We split the money fifty-fifty, minus expenses. The discretion is key, of course. The auction house can never know how we acquired the item, or they wouldn't touch it. So… how about it? You interested?

Didi and I looked at each other, and her eyes were huge and shining. Thirty grand to steal a basket? I didn't even have to ask.

I grinned at Gordon. Hell yeah. When do we leave?

We had no clue what we were getting into.

Okay, okay. The first basket. I'm getting there. Say, mind if we get some chicken nuggets? And maybe some fries and ketchup with that? Thanks, man.

So anyway—Gordon made it sound easy. The woman lives alone, away all day; the house is on a small road, pine woods on one side, corn fields on the other; a good chance the back door isn't even locked. We just sneak in, get the basket, and get out. How hard can it be?

Yeah, right.

We crack open the back door—and it's like getting punched in the face. The stench is unbelievable. Didi clamps a hand over her nose.

What the hell is that? But my face is already itching up a storm, my tongue suddenly too big for my mouth. Cats, I croak, and back away from the door. One cat, I can handle, if it doesn't get too close. But there's no way one cat could stink that bad, even with the windows shut.

Fine, I'll do it myself, Didi says, like it's my fault I have allergies. And she rolls up the bottom of her halter top so it covers her face up to her eyes and pushes inside the house. Even from where I'm standing, I can hear the cats start to meow, one after another, a whole damn chorus of them. A minute passes, then two, then three, and I'm getting nervous. What's taking so long? I peer inside the kitchen window, but all I can see through the frilly curtains is the cats. On the table, on the counter, on the floor. Cats everywhere. Damn, by now I'm really hoping I don't have to go in. Maybe the woman got new furniture and moved the basket to a different spot. But if it's there, Didi will find it.

Then I hear a screech and a loud curse—followed by hurried footsteps—and the back door swings open and Didi rushes out.

I scan her hands, but they are empty. No basket.

What happened? You couldn't find it? I ask, and she wheels on me. Oh, I found it all right. But the damn cat sleeps in it. Yeah, the one with the heart marking, except that photo was like ten years old. The cat is huge and vicious like you wouldn't believe. It almost scratched my eyes out. Didi points at her face, and sure enough, I can see three red, angry lines down her cheek. Blood trickles down her neck. Jesus. This is why I never want a pet. They're all killers at heart; it's in their nature. No way I'm going back in there, Didi warns me.

So we drive back to the farm to disinfect Didi's cuts and figure out our next move. Okay, so it's the cat's basket now. But the cat has to leave the basket some time, to eat and pee. What if we get another basket and swap it for the museum one? If they are similar, the cat won't care and the woman won't notice.

Let's try the antique barn, I say, and add stupidly, Hey, the scratches look badass on you.

Didi throws me a warning look—*don't mess with me, because I'm not in the mood*—but she gets in the car, and we're off.

The antique barn is a four-story wooden building crammed floor to ceiling with junk. The ugliest lamps, mugs, lawn gnomes, and watering cans you're ever seen, some genuinely chipped, faded, and bent with age, others obviously fake. Every floor is like a maze. Dozens of stalls with tall shelves choke full of stuff on both sides, with more stuff at your feet, hanging from the ceiling, and covering the walls. Anything from coins and buttons to bikes and TV sets, much of it covered with dust. Seriously, the place is one massive fire hazard.

But then we enter the wicker section, and my eyes almost pop out of my head. Because on the top shelf of the corner stall is a basket that looks just like Gordon's basket. It's a little smaller and a different shape, but the fancy loops and cross-patterns of wood and grass look awfully familiar. Same materials, same style. I'm no expert, but I would bet money the same hands made it. Which means it should be worth as much as Gordon's.

The seller isn't around, so I grab the basket off the shelf and spin around to show it to Didi. Except she's not there. She's two stalls behind me, wasting time looking at silver jewelry. Didi! I motion her over, and hold the basket out of view until she steps next to me. Her mouth falls open, and she snatches the basket from my hands. No way! Let me see it. How much is it?

We look for the price tag, but there isn't any. By now, Didi is positively glowing. You think the seller has any idea how much it's worth? she asks and licks her lips. I brush the basket with my finger, and can't help but laugh. Look at that dust. Is that how you'd take care of one-of-a-kind collector's item that's worth thousands of bucks? They don't have a clue, and we want to keep it that way. Come on.

We replace the basket on the shelf and walk over to the next stall, where another seller is polishing a set of spoons. She smiles broadly at us and explains that the seller we want stepped away for lunch, but he'll be back in twenty or thirty minutes tops, if we could come back then.

But when we do, we're in for a nasty surprise. The museum basket is now in a glass case on the counter, the wood polished so clean, it shines; and the price, when we ask about it, is nine hundred dollars. For a one-of-a-kind collector's item, it's a bargain, the seller tells us smugly. The thing is worth thousands.

And that's when I know we've been had.

Didi doesn't think the carpenter guy was in on it, but I have my doubts. An awful coincidence for him to show up right as we were walking away from the basket. At the very least, he must have been eavesdropping, because when we turned to leave, both Didi and I seething with disappointment, he was standing right there, and he kind of chuckled.

Normally, I would let it slide, not worth my energy, but I was already on edge. What's so funny? I snapped at him.

The guy smiled from ear to ear, and ran his hand through his hair. He fit right in with the surroundings too—old overalls stained with paint, gray tshirt with sleeves torn off, and ridiculous heavy work boots, even though it was close to ninety degrees outside. Oh, nothing, he said. Just a word of advice: if you see something you like, never show how much you want it.

He was talking to me but staring at Didi the whole time and smiling, and maybe if she didn't react, I could just shrug it off, but she blushed, her whole face turning pink, which never happens, and I'm not a very jealous person, but that really pissed me off. Thanks, I'll keep that in mind, I said through my teeth. Now can you move? You're blocking our way.

He did, with a nod at Didi, and I gritted my teeth but I kept walking, not worth it, we're never going to see the jerk again. But boy, was I wrong.

The next day was going to be a scorcher, ninety-eight degrees, so I got up early to finish the chores before the midday heat. The composter especially, because trust me, that stuff smells nasty even when it's nice and cool outside, but if you open it when it's hot and humid, you might as well roll in it like a pig, because it'll stay in your nose and mouth, and cling to your skin, and hair, and clothes all day. Not how you want to make it up to your fiancée after a fight.

I was cleaning the turkey coop when Didi finally emerged from the house. She wore a bikini and her big sunhat and carried a towel and folded beach chair she must have found in the house. I dropped my rake and rushed to help her, but she swung the chair open, plopped it down, threw the towel over it, and stretched on top in one smooth, fluid motion. Then she pulled her sunhat down over her face and proceeded to ignore me all morning while she suntanned. Not even a smile or a kiss. The turkeys circled her and the chair, pecking at the grass and making those strange turkey noises, but she ignored them too.

This stings, I thought to myself. I hate when we fight. It's not our honeymoon yet, and maybe the setting isn't exactly romantic, but it's an adventure, and we're supposed to have fun and make memories together. But I have my pride too, so I keep raking and pretend Didi's cold treatment doesn't bother me. The stupid turkeys are pecking at the chair now, but I figure, if Didi needs me, all she has to do is holler and I'll take care of them.

But the sound I hear is a crack—and then a gasp.

I turn, and Didi's chair is empty and she's on the ground, gripping a turkey by the neck.

The turkey struggles, feathers puffed up, and Didi's eyes grow wide, and I realize I got it wrong. She's not choking the turkey—the turkey's got her finger. And it's a tom, twice as big and ten times as mean as the rest. The beak is clamped around Didi's finger down to the knuckle. Or did the bird already bit through the bone? I definitely heard a crack.

But then Didi yanks her hand back, and I grab her wrist to check, and all her fingers are still there. Thank God, you're okay, I croak, and

I actually feel sick from relief. But Didi glares at me. Okay? I'm not okay. The fucker got my ring!

For a moment, I draw a blank. What ring? Then it hits me. The engagement ring I got her; the one I still owe Moe at the pawn shop three-hundred-fifty dollars for, although Didi doesn't know that's where I bought it. The turkey stands a few feet away, the head in profile and the neck extended like it's trying to make itself taller. One beady black eye stares back at me.

Didi gets to her feet with a huff. What are you waiting for? Catch it!

So I pick up the towel and stroll toward the bird, slow and casual, no eye contact, like I'm not interested at all—and then I lunge for it and trap it in the towel. I expect a ruckus, but once I have it swaddled nice and tight, so only the head sticks out, the turkey goes perfectly still. I can hear it growling, though, and it's unnerving. I didn't know birds can do that. The beady eye is giving me a death stare.

But no matter. I clutch the bird under my arm and turn to Didi, who is just hurrying back from the house. Now what?

Here, use this, she says, and hands me a big knife.

I blink. You mean… you want me to kill it?

She rolls her eyes. It has my ring. I want you to slit its throat and get it out.

I swallow. That's a little extreme, no? Maybe we should wait…

She scowls and grabs for the turkey. Forget it. I'll kill it myself.

The bird must sense the danger, though, a pure survival instinct, because as soon as I release my grip to hand it to Didi, it shrieks like murder and breaks free. It doesn't land on the ground, though, it's airborne and moving up. The huge wings flap awkwardly, the pear-shaped body bobs up and down mid-air, and I'm just staring, very confused, my fist still closed around the towel. Because turkeys can't fly, can they? But lo and behold, this fucker somehow makes it all the way up to the roof. And I realize: we're never getting the ring back.

Didi wheels on me, eyes flashing. You know what? Keep the stupid ring. I don't want it. And she marches up the porch steps and slams the door behind her, still clutching the knife.

I start after her, but stop. The situation is delicate. What do I say? I can't go in without a plan. I need to think it over. Didi might need a little time to cool off and reflect, too, and I wouldn't want to interrupt that. So I pick up the rake and get back to cleaning the turkey coop while I ponder my options.

Why rush it? It's not like we're leaving yet. We've got time.

Except we don't. Because an hour later, the carpenter guy shows up.

I'm still raking the floor of the coop and pondering the Didi situation, when a huge white pickup truck pulls up to the house. *Holzer Carpentry & Painting* is stenciled on the door, and country music blasts from the rolled down windows. The guy jumps down from the driver seat, but leaves the engine running and the music playing, which would annoy me even if he was a welcome guest, and he's not.

Just then, Didi rushes onto the porch, frowning at the noise—and stops short when she sees the guy. She's still barefoot and wearing only her bikini, and I have an impulse to grab the towel and wrap it around her. But I'm not fast enough—the carpenter guy is already walking toward her, after grabbing something from his truck.

Hey, Didi. It's Didi, right? he says, grinning from ear to ear. I got you something.

And he hands her a cheap and ordinary basket.

Didi blushes bright pink (again!) and starts to protest that she can't accept it, and why would he buy her anything, he doesn't even know her. But the guy only laughs and says it's nothing. And, by the way, if Didi likes baskets, there are two other antique shops a short drive away, not as big, but they have nice things. They are a bit hard to find, because the roads are not on the map, so the GPS is useless, but he could drive her if she wanted.

And this whole time, he's talking only to Didi, like I'm not even there. How did he find us? Did he follow us here? And what's with the gift? That's just weird. But then Didi runs to the house and returns in a short dress and sandals, and I snap back.

Actually, it's the rake that snaps, roughly in half. I was leaning on it too hard. I manage not to fall, though, and I march straight to the carpenter guy, the broken handle of the rake still in my grip, to let him know I mean business.

Whoa. Not so fast, buddy. She's not going anywhere with you. She's not interested, all right?

The carpenter guy finally looks me in the eye. That's up to her, no?

Now I'm getting really mad. Who does he think he is? I take a step closer and casually swing the handle I'm holding, in case he forgot about it. And I say, You don't get it. She's my fiancée. We're getting married. Now beat it.

But he doesn't budge. I'll leave when she tells me to leave, he says.

I feel Didi staring at me, practically burning a hole in my head, so I cool it and try a different approach. I even smile at the guy, although it hurts my face. Hey, what happened to your rule? Never showing that you want something?

The guy doesn't miss a beat. He turns back to Didi and says, Sometimes you have to break the rules and give it all you've got, because it's your only chance and you'll regret it for the rest of your life if you don't.

Didi sucks in her breath, her eyes huge like saucers.

Then she turns to me and says, Don't tell me what to do. You have no idea what I want. And look: no ring. And she lifts her hand to show me.

She doesn't wait for my response. She spins on her heel, grabs the guy's arm, and pulls him toward his truck. Come on. Let's go. I love antique stores.

I watch the pickup truck drive away, too stunned to form a coherent thought, my head buzzing like a swarm of bees. What just happened? It makes no sense. Didi is my girl. We have a connection.

I glance up at the roof, but the turkey is gone too, nowhere to be seen.

I hurl the rake handle at a storage shed and miss. I kick at a clump of grass and send it flying. But it's not helping. I'm still restless. I need something to do, anything.

I dig out a lighter from my pocket, grab the cheap basket, and light it on fire.

The wood crackles as it burns, and somehow that cheers me up. The smell is pleasant too.

Fifteen minutes later, the basket is nothing but ash.

I drag the beach chair into a shade to cool off. I'm shaken but amazed at myself too. Normally, I'm not an impulsive person. I don't fly off the handle; I don't lash out or break stuff or punch anyone in the face.

But I just set a thing on fire.

Damn. What else am I capable of? Maybe I need to stop holding back.

Sure, I could use another beer. And how about a shot of vodka to go with it? No, not to drink. I was going to change the bandage on my hand. I don't want it to get infected. That pig really did a number on me.

I thought I told you that part already. You want the details? Okay, picture this: Dusk is falling, the woods and the road getting darker, and Didi still hasn't come back, hasn't answered my texts, and I'm worried sick and seriously regretting I ever let Gordon talk us into coming to this damn town. But I can't just sit on the porch and wait for her. So to keep busy, I pick the lock on the storage shed and dig through the rows of shelves, the whole place as cluttered as the antique mall, like maybe the locals have a hoarding problem. I'm looking for another rake, but I find something much better.

Five more baskets.

I open the boxes one by one and can hardly believe my eyes. The same intricate loops and cross-patterns, but every basket is different. A whole collection. Jackpot!

When I hear a car in the driveway, I rush out of the shed, thinking it must be Didi—the carpenter guy dropping her off—and I don't even care where they went together, as long as he's gone and I can show Didi my discovery.

But the truck is red, or was red once, before the rust took over, and the whole thing shakes and rattles like it's going to fall apart. Then it stops—and a huge, black dog jumps off the bed in the back and charges in my direction. Only it's not a dog. No dog is that ugly. I stare at the massive snout, the flat nose, the small eyes, the shorts legs doing a weird little trot. I've never seen a wild pig before. Quick, where did I put my phone? I need a photo. I reach into my pocket.

Hands where I can see them! The voice sounds as rusty as the car. Or the first bullet goes through your knee!

I yank my hand out, and something drops on the grass. My wallet. But I don't dare pick it up. I put my hands in the air and slowly turn around until I face a rifle pointed straight at me. An old guy holds it. A baseball hat and a bushy white beard just about hide his face, and he's wearing a flannel shirt and cargo pants despite the heat.

Can I help you, sir? I say shakily, while the pig snorts and roots around my feet.

The man frowns and lifts the rifle so it's aiming at my stomach. You think I'm joking, son? You're trespassing on my friends' property. And stealing from them too, looks like. He says that with a glance at the open shed, the heavy lock dangling from the door with no key in it.

Oh, no, no, no, I quickly say. We're not trespassing. We're farm-sitting for the Millers while they visit with their grandkids. Honest.

The old guy cocks his head and glances at the dark house. We? I don't see anybody else.

Me and my fiancée. But she's… out at the moment.

The guy chuckles, but he lowers the rifle and walks over to the shed. He pokes his head in, and the frown returns. And the boxes? What do you want with them? And don't lie to me, boy. I've known the Millers for thirty years, and they don't let anyone near the shed.

I… broke the rake. I need it to clean the coop. That's what Bruce told me.

The guy scowls, but straps the rifle over his shoulder this time. You ever heard the saying, you break it, you buy it? You broke it, so buy a new one. Easy. Even the supermarket sells them. Don't go snooping around other folks' property. Just so you know, I'm still going to call Marcia, so your story better check out. Oh, and I'm going to take the boxes for now. No offense, but I don't trust you. And he stacks three of them one on top of the other and carries them to the back of his truck.

Take the boxes? My heart sinks. But he still has the rifle, and his giant pig keeps head butting me in the leg, snorting and chewing on something, and I can't think of any excuse to keep the boxes. Stop it, I snap at the stupid animal. What are you eating, anyway? I peer down at its jaw, the tongue working and the teeth grinding down on something—and it's a twenty-dollar bill. The pig is eating my wallet! Hey! Drop it! It's mine! And I grab the pig by the scruff of its neck.

It's like grabbing a rusty knife. I yelp in pain and let go. Then stare at the gash in my hand.

Come on, Pretty, the guy calls, unconcerned about my injury at all, and the pig spits out a wet, black mess that used to be half of my wallet and goes trotting to his owner. Up! The guy pats the bed of the truck and makes a step with his joined hands, and when the pig runs to him, he sort of tosses it up, and the pig is airborne for a moment before its hoofs hit the metal.

It's been a hell of a day. My wallet is in pieces, and my hand is stinging up a storm. But still, as I watch the rusted truck drive away with my baskets, I start laughing and cannot stop. The pig was called Pretty?

It's only when I'm drifting off to sleep that a fear grips me. What if Didi broke up with me and isn't coming back? But I won't let that happen. I've screwed up and let her down, but I can still fix it, I can still win her over. It's not too late.

And I make a decision: I'm getting those baskets. All of them. For Didi.

I wake up around midnight itching for action, although some of it may be mosquito bites. My hand hurts but it doesn't look infected. And still no sign of Didi. An urgency grips me. There's no time to waste. I need to get the baskets before I lose her for good.

The antique barn looks like a fortress at night, and I almost lose my nerve. But the padlock on the delivery door in the back easily springs open, and then I'm inside. The first floor has dim emergency lights, but the staircase is pitch black, and of course, I forgot to bring a flashlight. I always have a lighter on me, though, so I grab a tall oil lamp, light the wicker, and head up the stairs to the top floor.

The basket is still in the glass case on the counter, and I almost laugh in relief. Maybe my luck is finally turning. But the case is too bulky to carry, and I don't want to drop it and cut myself. Not a good idea to bleed when you're robbing a place. All I need is the basket. I carefully set my oil lamp on the counter and take the basket out of the case. I'm already turning to leave when a glint of silver catches my eye. A jewelry display. Wasn't Didi looking at it? I should get her something. Maybe not a ring, but how about this nice cuff bracelet studded with turquoise? Didi will love it. The stall is cramped, so I leave the basket in the aisle and hang the oil lamp from a hook high on the shelf, while I work the lock to open the display. It's jammed, though. Dammit. I kick the table in frustration—and the oil lamp swings left to right and flies off the hook, tracing a graceful arc in the air before it shutters against an record player and the oil spills on a stack of old magazines. Boom! Flames flare up, and I instinctively brace myself for an ear-splitting fire alarm and a deluge from the overhead sprinklers. But there's nothing, and the fire is already spreading, smoke curling and growing thicker.

So I grab the basket and run. I spot an ancient gas mask on a shelf and pull it on. It makes the stairs even darker, but I'm too much in a hurry to care. I burst out the back door, and I don't slow down until I'm inside my car parked two blocks away. By now, the entire top floor of the antique mall is in flames against the night sky. People rush out of their houses and run toward it, shouting and pointing, while a firetruck siren wails in the distance. It takes me a good minute to take off the gas mask, the dust mixed with my sweat making it stick like glue. Gross. Then I check the basket. Is it burned? Smashed? I expect the worst. But the basket is intact.

One down, six more to go, I tell myself and start the car.

It's still night when I get to the cat lady's house. My plan is to drive past it, then find a back road where I can park out of view and catch a quick nap. But her car isn't in the driveway, and I'm still high on adrenaline after torching a four-story barn, so I swerve into the driveway and drive to the back door. The plan is still the same: get in, grab the basket, get out. But in the gas mask this time. I don't think—I act. I don't dare turn on the main lights, but soft-glowing night lights in the outlets illuminate my path. Shadows shift all around me—the cats, dozens of them—but they stay out of my way. Could be the scary mask or the smell of smoke. But when I get to the prize basket, it's empty as well. Hell yeah! I snatch it and turn to leave. My stomach growls when I pass through the kitchen, and on impulse, I open the fridge. A huge casserole sits inside. I grab it too, plus a spoon from the dish rack. And then I'm out the door and driving.

Two baskets down, five more to go. For Didi.

The broccoli-cheese-and-bacon casserole hits the spot, but I'm too wired up to eat more than a few spoonfuls. I'm also running out of time, the night fading to dawn in the east sky.

The pig owner's house isn't hard to find. As soon as I see the reddish truck parked next to a squat farm house, I know I'm in the right place.

The windows are dark, the fields and woods silent, so I decide, to hell with it, I need those baskets—and I drive right up to the truck but facing in the opposite direction. I peer at the metal bed. If the guy moved the boxes, I'm screwed. But the boxes are still there. I drive two more yards and stop. All I need is to open the trunk, load the boxes, and get out.

That's when I see it in my rearview mirror. First the big snout, then the rest of the massive body. The pig is still in the back of the truck with the boxes! Now what? I need a weapon. I glance at the passenger seat. The gas mask is no good. But the casserole…

I leave the engine running and slowly get out of the car, my brain replaying random advice about what to do when a wild animal attacks you. No sudden movements. No fear, or the animal will smell it on you. And never, ever try to run. None of it awfully helpful, but I have an idea.

I set the casserole down on the ground off to the side and call in a whisper, Pretty! Come! I brought you something!

The pig snorts, the snout twitching, and the small, mean eyes stare at me—but then it jumps and runs straight at me, like it's aiming to ram into my crotch and knock me over. And I'm that close to jumping into the car and driving away, but I think of Didi and stand my ground.

The pig doesn't even sniff me once. It attacks the casserole, and the sight is not pretty.

I stare at the destruction, then shake myself and get to work. One box at a time, quiet and careful. The lid of the trunk barely closes when I'm done, but all the boxes fit. I slide behind the wheel and drive away slowly till I get to the road, then hit the gas.

I got them! I have all seven baskets!

Now I just have to find Didi.

Three problems, though. I've been driving for an hour, not paying attention, and I have no idea where I am. I'm almost out of gas and have only spare change. And my phone has enough juice for one last text.

And that's it. That's how I got here. No, my car isn't here. I ran out of gas and had to walk.

Listen, man. It's getting late. I thought Didi would show up. I texted her the address when I got here. But who am I kidding? She's not coming.

Wait? What are you saying? You knew who I was all along? And that I would be here? How? *You talked to Didi?* She was looking for me at the farm? When? Where is she? No, I won't calm down, man. I need to talk to her. She's safe? And I'm supposed to just take your word for it?

Get your hands off—okay, okay. I'm sitting down. Look. I'm calm. Not trying anything stupid.

A business proposal? You just tried to break my arm. Who are you, anyway? An Acquisition Specialist for Russo & Wells? What the hell is that? You identify new prospects and negotiate the terms? I don't follow. An… auction house in Manhattan?

Shit.

I still don't get it, though. The baskets are fake, man. They just look like some other baskets in a museum or something. What? They're the real thing? And worth how much? Wow. That's… that's a big number. Okay. But I'm not greedy. Make me an offer.

A trade? I would prefer cash, but I'm listening. Well, sure I'd like it to be fair. Risk of damage? I mean, yeah, the baskets in the shed were stored in plastic boxes, without proper ventilation. I don't know how long—months, years? What does that have to do with anything?

Whoa. Hang on.

You mean… Didi? I'm trading you the baskets for my fiancée? That's the trade?

Are you serious? But that's… kidnapping and… blackmail… and robbery. Oh, you think it's generous? Because… you could hold Didi in a plastic box for a month too.

Christ, Gordon was right.

Take the damn baskets.

I just want Didi back.

Moist
donalee Moulton

Someone is watering my plants.

I first noticed this with the peace lily. I had watered it mid-week. (I remember because book club meets on Wednesday, and it was my turn to host. A wilted lily would have been a greater topic of conversation than *Where the Crawdads Sing*.) The spathiphyllum consumes water like a hungover teenager. Yet when I went to water it two days post-*Crawdads*, the soil was moist, and a small puddle rimmed the inside of the planter.

I thought nothing of it at the time. Attributed the anomaly to weather or luck or the vagaries of light. But when the butterfly palm that sits beside the lily continued to send its leaves skyward long after they should have drooped in despair to the earth, I knew something more than light, luck, or low barometric pressure was the root cause.

After this, I made it a point to record the date and time I watered each plant. This was no small task. There are 26 plants. Within two weeks, 20 plants did not require me to water them even once a week – but they were not dry. Indeed, they looked healthier than under my green thumb.

Initially, I thought the watering spree might be an unexpected act of kindness, my husband rising to the occasion and lending a hand after 26 years. Who knew, perhaps dishes would be next. Despite that first rush of adrenaline and promise, however, my serotonin levels returned to reality. I worried Phonse might be in early stages of dementia, at times believing himself to be someone else. A gardener, clean freak, or alien watering can perhaps. But no, my husband was himself. He drew a clock without tremor or error, and he could recall eight of ten words

I put on a piece of paper. (The two words he forgot: laundry and anniversary.)

Even so, my husband was the most likely suspect – or helpful other. I spent some time with Google looking into disorders that could compel someone unknowingly to water plants without being asked. Google, surprisingly, did not have an instant answer to this question, but I persisted and finally concluded it could be a sleepwalking syndrome. I tested the diagnosis. Once Phonse was in bed and snoring soundly, I tied a cord to his wrist and mine. My husband didn't move, except to roll over yanking the cord and chafing my wrist. After seven days, I stopped the binding ritual and purchased a corticosteroid cream.

The plants were flourishing.

I finally decided the best approach was the direct approach. One evening following the six o'clock news, when Phonse was mid-scratch, I asked him if he had been watering the plants. That got his attention. "What are you talking about?" he asked.

"Someone has been watering the plants," I said.

"Don't be foolish," my husband said, but he paused. Perhaps this was reflection. No, it was Phonse solving the mystery. "You water the plants."

I could have pursued the discussion, albeit under duress, but my question had been answered. Phonse knew nothing about the plants. My daughter walked into the family room just as my husband made his pronouncement (he really should turn his attention to world peace). I decided to go for 0 and 2.

"Are you watering the plants?"

There is a look that only 16-year-olds can achieve. It is a cross between a stabbing constipation pain and a facial spasm. It means I am an idiot. Still, bodily consternation alone did not answer my question. I repeated it, although I anticipated the answer. Jasmine has never watered a plant. She might if a hormonal love interest gifted her with one, but I'm certain even that commitment would not last. My daughter simply doesn't deign to do housework. She gets that from her father.

The twitching stopped. It was accompanied by eye rolling, but I saw her lips parting and her tongue moving forward in her mouth. Jasmine spoke. "Nope."

And that was that. There is no reason for either Phonse or Jasmine to lie, just as there is no earthly reason for either of them to defy their DNA and water the plants. They have never done this before. Why would they start now?

Still, someone is watering the plants. I strolled through the house, poking a finger in every pot. A few could stand a little liquid libation, but most were contentedly damp – and not of my doing. I water the plants on Friday, unless I am hosting book club. The odd bit of greenery, like the lily, gets watered twice a week. This is an inconvenience, but it is preferable to a dead plant. Or a wilting one. Wilting plants always look like they are crying out for help. It creeps me out.

The question of who is watering the plants is more of a puzzle than a harbinger. Clearly no one is breaking into the house just to water my plants. That said, I now check the alarm system before I head to bed.

It occurs to me one humid, stultifying night about 3 a.m. that I am applying logic to a situation that may be logic proof. No one in the house is watering the plants and no one can get into the house to water the plants ('cause that's a thing). So maybe it's not someone but something.

I think instantly of my sister Joan. She's spiteful, and she's dead. Joan died a painful and protracted death from stomach cancer. I went to visit her in Alberta. I don't like that province. People smell like cows. Joan didn't smell like a cow, but she had numerous other bovine qualities many of which were directed at me with more than a hint of malice. Once, when I was in the second grade, Joan told all the kids at recess that I had lice. By the time we were back at our desks, half my class was scratching. One little girl, Sadie maybe, broke into tears. The whole class pointed at me and yelled, "She has lice." The teacher hustled me, at a distance, to the nurse's office. My mother was called. Joan grinned all through dinner. (I got back at her a week later by peeing in her bed just before her best friend arrived for a sleepover.)

Needless to say, my older sister and I did not like one another. That didn't change as we got older. There was more distance between us and fewer reasons to breach that span. I'm not certain if we disliked one another intensely enough for her travel 5,000 kilometres and haunt my house. But if she's here, dry plants would drive her nuts. I take some satisfaction in that.

There's nothing for it but to go full ghostbuster. I learn that smudging with sage can cleanse negative energy. (That would be Joan.) I'm not sure what smudging is, and I have only used sage in stuffing. (I do make a great buttery herb dressing with craisins.) I turn to Amazon. There are many options – sticks, incense, spray – but it will take at least two days to get a delivery. I don't have two days.

It takes a little more searching but I find a crystal shop near me (who knew). The shop sells sage sticks – dried bundles bound together for easy lighting and holding – as well as stones. I know nothing about stones but the nice man behind the counter says black tourmaline is an all-round protection against harmful spirits and energies. I buy a bracelet for $24.95.

Phonse and Jasmine won't be descending for several hours. I decide to do the smudging ceremony as soon as I get home. This ritual is an even better idea than I originally thought. Joan had asthma. The smoke will irritate her no end.

As directed, I open a few windows to prevent the smoke detectors going off then walk slowly through the house. I pay particular attention to those areas where there are plants. Part of the ceremony involves stating your intention clearly. "Joan, get the hell out," I say as I move from room to room and floor to floor. My bracelet jangles. I refuse to chant.

It is unclear how long it will take for the smudge ceremony to work or how often it should be performed. I repeat the ceremony for three consecutive days. At the end of day three, Phonse asks if I have burned supper. Jasmine wrinkles her nose in distain.

I toss the rest of the smudging kit in the trash. I turn back to Google looking for in-house camera equipment that is both affordable and easy to install. This takes about 12 minutes before I'm bored to tears. I make my way to Best Buy and return home with a mini camera tucked inside my jean's pocket. I'm pleased with myself for the purchase—$67.25 Canadian—and with having made the trip. This way, if it is Joan watering the plants, she won't know what I'm up to. There will be no unwrapping of a package post-delivery or reading a manual an evil spirit could peruse over my shoulder.

Instead, I have thumb-sized plastic disk in my pocket that contains a magnet. I pretend to clean the lamps and surreptitiously attach the camera. It's angled to clearly catch a full frontal view of the lily and the palm. If need be, I'll buy another camera.

I do a test run. Even though it's Thursday, I water both plants. On my afternoon walk, I look at the video. There I am clear as day. Joan is thwarted.

It's getting a little ridiculous the number of times a day I poke a finger into soil. Covertly, of course. It takes three days before I find moisture that is not of my making. I was beginning to wonder if Joan had caught on to the camera.

In anticipation of busting a ghost, and wanting to savour the moment, I treat myself to a latte at the local coffee shop and take out my phone for the official unveiling. The latte was pleasant; the recording was less enjoyable. In fact, the recording was downright boring. There were 12 hours of the lily and the palm doing absolutely nothing. Perhaps they swayed at one point. But at no point were they watered.

I'm at a loss. Perhaps Moses is coming down from on high to lend a hand. But no, I'd have caught him on tape. Family – dead or alive – is out. I order a second latte. Whatever is happening cannot be or have once been human. That leaves inanimate options.

My husband arrives home from work to find me on the roof. He does not think this is a good idea. It's my first time up here (one more than him). The view is quite lovely. I take a minute to breathe in the landscape. Perhaps I could meditate after all.

There are no holes in the slate tiles. Certainly none that I can see. After I climb down, I call a roofer. It takes him two days, but the professional concurs. There are no leaks in the roof. So nothing is leaking into the planters.

It must be the planters themselves. This house is new to us. We only moved in eight months ago. While the previous owners removed most of their belongings, they left a few plants, including the lily and the palm, and a ceramic spoon rest in the image of a basketball. I've read about gizmos that alert you when plants need to be watered. Perhaps there are gizmos that actually water them.

The lily sits in a standard plastic green pot that is tucked inside what looks to be a whiskey barrel made of distressed oak with faux metal bands. The word "HOME" is on an oval placard between the bands. I start with the planter. I remove the bands, the placard, the nails. There is no gizmo. I dig into the lily. There is plastic, dirt, leaves, and more dirt. I toss the lily into the trash.

The butterfly palm yields the same results and suffers the same fate. I hope Joan is happy.

I will not be undone by some unknown plant waterer. Of all the fates I have imagined, this is not among them. Over the next 12 hours, I remove all the plants from their pots and their planters. Then I remove everything from the house. I drive to the local dump – you don't want whatever is in those plants to be composted and leach into the groundwater. It costs me $75. I return the camera to Best Buy. Told them it was defective. So I'm only out $7.75.

Over the next several weeks everything returns to normal. My husband watches the nightly news and scratches on cue. My daughter continues to perfect her look of constipation and consternation. I host the book club, and no one notices the missing plants. I also called my brother-in-law in Alberta to say hello. It was a short conversation.

It is Wednesday. I have prepared devilled eggs and red velvet cupcakes for the book club. Eclectic comfort food. I take napkins and hand sanitizer into the living room. I put the eggs on a plastic tray reminiscent of van Gogh's *Sunflowers*. I paid $1.25 at the Dollar Store for the tray. The cupcakes are on a glass plate. I decide to add a bowl of olives to the fete. I know the expiry date has passed. I don't think it will matter, and I won't eat any.

I open the fridge door but can't seem to find the olives. I look behind the ketchup (which really needs to be wiped) and the peach yogurt. I remove ginger ale and Clamato juice (which I have never tasted in my life). I look in the cheese drawer and the produce crisper. There are no olives anywhere.

I repeat the search. To no avail.

Someone has been cleaning my fridge.

Hostile Takeover
Jill Hand

He had been watching me for six days. He was careful to keep his distance, but the same tingling sensation that alerted prehistoric humans when a big nasty beast with fangs and claws was eyeing them, crouching concealed in the shadows, waiting for the right moment to pounce, told me he was watching. On the seventh day, he pounced.

I was slumped on a wooden bench on the footbridge overlooking the harbor, picking at my cuticles, when he walked up, handsome as Satan on a Saturday night. He was decked out in rich-guy casual, the whole enchilada: massive gold wristwatch with more functions than a Swiss Army knife, straight-leg khaki shorts, premium sneakers, and a short-sleeve polo shirt with a pair of Ray-Ban Wayfarers tucked into the placket.

He asked, "Mind if I join you?"

"Go ahead," I said.

He sat, propping his left ankle on his right knee. He kept a respectful distance, not manspreading, not crowding me, calm, as if he just happened to be out for a stroll and decided to sit for a spell. He smelled good, like fresh laundry and spicy aftershave.

He pointed his chin at the boats bobbing at anchor in the harbor. "Nice day."

I agreed that it was a nice day. Just about every June day in Maine is nice, more than nice, heart-swellingly beautiful, with a cloudless blue sky stretching over picturesque coastal villages like this one, Boscomb Harbor. Seagulls mewed and swooped over sparking blue-gray water stretching to the horizon. The warm air had a fresh, salty tang, with just a hint of fish thrown in to keep things interesting.

Below us, vacationers were checking out the T-shirts on a rack outside a tourist trap called Harborside Treasures. Other vacationers were lined up at Down East Sweet Treats, waiting to buy ice cream. At a red-white-and-blue kiosk draped in fishing nets, a man with blond dreadlocks was selling tickets to Captain Andy's whale-watching excursions.

Happy couples walked hand in hand. A trio of adolescent girls, fairly pulsing with the restless energy of young animals, posed in front of a carved wooden mermaid figurehead. They were being baby birds, eyes open wide, lips pointed as if they were sipping through a straw. A fourth girl held up her phone, capturing the moment for posterity, or at least an Instagram or TikTok version of posterity.

You couldn't ask for anything more on a day like that other than to soak up the atmosphere and enjoy being in Boscomb Harbor. Not unless you were penniless and desperate. Then you weren't enjoying much of anything. I pulled the frayed sleeves of my hoodie over my hands to hide my bloody cuticles.

He cleared his throat. "Buy you a coffee?"

As pickup lines went, it was right up there with *Do you come here often?*

Before I could say no, he said, "I'm not trying to come on to you, honest. You just looked like someone who could use a cup of coffee."

"Okay, thanks," I said.

And that's how it began.

Once we were settled at a window-side table at the Spinnaker Café, he told me to order anything I liked. "I own this place," he said, gesturing to the ship's wheels and lobster pots and assorted nautical paraphernalia that made up the interior décor. He said it proudly, as if he were announcing that he was an astronaut who also happened to be a Formula 1 driver.

I said, "It's nice," causing him to beam with pride. He added, "I have a summer place, up on the Point. I actually own a few of the businesses here. I like helping the local economy."

When I made appreciative noises, he hurriedly said, "It's no big deal. I just wanted you to know that you can go ahead and order anything you like. Have the lobster eggs Benedict, or whatever you want, my treat."

I ordered the lobster eggs Benedict and so did he. We dug in.

He patted his lips with a paper napkin. "What brings you to Boscomb Harbor?"

I shrugged. "I dunno."

Unwilling to let it rest, he said, "I saw you on the Point, coming out of Alana Acosta's house."

The Point is Boscomb Harbor's version of the East End of Long Island. It's an enclave of what Mainers call "summer people," meaning people from out of state who own homes in Maine, and don't just spend a few days or a week there, staying in motels, shopping at L.L. Bean and visiting Acadia National Park. The Point at Boscomb Harbor is where old money and new money reside during the summer months, in well-tended homes with weathered silvery-gray cedar shingles, more or less in harmony.

Alana Acosta is Boscomb Harbor's very own celebrity. Every Maine town either has or used to have a famous person living there, at least part of the year. Bangor has Stephen King. Kennebunkport had the Bushes. Boothbay Harbor had Margaret Hamilton, who played the Wicked Witch of the West in *The Wizard of Oz*. North Haven Island had poet Elizabeth Bishop. Castine has chef Ewan Sylvester, star of TV's *Sylvester's Sizzling Kitchen Challenge,* and so on. It's as if a state law required every municipality to have its own A-lister.

My dining companion poked around in his fruit cocktail and forked a piece of cantaloupe into his mouth. He chewed, swallowed, and said, "Ms. Acosta has an interesting history. Her parents fled Cuba in the nick of time, just before Castro came into power. Word is, they were cozy with the American Mafia, stone-cold bad guys like Meyer Lansky and Lucky Luciano who turned the island into a criminal empire. There was gambling, prostitution, drugs, you name it.

"When it came time to vamoose, Hector and Beatriz Acosta filled the hold of a boat with gold bars and unset diamonds, like something out of *Pirates of the Caribbean.* They sailed to Miami and set up shop there."

I toyed with my eggs Benedict, pushing yellow yolk around in pieces of English muffin. From a speaker mounted in one corner, the Grateful Dead cheerfully informed us of what the Doo-Dah Man had told them.

He went on, "So anyhow, the Acostas kept on doing whatever they were doing back in Cuba, only in Miami. In the early sixties, they had a daughter, Alana. She was their only child, born late in their lives. She was fresh out of college when her parents died, but not before they used their ill-gotten gains to bankroll her first business, Acosta Cosmetics. It grew and grew, swallowing up dozens of companies that sold beauty products and vitamins and nutritional supplements, becoming Acosta Health and Fitness before finally morphing into the behemoth known today as ACOSTACO, which deals in everything from baby formula to five-star resorts. It's worth billions. *She's* worth billions."

I said, "Good for her."

He held out his hand. "I'm Caswell Lang."

I shook it, seeing him pretend not to notice my chipped nail polish and ragged cuticles. "Melissa Smith," I said.

He took a drink of orange juice. "I'm not being nosy, but I saw you leaving Ms. Acosta's house. Do you know her?"

He was definitely being nosy. I told him I'd gone there hoping to talk to her, but the butler wouldn't let me in, saying she wasn't receiving visitors. "I used to know her daughter. We were…close."

I let him fill in the blank about the nature of my relationship with Ms. Acosta's daughter, an only child, like her mother. She'd be in her early thirties now. No one had seen her in years. A rumor claimed she had joined a cult. Another rumor claimed she was a permanent resident in a high-end drug and alcohol rehab, possibly in California. Or maybe she was dead.

I took a deep breath, deciding to get it over with. "I was a blackjack dealer at a casino in Massachusetts. I lost my job. I was hoping Ms. Acosta would lend me some money, just until I get back on my feet."

My downcast eyes and tight lips let him put two and two together and conclude that I had been up to shenanigans at that blackjack table down in Massachusetts. Casinos take a dim view of that sort of behavior.

He considered that, nodding thoughtfully. "Ms. Acosta hasn't been seen around town lately. She's usually a very visible presence: in and out of the shops, eating dinner every night at the table reserved for her at the country club, hosting a booth at the library's annual book sale, but not this year. This year, she doesn't go out. She stays in her house. Is Ms. Acosta ill?"

He studied me, his perfectly groomed eyebrows raised in polite inquiry.

"I think it's some kind of neurological thing, Parkinson's or early-onset dementia. Maybe even a brain tumor. The butler wouldn't say, exactly. He wouldn't even let me past the front door. All he'd say was that there's a team of nurses that work for hospice, so I guess whatever it is, it's terminal."

Lang said, "I'm sorry to hear it. Where are you staying?"

When I told him I had a room at the Pinecrest Motel, he winced as if I'd said I was residing with the Hells Angels. The Pinecrest was a notorious rat hole, where shady locals get together to do shady things. Tourists who foolishly neglected to read the Yelp reviews before making a reservation took one appalled look and got out of there, fast. Staying at the Pinecrest Motel was tantamount to asking for trouble.

A waitress rushed up and freshened our coffee. At a smile and a nod from Lang she moved away, to circulate with her carafe among the other customers.

Lang said, "You can't stay there; it's not safe for a woman by herself. That is, if you're not with someone?"

I said I wasn't with anyone.

"In that case," he suggested, "Why don't you stay at my place?"

I said I couldn't. He said not to be silly, of course I could. He had several empty guest rooms and was rattling around all alone in his big house on the Point. I wouldn't be in the way and he'd appreciate having some company.

"No strings attached," he said firmly, and launched into a long story about how he started out with nothing and now here he was, through dint of determination and hard work, a wealthy man who owned a huge swath of forest up on the Allagash, as well as a considerable number of resort properties in places where the weather is warm all year-round.

His blue eyes gleaming with sincerity, he said, "Please, stay at my place, just until you get back on your feet. Then you can pay it forward and do something nice for someone who could use a little help."

I moved in to one of the guest rooms at Caswell Lang's house. A month later, we were married. Two months after that, he tried to kill me. It went down like this:

A few days into my stay at Lang's house, we were relaxing with glasses of wine at the firepit in the backyard. That's when I divulged that my name was not really Melissa Smith. It was Bea Acosta. I was none other than the daughter of Alana Acosta, Boscomb Harbor's own personal billionaire. I said I was christened Beatriz, after my maternal grandmother, but I preferred to go by Bea.

He said, "Wow, so you're the mysterious daughter."

I confirmed that I was indeed the mysterious daughter. I said that my mother and I had a parting of the ways, becoming estranged about ten years ago, when I graduated from college with a liberal arts degree. I had refused her demand that I apply to grad school and earn an MBA, so I could work for ACOSTACO.

Lang refilled my wine glass, his eyes wide at this revelation. I took a sip and said, "I used to write poetry. My English professors said it was pretty good. I had the idea of becoming a poet, professionally."

Lang's stunned expression made me laugh. "Yeah, how stupid was that? There's no money in writing poetry, not unless you're exceptionally talented, and even then, it would take years and years to make any sort of decent living out of it. I was good, but so are a lot of people. I'm not Maya Angelou. It took a while for that to sink in. By then, my mother had cut off my allowance and revoked my trust fund, hoping to make me give in and beg her for a job at ACOSTACO."

I drained the wine in my glass. "I stopped writing poetry. Whatever inspiration I used to have had evaporated, but I wasn't going to go crawling to my mother. I took any kind of job I could find. There's not much you can do with a liberal arts degree. I was waitressing and bartending and working in casinos. I was barely getting by. I was really depressed."

Lang put his arm around me and pulled me close. I leaned into him and we sat like that for a while in silence with my head on his shoulder, watching the flickering flames in the fire pit. Finally, he said, "I believe that everything happens for a reason. The universe brought you to me.

I've been alone for a long time. I don't care whether your name is Melissa Smith or Bea Acosta or Little Bo Peep. These last few days have been the happiest in my life. I'm all in. I love you. I want to marry you.

We gazed into each other's eyes. If it were an old movie, the camera would cut to crashing waves and exploding fireworks. Since it wasn't an old movie, we became very friendly, there beside the firepit, before finishing the wine and stumbling into the house and becoming even friendlier on the living room floor. The next morning, I moved out of the guest room and into the master bedroom.

We were married by one of Lang's tennis buddies, a guy named Brent. He wore a bowtie and was the preppiest of preppies. Brent was an attorney who specialized in trusts and estates. It's not generally known, but any lawyer in good standing with the Maine Bar Association can officiate at weddings.

Ours was a low-key ceremony, with Brent doing the solemnizing in his office in Damariscotta, with his paralegal and a summer intern acting as witnesses.

I had told Lang I didn't want a big wedding. He was on board with keeping it simple. Neither of us had any family to speak of. Lang had a couple of cousins with whom he wasn't particularly close. As for me, there was only my mother.

"I went to tell her I was getting married. This time, the butler let me in. A nurse had her sitting in a chair while she changed the sheets on her bed. She was bent over, moaning like a wounded animal. She didn't recognize me. I shouldn't have stayed away so long. Now it's too late."

My voice broke. Lang hugged me and said, "You didn't know she was in such bad shape. Don't blame yourself; it's not your fault."

Brent, the preppy tennis-playing lawyer, drew up our wills. Were Lang to predecease me I would be his sole beneficiary. If the reverse were to happen and I died first, Lang would inherit everything I owned, which amounted to the two-carat diamond engagement he gave me, and my clothes, all of which were from either Target or Walmart.

There were also his and hers life insurance policies, which Lang insisted upon. He and I were each insured for three million dollars, double indemnity in the unfortunate event of death under certain conditions, the foremost being as the result of an accident.

Six million dollars is not pocket change, although it's relatively small in comparison to the bonanza that was ACOSTACO. My mother was being cared for by a hospice nurse, which meant she wouldn't live much longer. As her sole heir, all that money would come to me. If I were dead it would come to my husband. Lang got busy making sure a fatal accident would befall his bride.

There was a popular song in the nineteen-seventies called "50 Ways to Leave Your Lover." You still hear it played occasionally on oldies stations. The point was that there were numerous ways to extricate oneself from a romantic relationship that had grown stale, all rendered in the form of humorous rhymes.

In terms of deliberately drowning someone by sinking them aboard a cabin cruiser, there are about a half-dozen ways to make that happen. Those include "crack the bellows, fellows," and "disconnect the pump, chump." Lang went for "pull out the plug, Doug."

By then it was mid-September. We'd gone out on his cabin cruiser, the *Maine Man,* several times by then. It was a pretty craft, with a small galley and a sleeping cabin and a head with a sink and toilet. We were about two miles out from Boscomb Harbor, chugging peacefully along, admiring the sunset, when Lang said there was a surprise waiting for me in our cabin.

He wasn't joking. There was a surprise waiting all right, but it wasn't sexy lingerie or a box of chocolate truffles tied with a red satin ribbon. The nature of the surprise became obvious when the cabin door slammed behind me. I tried the knob, but the door wouldn't open. I could hear Lang moving around, humming to himself. I pounded on the door. He hummed louder. Then I heard him move away. There was silence for a few minutes. Then water started trickling under the door. I pounded louder and yelled for him to let me out. No answer.

If Lang wasn't going to rescue me, then I had to rescue myself. I used a nail file to pull out the pins fastening the hinges to the door. Then I pushed the door open and walked out into a puddle of cold water. It was over my ankles and rising rapidly.

There was no sign of Lang. I hoped he hadn't taken the inflatable dinghy and skedaddled, abandoning me to my fate. If he had, my situation would be grim. I was far from shore in a rapidly sinking boat. The frigid Labrador Current runs through the Gulf of Maine, making the ocean temperature awfully cold. Although I'm a good swimmer, I doubted I could make it to shore without succumbing to a cramp or hypothermia. Plus, swimming at night in the shipping lanes is a good way to get run over by a freighter.

I breathed a sigh of relief when I found the inflatable dinghy where it was supposed to be. I put on an orange life vest, got in, and headed to shore as fast as the 10-horsepower outboard motor could go.

As it happened, I almost was run over, not by a freighter but by a cargo ship. I waved my arms and shouted. At what seemed like the last moment, a deck hand saw me. The ship stopped, a rope ladder was lowered and I climbed awkwardly aboard, trembling at the near-miss. Crewmembers surrounded me, talking excitedly in Portuguese.

"*Muito obrigada.* Thank you so much," I kept saying, shivering in the cold night air.

Where was Lang during all this? I told the police I didn't know, that I'd searched the boat for him and called out his name, but hadn't seen him anywhere.

That was a lie.

My murderous bridegroom had decided to celebrate his soon-to-be windfall by snorting some cocaine, his recreational drug of choice. When I departed the rapidly sinking boat Lang was sprawled on the deck, either dead or unconscious. I didn't linger to find out.

I had paid a visit to one of the shady locals who frequented the Pinecrest Motel, a scruffy dude who went by the charming name of Reptile. I made a purchase from him. What Reptile sold me was cocaine laced with fentanyl, a potent synthetic opioid.

"You want to be careful with this. A tiny bit—and I mean a *real* tiny bit—goes a long way," he said solemnly, as he handed me the little plastic bag.

"I'll be careful," I assured him.

A lobsterman found Lang's body floating near a buoy marking where he had set his traps. The cause of death was not drowning, but a drug overdose. The *Maine Man* was pulled up from the sea bed where it had sunk. The drain plug was missing. Evidently, Lang had pulled the plug, planning to escape in the dinghy and leaving me to drown, trapped in the cabin.

Luckily for me, he succumbed to temptation and decided to partake of the lethal mixture I'd swapped for his usual form of happy dust, which he customarily bought from his pal Brent, the preppy lawyer.

My mother laughed and addressed her butler, a big lug named Tony who used to be a prizefighter. "My daughter married a real sweetheart, didn't she, Tony?" Tony agreed.

Mom and I were sitting in the glass-walled conservatory at her house at the Point, looking out over the harbor. It was a gorgeous late September afternoon. The nurse had been dismissed, her role in the charade accomplished. There was nothing wrong with my mother's health. Lang's company had been in the initial stage of attempting a hostile takeover of ACOSTACO. My mother wasn't going to let that happen. She summoned me back to the United States from where I had been living, in a house she bought for me in France's Loire Valley. She laid out a plan and I followed through.

No more Caswell Lang. No more hostile takeover. I was the new owner of Lang's company. I kept the engagement ring as a souvenir.

The Story Never Told
Stormy White

It's a gray day, cloudy, drizzling rain. But cemeteries always feel gray to me. This funeral came fast, a car bomb three days ago and the burial today.

The facts are hazy, only speculation about the death of Bill Leer, a veteran of the Korean War who never talked about his role in intelligence and became a newspaper reporter everyone respected.

A bag piper is starting to play, and I sneak away grateful a few taxis are nearby because I'm afraid to use my car.

Intellectually, I've always known life must end in death. But now I feel it in my gut. How much time do I have?

My name is Parker Jackson and I'm a private investigator. The majority of my business comes from attorneys in private practice. Since they can't advertise and rely on referrals, I refer to them, and in return, they hire me when they need an investigator.

This catastrophe started as I was finishing a job for an attorney, Joe Moeller.

I had more respect for his secretary who should have gone to law school, but Moeller paid well.

The door to his office was open and I was in his waiting room listening to a young woman working hard not to cry.

I say woman, but she looked like a teenager. She choked, "What I've told you is privileged, right?"

Okay, I shouldn't have been ease dropping but it was Friday afternoon. The entire building was empty except for Moeller's office and whoever he was talking with was being tailed by an off-duty cop, Al Cherry. We recognized each other when I entered the building.

Moeller was showing her no sympathy. "Planning a crime is not privileged. And that's exactly what you're doing. Draft dodging is a crime. Maybe in California or New York, lawyers do that kind of thing but not here in St. Louis. Now get out before I call the police myself."

What a jerk. The kid was pregnant and trying to find a way to keep her boyfriend from being arrested for draft evasion. But why would anyone pay to have her followed?

As she stood to leave, Moeller demanded, "That's fifty dollars for the consultation."

Barely above a whisper, she protested, "When I made the appointment your secretary said the first thirty minutes were free. It hasn't been thirty minutes and I don't have fifty dollars." The tears were coming.

"It's only free if you stay longer than thirty minutes and pay for the extra time. Never mind, just give me what you've got."

She searched her purse and pulled out several one's and a twenty.

I couldn't stand it any longer. I knocked and walked in. "Deduct it from what you owe me."

I handed him a brown envelope. "Pictures. Your client's husband isn't screwing his secretary. He's screwing his sister-in-law and the waitress where he has coffee every morning."

As Moeller was eagerly going through the pictures, I slipped the girl my card. With eyes still tearing she managed a thank you and left.

As she rushed out, Moeller's secretary, Dottie, walked in with a grocery bag. She shot Moeller a dirty look as she unpacked coffee, sugar, and non-dairy creamer. She directed her comments to me. "I guess he decided not to help Sandy Venter. Too afraid he might anger the rich and powerful."

That got Moeller's attention. "What are you talking about?"

"The boyfriend she's trying to help. You know the young man whose father is hell bent his son will go into the army and begin his political career like his father and grandfather. They already have their campaign slogan claiming when our kids get drafted, they go. Which, of course, is pure bullshit. How many Yale graduates are fighting in Viet Nam?"

Moeller turned pale as it dawned on him the girl's boyfriend was Steve Burton, son of Senator Milton Burton. Then he turned red and demanded, "Why the hell didn't you tell me!"

"Why the hell didn't you read my note? It said boyfriend Steve B. supposed to report for induction September 30, 1965. Who else could it have been?"

Moeller ran his hands through his hair, and I could tell he was trying to think of a way to get involved. He could imagine his name in the paper. "But the girl looked so poor."

Dottie shook her head, "Heaven forbid we help somebody poor." She picked up a file. "After I file this at the courthouse, I'm going home."

"Could you wait while I think of something?"

"There's nothing to think of. No, I can't wait." She held up the file. "The statute of limitations runs Monday."

They both knew he would be lost without her. Still at fifty with no children, she felt motherly towards him. I could tell she regretted she hadn't made it clearer who Sandy Venter's boyfriend was.

I stood at the window and watched Sandy Venter walk to the bus stop. When she got on the bus, the guy tailing her, Al Cherry, ran to his car and made an illegal U-turn to follow.

I knew the gossip surrounding Steve Burton, son of Senator Burton and one of the heirs of the Burton empire. He was smart, handsome, and as adamantly opposed to the draft and the Viet Nam War as his family was for it.

The rumor was his father and older brother, already a state congressman, tried to keep the photos of Steve at anti-war rallies out of the papers. But it was news, and someone had published a picture of him at a rally in Boston.

Generally, I keep my mouth shut about politics to avoid conflicts with clients. Still Burton's father leaking to the press the date his son was supposed to report for induction seemed like an asshole thing to do. If the kid wanted to escape to Canada, he ought to have the same shot as the non-rich. Then again, I hadn't heard of many poor kids slipping into Canada. Couldn't help but wonder who was paying to have the pregnant girlfriend followed.

I make no judgments and offer no advice, but I do have a pamphlet with information on physical conditions which result in failing the physical for the army, beliefs of a conscientious objector, and questions asked at the Canadian border.

I live in St. Louis, but New Orleans is my favorite city. I'd live there if I didn't have to check on my aunt more frequently than I like. My office is above an antique shop on Olive Street in Gaslight Square.

Gaslight Square is a couple of blocks that are the closest thing in St. Louis to Bourbon Street. Lined with restaurants, antique shops, discotheques, bars with live jazz and folk singing, it is vibrant and diverse. The woman in a mink stole is no more out of place than the long- haired transplant from San Francisco. The white redneck thinks nothing of applauding and praising the black saxophone player whose kids he wants to shoot if they move to his neighborhood.

I used Moeller's phone to check in with my secretary, Kathy, who informed me I had an appointment at five with a John Doe. We call anyone we believe has given a false name John Doe.

Imagine my surprise when I found Paul Burton waiting for me. I was convinced Paul, Steve's older brother, like his father, could have kept Steve from being drafted. He could also afford to hire an investigator who had a posh office with an entire staff instead of a single secretary who imagined she was the next Joan Baez.

He shook my hand and smiled. Perfect teeth, deep blue eyes, expensive haircut, this guy wasn't planning on staying a state congressman.

"I got your name from my driver. You found his daughter who ran away. He thought she was in Haight-Ashbury, but you found her in Taos, New Mexico. You're good, discreet. I want you to find my brother. He's hiding and we think, never mind, we need to find him."

He held out an envelope bulging with bills.

This was wrong. Before I could answer, Kathy rushed over holding a record. "Sir, I know you meet a lot of influential people and thought you might be interested in some songs I've recorded."

She suddenly blushed as she realized her songs were anti-war and anti-segregation. This was Paul Burton who advocated prison for war protesters.

How many times had I told her to think before she spoke? I tried to help her. "I'm sure he can't accept something with copyright issues."

She quickly pocketed the record.

There was no question in my mind Al Cherry, the cop tailing Sandy Venter, had given him my name because he thought I had information from Sandy. I remembered the girl who fled to Taos and regretted taking the case. Her father was abusive and a bully.

I didn't take the envelope and he continued. "I need to find Steve before the 30th so he doesn't make a mistake he can never undo."

Before I could respond, the door opened and a slinky woman with big, brown, eyes and long, shiny, black hair walked in. She grinned, "I'm Laura, Steve's sister. I knew your aunt when I was at Villa. We need to find Steve before some hippie slut ruins his life."

She was followed by a tall, blond, blue-eyed, handsome young man who I guessed was her boyfriend.

As gorgeous as she was, the two things that flashed through my mind were how could she have brown eyes when everyone else in her family had blue eyes and why would she be so flirtatious in front of her boyfriend.

I'm sure she thought mentioning my aunt, letting me know she attended a posh Catholic school, and throwing aspersions on Sandy Venter would help convince me. She didn't know I took pride in being a fallen Catholic and liked hippie sluts.

"Wish I could help but I've got more commitments than I can handle."

Paul Burton's face clouded with anger, but his voice was civil. "This sounds like a cliché, but money is no object. Call me if you change your mind."

He paused and took a white envelope from his pocket. "Here. Dad's having a cocktail party tomorrow at five. Invitation only. I'll put your name on the list."

Laura took a pad of paper from her purse, scribbled something, and pressed it to her lips leaving an imprint of a kiss. "Here's my number."

She stepped close, very close, and handed me the paper. I could smell her Chanel perfume.

She cooed, "My private number on my special private paper. Call me even if you don't change your mind. Hope to see you soon." She saw me glance at her boyfriend and laughed, "Don't mind Jeffie. He's a pussycat."

I blushed out of embarrassment for boyfriend Jeffie who stared at the floor.

When they were gone, Kathy mimicked, "Call me even if you don't change your mind. I read she has four different colored contact lenses. What do you mean you have more commitments than you can handle? Hey, is that invitation for a plus one?"

I grinned, "We can find out. Just don't dress like a hippie slut."

That night I had dinner at the Three Fountains and walked around enjoying the ambiance of Gaslight Square. I couldn't believe it. I saw Sandy Venter slip into the Gateway Theatre and twenty minutes later come out wearing a blond wig and looking super pregnant.

What a clever girl. She couldn't very well hide being pregnant, but she could hide her identity by looking more pregnant. The gray-haired, distinguished looking man with a mustache she embraced had to be Steve Burton.

I couldn't help but think of Paul Burton's statement money was no object and spent Saturday morning doing research at the courthouse and moved to the public library when it closed at noon. It was interesting. Steve Burton must have been an afterthought of his parents. He was twenty-two, his sister, Laura, was thirty-three, and his brother,

Paul, was thirty-five.

Steve had obviously been his grandfather's favorite because Steve was the prime beneficiary of the trust. He was destined to become a rich man, all he had to do was survive to twenty-five. It was impossible to tell exactly how rich, but the family trust owned factories and farms worldwide.

Ironically, Steve whose politics were the exact opposite of his politician father and brother, was the most photogenic and charismatic of the family. Still the folks that voted for Milton and Paul Burton wouldn't forgive any leniency to a draft dodger.

Because some facts never make it into print, I called my friend on the St. Louis police force. He informed me the rumor was a fair number of the police department served the Burtons more than the public. But the only member of the family he was personally acquainted with was Laura.

When Laura was pulled over for DWI's she was driven home, and her drugs returned. When police responded to complaints of assault, she was taken to her parents' mansion where she sobered up and whatever male she had abused took a cash settlement and filed no charges.

His assessment was, "Laura can do no wrong in her father's eyes and her brother Paul hates it. Paul hates his younger brother too. Everything he's had to work for just falls into Steve's lap. At Yale, Paul got academic warnings while Steve got A's. Steve goes scuba diving, mountain climbing, even climbed K-2, while Paul's only exercise is getting in and out of a golf cart."

The more I discovered about the family, the more I knew there wasn't enough money to get me involved.

But Kathy was excited about the cocktail hour at the Burton mansion. I have to admit I was curious. I don't get invited to a lot of rich folks' 'cocktail parties. Kathy looked good in a sleeveless black chemise dress with her long, brown hair in a bun. I looked pretty good myself in a dark gray tailor-made suit I had taken in payment for a job well done.

A long, tree-lined driveway led to Milton's three-story stone mansion. I had to show the invitation three times to gain access. I recognized the security as off-duty cops.

Kathy and I mingled, ate stuffed mushrooms, and drank California wine. Surprisingly, Milton Burton's wife, Claudia, was the only Burton present. She looked unhealthy to me, thin and pale.

Nothing creative about the inside of the house, just an ordinary rich person's living room with French doors leading to a patio and rose garden which were kept open to let out the smoke. A few light sprinkles of rain, a lot of conversations that made me cringe, and it was time for us to leave.

By eight, Kathy, hair down, was at McConnell's Bar singing and hoping to be discovered, and I had changed to a cheap sports jacket and was going up the stairs to my office.

Huddled at my door was Sandy Venter sobbing. Her pants and oversized white shirt were blood splattered.

"They're dead. Murdered. Blood everywhere. They're going to think that …"

Situations like this are fraught with pitfalls. I'm not an attorney so there's no privilege. I can be forced to testify. Destroying evidence and tampering with evidence are crimes. I went downstairs, looked around, locked the door to the sidewalk, and returned to the sobbing girl.

"Who? Where?"

"Steve's brother, Paul, and Laura's boyfriend, Jeffie. The Gateway Theatre in the prop room."

So many questions. But the smart thing for me to do was get to the scene if I could. The smart thing for Sandy was to pull herself together before she talked to the police. Once something is said, it can't be unsaid.

I pointed out the restroom and a stack of clothes hoping she would clean as much blood off her as she could without me telling her. I asked, "When's the baby due?"

Even in her emotional state, the mention of the baby made her smile, "End of November."

A crack of thunder made me jump and I grabbed an umbrella. The storm had finally arrived. The crowds were gone. The pounding rain had even driven the panhandling bums inside.

The Gateway Theatre, a theatre in the round, was what I considered a step to becoming a more cosmopolitan St. Louis. It was above the Three Fountains Restaurant, but there was no performance tonight. A single cop wearing a yellow raincoat was standing in the doorway.

Usually, three policemen show up for a purse snatching. Murder and only a single cop?

I saw Bill Leer approach the officer who shook his head. Bill walked away and I caught up with him as he rounded the corner.

I knew Bill as one of those rare news reporters you can trust. He was tall, thin, and his face never showed what he was thinking. But if he said something was off the record, you'd never see it in print. Besides being honest, he was a damn good reporter.

He jumped when he saw me. "Parker, what did you hear? I got a tip Milton Burton was seen using the phone at the Three Fountains and a little later an ambulance drove away with no sirens. There's a rumor folks are paying cops to keep Gaslight crime out of the news."

That was probably true. News of crime hurt business and Gaslight Square had developed like a dream and could fade away just as fast if people thought it wasn't safe.

I nodded. "I heard something happened in the theatre prop room."

We both knew the back way in and went up the stairs. The door was unlocked and only a single light bulb lighted the room. Barely breathing, we tiptoed in. It looked like I thought a prop room should look, furniture stacked up, shelves with lamps, vases, a few dishes, a few tools, and a rack with clothes.

We both stopped and stared at a huge pool of black blood. As our eyes adjusted to the dim light, we saw more blood. Too much blood for a human to lose and still be alive.

Partially covered by congealing blood was a piece of paper. I used my handkerchief to pick it up. It was from Laura Burton's notepad. Had Laura Burton been here or someone with a note from her? Beneath the blood, I could read, "Gateway T. prop room, Sat. at 4."

"What the hell are you doing here!" Senator Burton stood in the doorway accompanied by off duty cop Al Cherry carrying a bucket and rags. They were both wearing medical overalls over their clothes.

Al unzipped his overalls and pulled out a revolver and handcuffs. "I can arrest them for trespassing."

Bill acted perplexed. "That would be an interesting story. Even more interesting trial."

Cherry grinned, "I could just shoot them and say I thought they were burglars. Then we wouldn't have to clean up this blood."

My heart was racing. Cherry might not be joking. I knew he had been disciplined twice for shooting unarmed suspects. I cleared my throat. "Our witness has instructions to call the feds if we don't check in."

Cherry laughed, "They ain't got no witness." Then a worried look came over his face. "Do they?"

The Senator sank down onto a chair. "Just clean." He looked at us, "My son's gone. My beautiful daughter is…." He stuttered. "Is not herself."

He paused and his jaw tightened. He had made up his mind. "Get out. My son was killed in an auto accident tonight." He looked directly at Bill. "If you or your paper ever print anything different, I will sue you into oblivion. And then…" He paused.

His face was twisted with hate. For years he'd worked to build a power structure and now he could see it diminishing. It could even be destroyed. And Bill could make that happen.

Milton Burton spoke softly as he glared at Bill. "And then I guarantee you will know the pain of losing children before you die. Twin daughters, right?"

Milton looked at me with eyes as cold as any reptile and hissed, "Tell the slut she's safe as long as she keeps her mouth shut."

I saw the look Milton gave Don Cherry. It said we'll take care of them later.

I'm not embarrassed to say I ran down the stairs and back to my office with Bill right behind me. As I was unlocking the door, a gray haired, athletic man with a bloody sleeve came up.

"She's in there, isn't she?"

Sandy Venter embraced the gray-haired man who pulled off the wig and gently cradled her. I pulled the shades, and they told their story as Bill and I sat still shaking.

Sandy and Steve met his senior year at Yale. It was love at first sight. Sandy was a freshman at Vassar and hated it. By April she knew she was pregnant and hated the idea her identity and respectability should come from having a husband. She also knew she would be a pariah in her hometown of Hannibal, Missouri. So, when Steve graduated in May, they travelled the east coast working against the Viet Nam War.

In August, when Steve introduced Sandy to his family, his father pulled him aside and told him not to make a scene, but they knew about Sandy. He'd arranged to have a warrant for her arrest issued alleging prostitution. He was adamant neither he nor his brother, Paul, were prepared to tarnish their careers to help him avoid being drafted.

Steve swore to his Dad he would never forgive him, never wanted to see him again, and fled the estate.

Since that day in August, Sandy and Steve hid trying to figure out what to do. They wore various disguises and took odd jobs. Steve's car had been towed and impounded. They planned to leave St. Louis but wanted to give Steve's family one last chance. After all, Sandy was about to have his father's grandchild and he knew his mother was not well. They agreed to meet in the prop room at the Gateway Theatre.

But his mother didn't come. Only Milton, Paul, Laura, and boyfriend Jeffie came to the meeting. Unfortunately, Laura was intoxicated, and Paul was angry because they had just finished paying off two police officers she had attacked when they stopped her for drunk driving.

Suddenly, wild-eyed, Laura picked up a screwdriver and went berserk stabbing Paul and screaming all he cared about was money.

Her boyfriend, Jeffie, grabbed her arm, and she dropped the screwdriver. She picked up a box cutter, slashed his throat, and returned to stabbing Paul. Steve attempted to grab her, but she cut him in the shoulder. Finally, she collapsed exhausted and silent.

Paul and the handsome blue-eyed boyfriend lay dead. Sandy and Steve ran down the stairs and in opposite directions fearing they would be followed.

After they finished telling their story, we sat numb.

Was it possible Milton Burton was going to cover up the murders of two people? Could he? Bill's mind was working faster than mine, and he gently questioned Steve and Sandy.

"Who knew about the meeting?"

"Was anyone but the five of you in the theatre?"

"Did you see what happened to the bodies?"

My office consisted of two rooms and a bathroom. The walls were exposed brick and Kathy had decorated with a sofa and comfortable chairs. Five filing cabinets housed my camera equipment and files. It felt safe. Damn, why hadn't I taken a camera?

Steve and Sandy huddled on the sofa answering Bill's questions. Then Bill went to my desk and made several calls.

He cleared his throat and announced, "The senator's office put out a statement his son, Paul, was killed in an auto accident this evening and on hearing the news, his daughter collapsed and was hospitalized. There's nothing about the boyfriend, Jeffie."

He paused and his voice got low. "The friend who tipped me off about Milton Burton making a call from the Three Fountains and an ambulance arriving is dead. They found him in a parking lot shot in the head. Cops are saying it was a robbery."

I didn't feel safe anymore.

What scared me most was Steve knew his father best, and he was more frightened than any of us. He choked, "We need to get out of town."

He was right. I reached in my pocket for my wallet and felt a paper, the blood-stained note from Laura's notepad. I had stuffed it in my pocket when Milton Burton walked in. I took the small bills from my wallet and five hundred dollars from my safe and gave it to Steve.

Bill nodded and offered to give them a ride to the bus station in downtown St. Louis.

I muttered, "We should get them out of St. Louis. I can give them a ride across the river to Alton, Illinois, and they can take the train to Chicago."

Four days later, I caught up with Bill at the memorial service for Paul Burton. He whispered, "They cremated Paul the next day."

I nodded. "Got a call from Sandy. She and Steve are in San Francisco talking to some lawyers. As it turns out, the toes he lost on K-2 from frost bite qualify for a medical deferment. All that heartache could have been avoided by a minute of research. Are you coping?"

He swallowed. "I can't sleep. And when I do, I have nightmares. A police car drives by my house every day. I won' let the twins go anywhere." He sighed and grinned his crooked smile. "It's ironic that Milton Burton's threat is the only thing he's ever said that I believe."

I looked up as Laura Burton in a black suit, short hair, and looking the picture of sophistication began her eulogy. I felt light-headed and my mouth went dry.

Bill whispered, "They claim she dried out at Missouri Baptist and has gone on the wagon. The governor appointed her to take her brother's seat."

"Does she know we know?"

Laura finished her eulogy, and I caught her glance at Bill and me. The same cold, reptile look her father had.

He was trembling as he answered, "Does that answer your question? The cop who was at the door that night killed himself day before yesterday."

Loose ends were being tied up. I knew it was only a matter of time before Bill and I came under scrutiny.

Bill whispered, "My wife and the twins flew to Kansas City where her brother picked them up. He's driving them to Seattle."

As I sit in the taxi trying to determine if anyone watched me leave, I recall my last conversation with Bill. His family wasn't here so I'm guessing they're safe in Seattle.

I'm suddenly overwhelmed with anger. Damn Milton Burton.

Then an idea.

No way to prove Paul Buton was murdered. But what about Jeffie?

I am good at what I do. I had only a name, Jeffie, and the knowledge he must have been seen with Laura Burton. Found his picture from a guy in the Square who takes photos and tries to sell them. Then I found pictures of Laura and Jeffie at fundraisers.

The next step was nerve wracking because I wanted info about Jeffie but didn't want it getting back to the wrong people I was asking. Laura never went anywhere without a date, and Jeffie had been her date enough times to leave a trail. A little bit here, a little bit there, and I had him.

Jeffie was Jeffrey Combs from Watervliet, Michigan, high school basketball star, and brother to two sisters. His parents and sisters were sick with worry because they hadn't heard from him.

An anonymous call and they began their search in St. Louis. They were relentless. It became a project for the local high school. They even got a statement from Mrs. Claudia Burton she had expected Jeffie to be at her cocktail party with Laura the night her son Paul died.

Not exactly sure what my plan was except to give the senator something to worry about other than me.

I was having a conversation with my cop friend who told me a body found in an abandoned building in north St. Louis was thought to be Jeffrey Combs when Kathy walked in and heard the name Laura.

Not sure whether it was divine intervention or a death sentence, I froze at her words.

"Are you talking about Laura Burton? State congressman bitch?

Tried to do her a favor by letting her know I found her note that said Saturday at 4, Gateway T, prop room which had to be Gateway Theatre. I mean it was Wednesday so she wouldn't miss the Saturday appointment. You'd think she'd say thank you for being reminded. I said I hoped she hadn't hurt herself, and she said, 'what the hell are you talking about?'"

I gasped. She was talking about Laura's note with Paul and Jeffie's blood I had picked up and put in my jacket pocket. I rarely ask Kathy to do un-secretary-like chores, mostly because she refuses. But hiding out like I was, I had asked her to take my sports jacket to the cleaners. She must have found the note.

Kathy continued, "I told her I saw the blood on the note. Then she accused me of trying to blackmail her."

"What did you answer?"

"I said screw you, bitch. Then I thought maybe it was a past appointment and there really was a lot of blood. When she asked who this was, I thought ah oh."

I choked, "And you said?"

Kathy grinned, "I said 'That's for me to know and you to ponder.' Thought I'd be clever and added, 'Really a lot of blood. Your paper, your fingerprints.'"

Kathy waited for effect and continued proudly, "She started screaming I know who you are. Go back to your cows you ignorant, pregnant hippie slut. My father will take care of you."

"Uh?"

"Yeah, that was my response. I think the alcohol and drugs did something to her brain. Sorry, I didn't mention it earlier. I put that note in the safe."

I sat for almost an hour trying to figure out if I was slipping down in Milton's list of dangers or rising, especially with Jeffrey Combs' family claiming he had been last seen alive with Laura Burton and demanding she be questioned.

I had my answer when I left the office as the sun was rising. There stood Al Cherry grinning like a Cheshire cat holding a sawed-off shotgun.

"Never got to take care of your reporter friend. But this makes up for it."

I stood frozen and didn't even flinch when I heard three pops. Cherry crumbled to the ground. The back of his head nothing but a bloody mass.

Standing there holding a revolver with a silencer was a raggedy bum who grinned Bill Leer's grin. "Good work on Jeffrey Combs."

I managed a "Thanks. Who was in the car?"

He smiled, "Body donated for medical research but no medical school wanted it."

I choked, "Are you coming back?"

"Soon."

Murder by Alternate Facts
N. M. Cedeño

"Sorry to disturb you so early, Arlene, but Terri Coldwater died last night. The sheriff sent me to notify you." Deputy Gilman McDonald, a towering twenty-six-year-old Black man, stood in his gray sheriff's department uniform on my covered porch.

I recognized his uneasy tone of voice. He'd sounded similarly uneasy the day he'd ended our six-month relationship in high school. Gilman looked commanding in his pressed uniform. His face with its full-lipped mouth and perfect cheekbones always had movie-star-like symmetry but, in the years since I'd last seen him, had gained gravitas and firmness of purpose. Standing with my blond hair in a tangle on my shoulders, I wished Sheriff Calderón had sent a stranger to notify me. I clutched my robe over my cotton pajamas against the morning chill and said, "May she rest in peace. We've lost a great poet, but she deserves peace."

"Amen to that," Gilman said, staring at me with more concern in his eyes than I thought the situation might warrant.

The silence stretched for a moment and the hairs on the back of my neck prickled. Then it hit me. Why had the sheriff sent Gilman in person? A phone call would have sufficed to tell me about Terri. At the age of 22, Terri was ready to die after five years of constant pain in a crushed body. Everyone in the town of Oak Hollow, Texas, knew Death was coming for Terri, and many had wished he would be merciful and hurry up. For her part, Terri had born the pain with determination and gallows humor. With her body broken, but her mind sharp, she dictated three books of uninhibited, soul-rending poetry from her hospice bed, knowing her time was short. I realized I was holding my breath, waiting for Gilman to relay whatever else he had to say. "What is it, Gil?"

He stepped closer and said softly, "Jack Almond was found dead this morning, too."

I grabbed the doorframe and Gilman reached out, prepared to catch me if I collapsed. I waved him off. "Jack? What happened? He didn't kill himself because of Terri, did he?"

"The cause of death hasn't been determined."

"You mean someone might have killed him?" I asked, clutching the doorframe so tightly my fingertips went white.

"The sheriff says we shouldn't speculate. Doc Morales is examining the body. Sheriff Calderón sent me to tell you to be on your guard, in case someone is looking for a twisted kind of vengeance." He pivoted on the porch, turning to glance behind him, as if he expected to see an attacking horde instead of an empty, neighborhood street. "You need to be alert for threats. I've already checked the area around your house once."

I fought to breathe evenly as my heart began to race. "The sheriff thinks the threats will start again. And the vandalism." I remembered the vitriol aimed at me after the wreck that had injured Terri and Jack, in spite of the fact that I'd merely been the Good Samaritan in the whole scenario. On bad days, I wished I'd been the Levite.

Gilman turned back toward me and put a hesitant hand on my shoulder. "You're the only hero in the whole mess, Arlene. The sheriff's department knows that. Until we know what happened to Jack, be vigilant and mind your surroundings. Don't go out alone after dark. You could call me if you need an escort someplace."

I gave a shaky laugh. "Your mama didn't approve of us dating. What would she say if I started calling you again? Besides, where would I go? This town rolls up the sidewalks at sunset."

Gilman chuckled, and squeezed my shoulder. "Watch yourself. Okay?" He glanced around the neighborhood again, as if he needed to set me an example, and took his leave.

I could still feel the warmth of his hand on my shoulder as I closed the front door. My phone, plugged in to recharge in the kitchen, rang. I rushed to answer it. "Hello?"

My Aunt Amy's worried voice replied, "Arlene? Are you okay? I just heard about Terri."

"I'm okay. Did you hear about Jack?"

"What about Jack?" The pitch of her voice, always girlish in a way that belied her age, rose even higher.

"He's dead too." I said, cringing as I heard her gasp.

"I thought Jack had his survivor's guilt under control."

I shuddered, wishing Gil had stayed, feeling isolated in my house. "It may not be suicide. The sheriff advised me to watch my back."

Aunt Amy was quick to accept the implications. "Murder? Oh no! Don't come to work. I'll manage the store without you. Stay home and keep your door locked."

"If I sit here, I'll have too much time to dwell on the past, and every noise will scare me. I'll worry myself into a panic attack. I need to work. Besides, if Jack was murdered, I'll be safer there with you."

"Of course, you're right. Come in. You can redo the front window display. That will keep you busy. Though, I expect half the town may visit from morbid curiosity today. They'll ask questions."

"Which I won't answer, just like every day for the last five years. I'll be there soon." We ended the call. I pushed bad memories aside and ate breakfast before slipping into my favorite capri pants and a comfortable t-shirt and brushing my blond hair into a pony tail. A constant state of anxiety settled over me as I realized that right after Jack's and Terri's names, my name would be the next one on the lips of every person in town.

*****

I parked in the lot outside Aunt Amy's flower shop and shook away my visions of the wreck that had started everything. The memories had been playing liked a looped video in my head as I drove. Schooling my face to project composure, I walked into the shop. The scent of a blooming garden met me as I entered the store. Inhaling the perfumed air, I smiled in relief at the sight of my aunt wearing her favorite floral print blouse and felt safe.

Aunt Amy, solid and squat at barely five feet tall, with blond hair beginning to show streaks of white, met me at the door and hugged me. "Please tell me no one has called to harass you." Her girlish voice was filled with concern.

"Not yet," I said.

Amy's brow creased. "Hopefully, no one will dare this time." She hugged me and led me to the counter to allow me to put my purse behind it. "I wish I could offer something better than 'this too shall pass,' but I can't. All I can offer are the new orders of roses to be unpacked and plants for the window display."

The bell on the shop door jangled, and Dora Plein entered dressed in somber colors—a maroon pullover with black slacks—befitting the task of selecting funerary flowers. Dora gave me an accusatory look from protuberant eyes under thick black bangs, as she did every time we crossed paths, to make sure I knew that she still blamed me for her cousin Mitchell Cattleman's death in the wreck.

"I'm here to order flowers for Terri's funeral," she said to Aunt Amy, glaring at me as she spoke.

I could feel her wrath from across the store, but did my best to ignore her.

As Amy dealt with Dora, the bell over the door jangled again, and Deputy Gilman McDonald strode into the store. He radiated urgency as he marched toward me.

"Arlene, we have a problem," he said.

"What's wrong, Gil?" I asked. Distracted, my grip on a handful of roses slipped and a large thorn stabbed into my hand as I tried to catch them. I winced and dropped the roses onto the work table.

"Terri didn't die of natural causes and neither did Jack. They were both murdered."

"What? How? Who?" Sentences refused to come out of my mouth properly.

"Terri was suffocated. Jack died of a gunshot wound, and the doc says it couldn't be self-inflicted. The sheriff is concerned for your safety. Have you seen anything unusual or experienced any new harassment?" He stood with his hands resting on his gun belt.

I glanced at Aunt Amy who stood frozen at the register holding Dora Plein's credit card.

Dora said, "Jack Almond is dead? Well, then justice has finally been served!" A look of malicious triumph lit her face.

I'd had enough of her. "Well, Deputy McDonald, Ms. Plein tries to kill me with her eyes every time she sees me, so that's not *new* harassment."

Gilman walked toward Dora. "Ms. Plein, perhaps you have an idea about who might have felt it was wrong for Terri and Jack to survive that wreck. You've been quite vocal over the years, saying your cousin Mitchell should have survived instead. Maybe you need to have a word with the sheriff."

Dora backed a step toward the exit as one hand fluttered to her chest and clutched at her maroon pullover. She spluttered, "I have no idea what…That is, I don't know anything about Terri and Jack. Er, I have nothing to do with this."

"Given the opinions you've posted online over the last five years accusing Arlene of letting Mitchell die and suggesting that Terri and Jack somehow caused the car accident, I think you have plenty to do with it." Gilman gave her a scornful look. "What if someone believed you and decided that Terri and Jack should die? What if Arlene is next?"

Dora shook her head in vehement denial, causing a few strands of her bobbed, black hair to adhere to her thickly-applied pink lipstick. "No, I haven't posted anything in ages, well, in at least six months. Besides, we all saw those leaked therapy notes someone posted online three years ago. Jack admitted to the counselor that he might have distracted Carlos! I haven't been talking to anyone…except that researcher who contacted me two weeks ago. He said he was interviewing people about the accident to write a true crime novel, a book to show what truly happened and to expose the people responsible for Mitchell's death." She brushed her hair off her face as her frog-like eyes darted back to me.

Gilman pulled a notebook from his pocket and flipped it open. "Two weeks ago? What researcher? I need a name. The sheriff's department needs to see any messages you exchanged with this person."

Dora raised her chin indignantly. "I don't see what that has to do with the sheriff's department. Why should I give y'all my messages?"

"So you would rather withhold information in a double homicide investigation?" Gilman turned his head away from her and spoke into the radio on his shoulder, letting the dispatcher know he had a witness, Ms. Dora Plein, who was refusing to divulge information related to a double murder.

The radio on his shoulder crackled as a voice requested his location. "Amy's Florist Shoppe on Main."

The voice responded, "Sheriff Calderón is in route to your location."

Even before Gilman could acknowledge the response on his radio, Sheriff Calderón walked into the shop and all talk ceased. He removed his cowboy hat and nodded to me and Aunt Amy.

I nodded back, suspecting he'd been getting coffee next door. He stopped at Jason's Café and Bakery for coffee on a regular basis.

The sheriff had an authoritative presence which combined with his gravelly voice and piercing eyes to make him seem larger than his five-feet six-inch wiry frame. He approached Dora and said, "Ms. Plein, please tell me you haven't broken that court order and taken to slandering and libeling Arlene again."

Dora said, "I told strictly the truth! Arlene could have pulled Mitchell from the wreck. She chose to save Jack instead. She let Mitchell die by choosing to leave him behind. That's the truth." She compressed her pink lips and crossed her arms on her chest.

Sheriff Calderón stepped right in front of Dora. "I'm going to remind you again, Ms. Plein, to think about what *Mitchell* would have wanted. Besides, Mitchell died before the train hit his car."

"According to her!" Dora shouted as she pointed at me. "How do I know he was dead before the train hit? Terri certainly wasn't, and she left Terri to die."

The sheriff turned his exasperated face to Gilman. "What's this about withholding evidence?"

Deputy McDonald quickly summarized what Dora had said.

Sheriff Calderón said in an even voice, "Well, Ms. Plein, as a potential material witness to a double homicide, you'll be joining me at the sheriff's office, while we await a warrant to search for those messages."

Dora Plein raised a hand. "That's not necessary, Sheriff. I have the messages here on my phone. You can read them. You'll see that they have nothing to do with murder. Just the facts." Dora removed her phone from her faux-designer purse and unlocked the screen. She accessed her messages, then handed the phone to the sheriff. "There. See."

The sheriff scrolled through the messages. "Well, this is interesting." The vertical line above his nose deepened as his eyebrows came together into one ominous line. "Have you been making videos, ma'am?"

Dora's nose crinkled in confusion. "Videos? I don't know what you mean."

"We received a call last week from Terri's mother, Loretta Coldwater. Someone released a video on one of the popular communication apps that all the kids are using now, and it spread like wildfire through Oak Hollow High where Loretta's youngest boy, Jonah, who's a junior, saw it. The video suggested Terri and Jack distracted Carlos Serrano while he was driving, causing the head-on collision with Mitchell Cattleman and his children at the railroad tracks. The words over the images in the video match what you've written here word for word, like someone cut and pasted this message." He glared at her. "The video suggested Terri deserved her injuries and that Jack escaped justice. You wrote this email two weeks ago. The video went out last week. And this week Terri and Jack were both murdered. You don't see a connection, ma'am? I do."

Dora's voice rose belligerently as she spoke, "If Jack was murdered, then someone finally got justice for Mitchell. You should have arrested Jack years ago. Jack should have stood trial for Mitchell's death!"

The sheriff snorted in disgust. "Survivor's guilt, Ms. Plein. Jack blamed himself for the accident even though he *wasn't* responsible. He convinced himself that he might have somehow distracted Carlos, though he didn't know what he might have done, or if he did anything at all. The investigation blamed both drivers, Mitchell and Carlos, equally, not the passengers."

"Your investigation, you mean. I won't listen to these lies." Dora put her hands over her ears in a melodramatic gesture.

Aunt Amy and I exchanged a glance, both rolling our eyes. We knew that Dora Plein preferred her own 'facts' over anyone else's. She decided what was true based on what she wanted to believe.

I noticed Gilman watching me. His posture was tense, worried. I raised my eyebrows questioningly at him.

He turned away, pretending not to see me.

What could he be worrying about? A thought hit me. "Sheriff, did that video mention me?"

The sheriff gave Gilman an irritated look, but Gilman shrugged as if to say "I didn't say anything."

"Sheriff?" I said again.

Sheriff Calderón looked at his feet for a moment before nodding reluctantly. "I'm sorry, Arlene, but, yes, the video mentions you."

"What does it say?" I asked.

"It says that you saved the wrong person. Let's leave it at that." The sheriff said to Gilman, "Please escort Ms. Plein to the sheriff's office and take her statement about her communications with this so-called researcher." He handed Dora's phone to the deputy. "Collect the messages for evidence."

Aunt Amy quickly finished charging Dora's credit card and handed it back to her. Then, Gilman directed Dora out of the shop to his patrol car.

"Okay, Sheriff, she's gone. What else did the video say about me?" I asked again.

He walked over and stood next to me. The corners of his eyes crinkled and his mouth pinched in sympathy. "The video suggests that you witnessed the car wreck instead of arriving after it, that you might be the only one who knows the truth, the only one who could place the blame squarely on the teenagers—Carlos, Terri, and Jack—and clear Mitchell Cattleman's name."

A buzzing filled my ears, and the world wobbled. I grabbed the work table and ordered myself not to faint. "They must know I didn't see the wreck! It's in my witness statement."

The sheriff said, "Breathe, Arlene. I don't want you passing out."

"I'm fine," I said in a shrill voice. "Why would they think I saw the wreck?"

Sheriff Calderón infused kindness into his gravelly, rumbling voice, "The video's narrator accuses my office of preventing you from giving public statements or interviews. Someone thinks we silenced you and that, free of my influence, you might reveal more about what happened."

I covered my face with my hands. "Why do they keep inventing these lies? I don't talk about the wreck because I don't like to relive that night."

"Facts and truth don't matter to people who are invested in proving what they want to believe." The sheriff patted my shoulder and stepped away. "Dora Plein would be my prime suspect in the murders if I didn't know she was playing bingo at the Volunteer Fire Department Fundraiser at the time of Terri Coldwater's death. While she could have killed Jack, I believe we are looking for a single murderer. Witnesses and security video place a vehicle—a rusty-fendered, blue Ford Focus— near Jack's house and outside Oak Hollow Hospice Care."

"Who is nuttier about rewriting the history of Mitchell Cattleman's death than Dora?" I asked, bemused by the thought. "His wife and kids relocated to be near family in Iowa and are still there. Unlike Dora Plein, Mrs. Cattleman never blamed me for Mitchell's death. The kids are only, what, nine and twelve years old now? They're too young to be seeking revenge on their own."

The sheriff tapped his fingers on the work table full of roses. "Last I heard, Monica Cattleman was engaged to be married again, putting the past behind her. I'll check on her, but I doubt she had anything to do with this. Maybe we'll get a lead from Dora Plein's messages with this 'researcher.'"

Sheriff Calderón admonished me to be careful and asked Aunt Amy to keep an eye on me before taking his leave.

*****

The day passed quickly as customers streamed into the shop to order flowers for the upcoming funerals. A few offered me a sympathetic smile and condolences. Several, including a reporter, tried to ask questions, but Amy interrupted, saying we didn't want to discuss the deaths.

Payton Coleridge, the young man Aunt Amy had hired recently to help run the shop while she ordered inventory or while I did the accounting in the back office, arrived at two for his shift. He helped at the cash register until we closed the shop at six o'clock every night, Monday through Saturday.

Payton, an art student with a chubby, acne-blemished face and bleached hair that flopped into his gray eyes, was new to town, which should have been a relief for me, since he didn't have a position on what I should or shouldn't have done the night of the wreck. However, barely a week after he started working at the shop, he inquired about the wreck, saying everybody he met asked if I talked about it. In the last two months, he'd tried at least once a week to question me, but never in Amy's presence. Amy didn't know that when she left me with Payton while she worked in the back office, she was leaving me with the person most likely to harass me for information. I always shut down his questions telling him I didn't want to talk about it.

During a lull between customers, Payton said, "I heard Jack killed himself because he felt guilty for causing the wreck."

"Nope. Jack was murdered."

Payton leaned across the register counter toward me. "How do you know?"

"The medical examiner said so. Now drop the subject."

"I heard Terri and Jack should have been arrested for causing the wreck."

"Dora Plein concocted that story. It's a lie." I clenched my hands, fighting off a wave of disgust. "Jack and Terri were innocent passengers in a wreck caused by negligent driving."

"You believe that?" Payton asked, raising one eyebrow. "That's the sheriff's version of the wreck, but I read online that it's a cover-up to hide the truth."

I threw my hands in the air in annoyance. "Cover-up for what purpose? There's nothing to hide."

"To hide the truth." Payton tossed his head to get his bleached hair out of his eyes.

"Why bother to hide the truth? The people responsible died in the wreck." I tried to inject some sarcasm into my voice.

He ignored my sarcasm. "Not Jack and Terri. Maybe the sheriff was paid a bribe to protect one or both of them."

"He wasn't bribed. Jack and Terri didn't cause the wreck." I was frustrated and irritated with myself for responding to his questions. If he kept this up, I'd be yelling at him soon.

"But how do you know? Can you prove it?" He lowered his voice to a conspiratorial whisper and hissed, "Did you see the wreck happen?"

"NO! But neither Terri nor Jack had any memory of doing anything to cause the wreck. Terri was an open book. Her emotions are in her poetry, and you won't find guilt there. Jack blamed himself for surviving, but he knew the wreck wasn't his fault."

"But I heard there were therapy records where he confessed—"

"Wrong." I cut him off. "He didn't confess to anything. He wondered if he could have done something to cause the wreck because he blamed himself for surviving. But he had no memory of doing anything. HE WAS INNOCENT." I inhaled deeply to calm myself and breathed in the heady scent of dozens of flowers. "Please stop talking about this.

The sheriff's report contains all the facts. If you want to read another independent version of the accident investigation, get the National Transportation Safety Board report regarding the train. The NTSB team independently found the same results as the sheriff's accident investigation." I ignored Payton and began rearranging the window display.

As I reached for a fern in a hanging basket to place in the display, Payton put it in my hand. He was right behind me. "Thanks," I said in a flat, discouraging voice, then hung the basket from a hook in the ceiling.

"Do you ever wonder if those kids blame you because they're growing up without a dad?" Payton asked.

My heart twisted in my chest as I remembered the children's terrified faces. "No. Stop asking questions."

"But you could have saved their dad. You passed by him to get Jack."

I froze as the smell of smoke replaced the sweet scent of flowers and the heat of flame overrode the air conditioning in the shop, taking me back to the wreck. "No."

"No? You don't feel guilty?" He put his pudgy, acne-covered face right in front of mine.

"Mitchell Cattleman was dead before the train hit, slumped over the steering wheel, eyes open and staring. I couldn't have saved him." I said in a soft voice, seeing the man as he had been when I pulled his crying children from his car.

"What? I never saw that online."

"It's in the sheriff's report," I whispered.

"But the sheriff's report is a cover-up."

"I WAS THERE! I KNOW WHAT I SAW!" I shoved some succulents onto a shelf in the window and stared at the parking lot. "I don't want to talk about this." My eyes fell on a blue car parked a few spaces from the shop door. The front fenders were rusty. A jolt of fear hit me. I stomped away, hoping to put some distance between me and Payton. He had goaded me into saying more than I'd intended. I'd never seen him drive a rusty, blue Ford, but suddenly I didn't feel safe standing close to him.

"Wait, Arlene."

I didn't stop.

"Stop, Arlene, or I'll shoot you."

I turned to find Payton with a gun dangling from his right hand. It was pointed at the floor, but Payton's pale, pudgy finger was curved around the trigger. "What are you doing?" I asked.

"Trying to get you to tell the truth. *Everything* I read about the wreck in the online discussion group says that you are *lying*. Why are you lying?" Payton stood a few feet from me, with his jaw clenched and his bleached hair flopped over one contemptuous eye.

"I'm not lying about what I saw. None of the investigators had any reason to lie. If you want the truth about the accident, read the investigation reports, not speculative posts and opinion pieces on the internet that are based on rumors and wishful thinking."

Payton shook his head in disbelief. "What does the sheriff have on you? Is he blackmailing you so that you support his version of the story? Is that why you didn't give interviews?"

"I didn't give interviews because I didn't want to relive that night. Besides if I gave an interview, I'd have to admit the split-second choice I did make: between saving Jack or Terri. The train was coming. I didn't have time to check who was alive or dead. I had to choose one person in the back seat where the doors would still open easily. Carlos, in the driver's seat of the second car, was pinned by the steering wheel, and Mitchell Cattleman was dead. I'd already saved the kids. I only had time to grab one more person. Jack groaned, so I chose him and left Terri because I knew he was alive. I didn't want to have to say that on television. Terri's mother already hated me for leaving her daughter to get crushed by that train."

"So that's the cover-up?"

"There's no cover-up. It's in the report."

He sneered, "You're lying for the sheriff or protecting yourself maybe."

"Okay. Fine. I'm protecting myself. I didn't give interviews because everyone decided I did the wrong thing. Terri's family hated me because I didn't rescue her. Dora and her family hated me because I didn't rescue Richard Cattleman, despite the fact that he was dead when I arrived. Carlos's family hated me because I didn't pull him out of the wreck instead of Jack. I did the best I could! I couldn't save them all before the train hit them! I got vicious phone calls, texts, and messages. My house was vandalized. My car tires were slashed. If I explained how I chose to save Jack, I would have given them more ammunition to attack me." Tears streamed down my face.

"You're still lying. I want the truth. I *deserve* the truth."

"What does this tragedy have to do with you? Why do you care what happened?" I asked.

Payton smirked, apparently pleased that I'd asked and not in the least worried about how upset he'd made me. "My mom raised me alone. I asked her about my dad when I was growing up, but she said she hadn't told my dad about me because she didn't want his help raising me. She finally told me his name six months ago when I turned twenty-one. So I started searching for him, and found out he died in an accident."

"Mitchell Cattleman was your father?" I felt like I'd been hit in the chest. I could barely inhale.

Payton's smirk vanished. "My mom met him while they were in college. Anyway, I researched the wreck and discovered that my father was killed and that the people responsible, Jack and Terri, were never arrested. The murderers deprived me of the ability to meet him."

"Jack and Terri were victims in a car accident, not murderers. Your mother deprived you of the chance to know your father and deprived him of the chance to know you. You should have grown up knowing him." I searched for a way to escape him, but I'd have to pass him to reach the front door. Aunt Amy was ordering inventory in the back office with the door closed. I couldn't reach the office door before

Payton could shoot me.

He raised the gun and pointed it at me. "Don't you dare blame my mom! She thought I'd have years to get to know my dad. She didn't know those teenagers would kill him!"

I raised my hands and stepped back from the gun. "I'm sorry you didn't know your dad. Neither did I. My dad died of cancer when I was two, and my mom died of a blood clot in her heart when I was seven. At least you had your mom."

"That's why Amy raised you?" he asked curiously, lowering the gun a fraction.

I nodded, keeping my eyes on the gun. "What are you going to do with me?"

"As soon as you tell the truth on video for me, and I'll let you go."

"I don't know what you want me to say. I could invent something, but it wouldn't be the truth." My knees began to shake. "Two cars collided nose to nose on a hill on an unlined, unlit county road on a dark night. Both drivers took the hill close to the middle instead of on their side of the road. The wreck occurred over train tracks. When I came upon the scene, a train was coming. I saved Mitchell Cattleman's two children and Jack Almond before the train hit the two wrecked cars. Terri Coldwater survived with catastrophic injuries. Carlos Serrano died. Mitchell Cattleman died before the train hit."

He looked at me like I'd lost my mind. "What is wrong with you? If I shoot you in the shoulder, would that make you tell the truth about what you saw?" Payton raised the gun and steadied it with both hands, aiming at me.

"NO, PAYTON! DON'T SHOOT!" I screamed, hoping Amy would hear. I flinched, expecting him to shoot.

"Tell me the truth," Payton insisted, walking toward me.

"Stop, Payton. Drop the gun!" Aunt Amy's girlish voice called from the back of the store. "I called the sheriff." She stood in the office doorway holding a shotgun, aiming it at Payton.

Payton swiveled his head toward her, but kept his gun aimed at me.

Realizing I was in range of being peppered if Amy fired the shotgun at Payton and that Payton wasn't watching me, I slid toward the front of the shop, out of the line of fire of both guns.

"I only want the truth, Amy. Arlene can tell the truth and clear Mitchell Cattleman." Payton sounded annoyed with both of us, but not afraid.

"Put the gun down. Deputies are coming right now." Amy walked steadily toward Payton.

Through the front window, I saw a sheriff's department car enter the parking lot and stop. Deputy Gilman McDonald jumped out, raced toward the store, and peeked in the window. I caught his eye, relieved to see him.

Gil unholstered his sidearm and entered the store, causing the bell on the door to jangle which drew Payton's attention.

"Drop the gun," Gilman said, aiming his own weapon at Payton.

As the hand holding the gun dropped to his side, Payton shook his head in disappointment. "You're ruining everything. I need Arlene to tell the truth. That's all. Then my mission will be complete. This is the last part of the plan."

"What plan?" I asked.

He stared at me as if I was being intentionally obtuse. "The plan to get justice for Mitchell. Duh."

Gil motioned for me to come to him, so I did.

As I ducked behind Gilman's protective frame, he said to Payton, "Drop the gun."

"It isn't loaded." Payton dropped the gun. "I was only supposed to scare Arlene into telling the truth. Failing to save Mitchell isn't the same thing as killing him. We debated it, and decided she didn't need to die."

I asked, "Who made the plan?"

"The online group: J4M, Justice for Mitchell. You're all enemies of justice," Payton said, pointing an accusing finger at us.

"Put your hands up," Gil said as he stepped forward to kick the gun away from Payton.

Payton complied, shaking his head solemnly. "I'll be released before you can finish booking me. We discussed it online. The Feds will see that the sheriff's department is corrupt and that our plan was the only way to get justice. We're uncovering corruption. You can't arrest me."

"We'll see about that." Gil handcuffed Payton as two more sheriff's department cars roared into the parking lot.

I ran across the shop and hugged Aunt Amy.

Sheriff Calderón walked into the store a moment later and conferred with Gil for a moment before Gil led Payton out of the store. Then the sheriff joined Amy and me at the register counter. "Arlene, dispatch said he was holding a gun on you and asking questions about Mitchell Cattleman. What happened?"

I explained what Payton had said about being Mitchell Cattleman's son and the online group J4M.

The sheriff almost ground his teeth as he clenched his jaw. "That video last week was labeled 'a J4M Production.' We'll have to see if Payton produced it, or if it was someone else in the group. If Payton thinks he'll get away with this, he's as crazy as Dora Plein. If the search of her electronics reveals she is part of this online J4M forum or had any knowledge of a plan to murder Jack and Terri, we'll arrest her too."

I remembered the blue car I'd seen. "There's a rusty blue Ford in the parking lot."

Sheriff Calderón said, "The crime scene unit is coming to process it for evidence. I received information on my way here that a blue Ford Fusion is registered to Payton's mother. He may have driven her car to commit the murders. We found fingerprints on the door to Terri's room at the hospice that didn't match any already in the system. We'll compare the prints with Payton's."

"I wish I could have made him believe me," I said. "He's been asking me questions about the wreck for weeks, and I refused to answer. Maybe if I'd answered his questions before…"

"Nothing you could have said would have changed his mind. He was too brainwashed by the lies," Aunt Amy said as she put her arm around me.

"Your aunt is right," said Sheriff Calderón.

I wanted to believe that they were right, but I had a sinking feeling that I should have tried harder to stop the lies from drowning out the truth. Payton believed he was working to get justice for his father because Dora and her supporters insisted that their version of events was true and proclaimed it far and wide. As a result, Payton was absolutely convinced that Dora's version was true.

I wished that I could have saved all the victims. While I no longer blamed myself for being unable to achieve the impossible, it still pained me to revisit the memories. Attempting to avoid that pain had silenced me for five years. What if I had talked about the wreck to anyone who asked? Would it have made a difference? If I'd given interviews, would my statement of the truth counterbalance all the lies? Or would Payton still have believed I was lying? Like Dora Plein, would he have believed want he wanted to believe, even with all the facts laid out for him?

I didn't know the answer to any of those questions, but I knew I couldn't allow a smear campaign to tarnish the victims or question my actions unopposed anymore. The people who hated me would probably still hate me, but at least I would know I'd done everything I could to make sure everyone had the facts. Whether people chose to believe me was beyond my control.

Keeping Secrets During Wartime
Maroula Blades

Since I can remember, I have spent pleasurable hours at my grandpa's house in *Zehlendorf*, Berlin. Grandpa, a vivid old man, loved cooking and baking cakes and biscuits. *Rouladen* was his favourite meal to prepare—a classic German dish of sliced, rolled beef served in spicy brown gravy stuffed with bacon and caramelised onions. He'd baked a fabulous apple strudel too, dressed with vanilla sauce. Over the past month, I have always had a glass of walnut liqueur after dinner. He had bought the liqueur last year at the Christmas market in front of the picturesque Charlottenburg Palace in Berlin.

As I entered Grandpa's house last Sunday, it felt different. He looked solemn. He wore a wool V-neck blood-red pullover that matched his oxblood-coloured brogues. An envelope with my name printed on the front sat between a tub of honey and the sugar bowl.

"Hello, Grandpa, what's wrong?"

"I'm mourning."

"I'm sorry; did one of your friends die?"

Grandpa shrugged his shoulders.

"I'm glad you're early. I have a few things to tell you, but we're waiting for other guests, Mr. Davis, a retired army medic, and Mr. Rankin, who is a police officer and my fishing partner; he's off-duty today."

"Oh."

Grandpa poured green tea into mugs that had glazed watercolour landscapes on them. I spooned two heaping tablespoons of honey into my mug. While I was doing this, the doorbell rang. Grandpa left his chair with his walking stick and moseyed through the corridor to the front door. His guests had arrived.

"I know you're all wondering why you're here," says Grandpa. Please take a seat. "Help yourselves to tea, cheesecake, or biscuits."

"Thank you, Mr. Reinhardt," said Mr. Davis. "I'll take a piece of cheesecake."

Mr. Rankin, the off-duty police officer, smiled, pointed, and said, "Two of those chocolate chip cookies will do, thanks."

Once everyone was served, Grandpa got up, went to the cupboard, and took out a burgundy leather photo album. The book's pages were tatty. Water stains and mildew plagued the sheets.

"This was in the attic for years; it's damp up there. The roof and walls need insulation. Vermin infests the place."

I shuddered. Grandpa flicked through the album and then stopped at a large photograph of a young woman dressed for spring.

"Wow, doesn't she look like my mom?"

"This is Lottie, my twin sister."

Her sculpture-like features were like my mother's. Dad teases Mom sometimes by calling her saccharine sweetness because of her chiselled bone structure.

"Grandpa, I thought you were an only child; Mom did too."

Tears swathed the old man's eyes.

"No, I'm not, Susanne; Lottie died years ago."

Mr. Rankin, the police officer, tapped his fingers on the table. His eyes flicked over the clock on the mantelpiece.

"When the Red Army, the Soviet troops, invaded Berlin in 1945, the soldiers reigned terror in many districts before the other allies arrived, after which they divided the city into four sectors." Grandpa paused for a few seconds.

"That's common knowledge," said Mr. Rankin in a gruff tone.

"A part of the house served as a grocery store back then. We grew our own vegetables and fruits, and the milk came in large metal churns from the dairy up the road."

Grandpa turned to a page where a mottled, sepia-coloured image of the shop appeared; two young people, a man and a woman, served customers from behind a makeshift counter. Under the photo, someone wrote, *The Twins.*

"I wasn't in the army because of a club foot. So many of the soldiers were around fifteen with little training and were ordered to the front lines to fight." Grandpa sighed.

"So, you helped your parents out in the shop during World War II?" Asked Mr. Rankin.

"Yes, that's right."

"Having a food shop during those dark days must have been a blessing for the family," I said.

Grandpa nodded and continued, "We had a root cellar at the bottom of our field where we stored vegetables and fruits. We could store food for weeks or months."

The doctor added, "A root cellar is a great alternative, even now, to having a fridge. If you're poor and live in a rural region, root cellars are fantastic for storage. Nowadays, organic farmers are implementing root cellars because they're environmentally friendly, too."

Mr. Rankin rolled his eyes and then yawned, stating, "I have to be going soon."

Grandpa's face flushed. The off-duty police officer fidgeted, and Mr. Davis frowned at him.

"Yes, sorry. As the troops invaded the area, we heard shouting and screams from women along our road. Lottie ran upstairs and locked herself in the attic. There was a thump on the door, so I opened it. Five Soviet soldiers entered. I raised my arms above my head like this," Grandpa showed. "One soldier pushed me outside into the garden; the others searched the house."

"Good God. Yes, women suffered atrocities when the Soviets took Berlin. As an American allied doctor, posted here in 1958, I had read reports dating from April 1945 on the Russian occupation, which were terrible."

"Carry on, Mr. Reinhardt," said Mr. Rankin, after which he cleared his throat.

"It drizzled; the waiting was painful. My only worry was for my sister. Our parents had gone out to buy coal for the oven heaters."

Grandpa took a sip of tea.

"I heard nothing from the garden. Finally, the soldiers came out. I stared deeply into their faces to learn what might have happened. Their expressions looked the same as when they arrived."

Mr. Rankin snapped, "And what happened to Lottie?"

"I waited until the soldiers were out of sight and then scrambled into the house to the living area. The dining room's furniture was overturned, books scattered the floor, and they rolled the rugs to the side."

"What a horrendous ordeal!" Said the Mr. Davis.

"I ran upstairs; the rope ladder to the attic was gone. I had to balance on a chair with a large book pile to reach the attic hatch. I pushed with force, but the door didn't budge. Lottie, I cried, but there was no response."

Grandpa pursed his lips. His hands trembled.

"Are you fine?" The doctor asked, "You don't have to say anymore."

"Oh, but I must tell you what happened; it's burning me. I can't stay silent anymore."

I took a plaid green blanket from the sofa and laid it across Grandpa's legs. Grandpa continued, "As I tried to enter the attic, Daniel, our neighbour, knocked on the door. He told me of an accident up the road. A Russian convoy truck had collided with two people on a tandem, drawing a coal cart behind them. It was my parents. I broke down and told Daniel about the soldiers and Lottie. He said, First, let me help you open the attic door, and then we'll go to the hospital to see about your parents."

The cheesecake was sticking to the roof of my mouth. It became tough to swallow.

"Even with Daniel's help, I wasn't able to open the hatch. An apple tree grows near the house. I got on a branch and then inched up the iron ladder attached halfway up the rear wall. Chimney sweepers used it back in the day. It took me time to haul myself up the rungs. My arms were muscular in those days from lugging produce."

"Susanne," said Mr. Davis, "please stop chewing your thumbnail; you'll damage the side of the cuticle."

"Sorry, Mom calls it a sick habit; Grandpa, go on with the story."

"Should I follow you? Daniel asked. No, thanks," I told him. I wanted him to leave because I was afraid of what we'd find. Daniel loved Lottie; he wanted to marry her. He told me this one Sunday afternoon as we sat on the bank of the Havel, drinking our first beers while fishing eels. The eels were easy to catch as they swam near the banks under the shadows of weeping willows."

"It's understandable that you wanted him to leave," said Mr. Rankin.

"I smashed the attic window and climbed in. My eyes had to adjust to the dim light. A limp shadow of a person floated above the floor. To my horror, it was my lovely sister. She had hung herself. My legs gave way; I fell to the ground and wept."

"Oh, Grandpa, that's so awful."

"Yes, Susanne," said the retired doctor. "It is tragic."

I ran to the elderly man and hugged him; tears were streaming down his wrinkled cheeks.

"Before Lottie committed suicide, she pulled up the rope ladder and pushed a wooden trunk across the hatch."

Mr. Davis blew his nose and wiped the moisture from his eyes with a fusty white handkerchief.

"After what seemed like ages, I left the attic by the rope ladder. As night fell, I walked dazed to the hospital. Once there, a nurse took me to the basement mortuary. Sterile linen covered my parents; the nurse drew the sheets back. I identified them, gasping at the sight of their broken bodies."

"No wonder it sounds hellish," said the doctor.

"I told no one how my family died; I couldn't face it. For two years, I lived and slept in the barn with the chickens. After which, I plucked up the courage to live in the house and opened the store again."

"You're strong-willed, Grandpa; many would have crumbled in such a situation."

"I continued to live and work alone here for nineteen years until I married your grandmother, who was much younger than me, in 1964. She was an American-born army nurse who worked at the US compound with the doctor. Mr. Davis, do you remember when you introduced us to one another at the Thanksgiving Ball held in the officers' mess hall?"

"Her name was Lynn Stovall back then. She matched her cocktail dress, which had an embroidered leafy motif around the neckline, with a peach silk scarf."

"As you well know, she died from pneumonia last autumn."

Mr. Davis composed himself and said, "How you've suffered. I'm so sorry."

The doctor held Grandpa's right hand on the table.

"Mr. Davis," said Mr. Rankin.

"Yes."

"Why did you stay in Germany when the US troops withdrew in 1994?"

"I'm quite taken with Berlin, especially in this part of the city where I was stationed. The people are friendly, and *Zehlendorf* is rather green. Plus, I was up for retirement, and I've made Berlin my home."

"I see."

Grandpa straightened in his chair, announcing, "And now, for the reason that you're all here," Mr. Rankin's face was alert; he shifted in his seat, saying, "Yes, go on."

"I'm sorry, Susanne; you should know this, but you'll understand," Grandpa said quietly. "Lottie is still up in the attic." Grandpa blows his nose and says, "I couldn't move her, and I wanted no one to take her."

"What?" The police officer shouted, "I need to make a call."

"No, Lottie belongs here; you can't let them take her away. I thought you'd understand. Please. When you caught fish, you always threw them back into the river. You said you didn't want to take them from their home."

"Mr. Reinhardt-George, Lottie deserves a proper burial," the doctor said, his mouth wide open. "It's the decent thing to do; you owe her that much, don't you think?"

"No, no, that won't do; she belongs here, period. There's no need to disturb her. She is fine up there; Lottie has all she needs."

"You're not making sense, Mr. Reinhardt," said the police officer. "This is no laughing matter."

"Who's laughing?" Grandpa's top lip curled.

He made a face I'd never seen before, and it frightened me. Mr. Rankin lunged forward and leaned on the table to face my grandfather.

"An independent psychiatrist is being called in to assess your mental condition. Mr. Davis, as you witnessed the account of these historic events, make a statement at the station."

The police officer's authoritarian tone scoured my ears, and then it reeled in my head.

"By all means," grumbled the Mr. Davis, lowering his head.

"You must come too, Susanne."

I didn't have the strength to say or do anything.

Sirens surrounded the house—a house I used to love as the love I had for my grandpa waned. Two uniformed officers entered the house. They introduced themselves. The lawmen hurried to the attic, led by Mr. Rankin. He was in investigative mode. We waited for a short time in silence as Grandpa sobbed on his sleeve. Mr. Rankin returned with a grave look on his face and said, "Susanne, I'm sorry; I don't want to alarm you further." He paused and then said, "But we have found out there are, in fact, two corpses in the attic. We will have to do thorough tests to identify the deceased persons."

"What, there are two of them?"

"It's dark up there; we'll need spotlights. We have found a man's black shoe near the hatch and a skeleton, dressed in male clothes, slumped over a trunk."

"Good God, anything else?" Mr. Davis asked.

"I'm guessing, but I think it's Daniel. There has been significant vermin activity. The floor looks as if it's moving. We must bring in the pest control people. That's all I can say for now."

"I told you who one is," screamed grandpa while taking a swing at Mr. Rankin. "Lottie must stay."

An officer rushed to secure handcuffs on grandpa's wrists as he mumbled, "I trusted you, all of you, to look after Lottie. I wish I had never told you anything."

Death Arranged for the Archbishop
Mary Jo Rabe

Timotheus Hoppenstedt frowned and bent down the brim of his oversized, black fedora to cover his forehead and eyebrows on this chilly, wet Monday afternoon. He couldn't stop moving his scrawny, cold fingers over his cell phone. He wanted notification that he was getting his job back. Failing that, he wanted to hear from the auxiliary bishop.

Viciously indifferent automobiles, vans, motorcycles, and mopeds in the Pfaffengasse roared by, taking no notice of him. The street was a favorite shortcut for too many vehicles. Even the steady rain couldn't clear away the stench of motor exhaust. Timo coughed and shivered. He needed a drink.

The auxiliary bishop might think it unnecessarily risky for Timo to rest his bony backside here on the low brick wall at the intersection of the Pfaffengasse and Stolzstrasse. A few meters to his right, the slippery cobblestone path to the cathedral began, and tourists rushed around in both directions.

The employees of the chancery office would see him. It was five in the afternoon, a time when most of them surged out of the building and headed home. Some rushed to the underground employees' garage where he used to park his BMW, others to the streetcar stop at Oberbirken with its crowded wooden bench wrapped around an aged and dying linden tree, still others past the cathedral to various downtown bus stops.

Timo didn't want to go home. For the past month, he had spent far too much time brooding at home.

On the south side of the intersection the gargantuan, five-story, red sandstone chancery office building not only took up an entire block but also blocked out any haphazard rays of sunlight. He used to think the building was a magic castle where all his dreams came true. Now it was just a cold-hearted, stone monster that tossed him out onto the street.

On the north side of the intersection, residences of the bishops and priests who worked in the chancery office lined up contemptuously along the Pfaffengasse, each one rebuilt quickly, inefficiently, and identically in the 1950's after having been pulverized during a bombing rain in November of 1944.

Timo kept jerking his head back and forth. Looking to the right he saw the chancery office, looking left he could stare at the residence of Auxiliary Bishop Dr. Gabriel-Thomas Tellheim-van Enz, whom he intended to visit as soon as the good bishop left his office and went home. The bishop's corner office was up on the third floor of the chancery office building, lit up, easily visible from a discrete distance.

However, giving it more thought, even if homeward-bound employees did see him, due to his current circumstances no one would acknowledge him, much less try to talk to him. They no longer saw the most powerful layperson in the archdiocese, the finance genius the archbishop had elevated to the same level as the vicar general.

They would feign a busy tunnel vision and walk past a balding, gaunt, sixty-year-old man in a somewhat baggy, wet, brown suit, who had lost at least ten pounds during the past stressful month. Even the incompetents he personally had hired and the subordinates he had promoted averted their eyes as they marched past him toward the cathedral. So much for loyalty.

Fortunately, he didn't need the loyalty of Bishop Tellheim-van Enz. They had certain overlapping interests. Timo wanted his job back and he wanted to get back at the archbishop who had removed him from his position of honor and authority. The ambitious auxiliary bishop wanted to become the next archbishop, sooner rather than later.

How did it all come to this? Timo honestly didn't know. Thirty years ago, Herr Demeter hired him for the personnel department even though his grades in law school weren't that impressive and he had already been fired from two jobs because of supposed incompetence.

The next twenty years went by with only a few unimportant glitches. He then got along well with Herr Demeter's successor, Herr Ruppel. Until the catastrophe last month. But he didn't want to think about the past. The humiliation hurt too much. He stared at the bishop's office windows and pushed his hat to the back of his head.

At the same time, Auxiliary Bishop Dr. Gabriel-Thomas Tellheim-van Enz sat at his elegant, oversized desk and glanced out his office window. Once he achieved his goal, he was going to miss this magnificent office with windows to the west and north. He could see the cathedral in one direction and look down the street and see his house in the other, both panoramic views giving him a sense of pleasant anticipation.

The only flaw in the scene was that miserable lawyer Timotheus Hoppenstedt skulking around the path to the cathedral. What a loser. Still, one had to work with the material one had at hand.

The new office, the one befitting him, which he would occupy as soon as his actions were successful, was slightly smaller and located at the other end of the chancery office building. It was also the traditional office of the Archbishop of Fredburg. Sheltered from the internal noise of the chancery office and from the traffic on the Pfaffengasse, it offered a splendid view of the downtown Burgberg mountain.

That office indeed would do. Every time Bishop Tellheim-van Enz was in his future office, in his mind he started replacing the furniture.

His current office, however, was completely satisfactory for the time being. He was slowly filling it with the style and substance he deemed appropriate.

His secretary Frau Pauli was industrious and discrete. More importantly, she acquiesced to all his quirks, like always needing fresh cut flowers in his office. She dutifully brought new ones from the farmers' market around the cathedral every day. Today his office was filled with the fragrance of roses. A satisfactory working atmosphere.

The modest and humble lifestyle of the previous and current archbishops was, obviously, simply not to his taste. His huge desk was art-nouveau solid mahogany. Fortunately, the previous archbishop had been too busy with his second job as chairman of the German Bishops' Conference to take note of what kind of furniture Bishop Tellheim-van Enz ordered.

As a matter of tact and tactics, Bishop Tellheim-van Enz let everyone believe that the solid gold crucifix on the wall was just gold-plated. It had certain sentimental value as a gift from his sympathizers in Opus Dei after their machinations got the pope to select him to become auxiliary bishop. Naturally, Bishop Tellheim-van Enz couldn't officially join Opus Dei, what with the Archdiocese of Fredburg's liberal and progressive tendencies. But the members understood that he was one of them in his heart.

Auxiliary bishop was a fine stepping-stone to better things; he already found opportunities to make political and societal connections. However, only the position of archbishop would give him power, and, more importantly, access to money.

Just because previous archbishops had insisted on using the substantial church tax revenues for various projects helping the poor didn't mean that he had to. He would steer the archdiocese back in the direction approved by Opus Dei. Once he did that, his chances of becoming a cardinal would be excellent, as would chances for future, even more powerful positions in the Vatican.

Fortunately, Bishop Tellheim-van Enz was flexible. He had to be. Life was never predictable. After the previous archbishop died, the bishop's council was supposed to elect his colleague, the seventy-year-old auxiliary bishop, who would then serve until he turned seventy-five, when he would be forced to retire.

At that point, Bishop Tellheim-van Enz would have the right age and sufficient number of years experience as an auxiliary bishop to be the perfect candidate for archbishop. His friends in Opus Dei would make sure that he was on the candidate list from the Vatican, and the members of the bishop's council, whom he had been flattering and bribing ever since he became auxiliary bishop, would elect him.

Instead, the old auxiliary bishop removed himself from consideration, citing health issues. The bishop's council surprisingly elected the youthful head of the church court as the next archbishop. Archbishop Schlosser was even younger than Bishop Tellheim-van Enz. There was no way Bishop Tellheim-van Enz could succeed him, unless the good archbishop met a more timely demise.

Bishop Tellheim-van Enz stood up and stretched. Some of his admirers, of whom there were a sufficient number for the time being, worried that he was too thin, but he ran almost every day for the express purpose of maintaining the same athletic physique he had had as a theology student.

Frau Salbei, his obedient housekeeper whom he inherited from his predecessor, was willing to cook healthy meals and desserts completely devoid of sugar. He prudently drank only mineral water, though did indulge in the few sips of wine at Eucharist services.

Since no one was around, he pulled out the hand mirror in top drawer of his desk. His full head of thick, dark-brown hair was speckled with some attractive streaks of gray. His appearance was perfect, except that the lack of subcutaneous fat had certain unfortunate consequences for his face. The wrinkles were increasing in number and depth.

There was no way he could get away with cosmetic surgery at present. Such obvious vanity would prevent his imminent election to the position of archbishop soon after the current one suffered his unpredictable accident.

It was raining harder, but probably time to be on his way home. Herr Hoppenstedt would no doubt follow twenty steps behind him and then knock on his door, while acting as if he didn't know whether the auxiliary bishop was there or not.

Of course, he did have to invite Herr Hoppenstedt to supper, since they had serious detailed planning to do. Fortunately, he had warned Frau Salbei that Herr Hoppenstedt would come for some pastoral counseling this evening, perfectly understandable considering the difficult situation in which Herr Hoppenstedt found himself.

Claiming he wanted to save Frau Salbei some work, because he could not know how long the counseling would take, he had suggested that she prepare an especially modest repast and then take the evening off. She had nodded gratefully.

As on most late afternoons, Director of the Diocesan Archives Dr. Frank Wetzel peered over the sixteenth century medieval investiture transcript from Konradingen that he had spread out over his desk. He had been working on an annotated edition for years now.

His sixty-year-old hips twinged ominously as he stood up to go turn on his office light. He preferred to work by natural sunlight, but the archives were half underground, it was November, it had started to rain, and at five in the afternoon, it was too dark to work without artificial light.

Now that he was up, he shuffled over to the reading room to see if any archives users were still there. No, nobody. No local historians. No hobby genealogists still peering at baptismal records on the microform readers and hoping to discover they were descended from royalty. Even the young priest who needed help deciphering old handwriting for his dissertation had left for the day. Maybe Frank should also go home and change into some comfortable clothes.

He was a short man who tried to get people to take him seriously by always dressing in professional attire, coming to work every day in a suit and tie. He didn't consider himself an athlete but was a passionate hiker. Up until last year, he always hiked up and around the Burgberg for an hour before supper. Most weekends he spent on all-day hikes throughout the Black Forest.

Hiking had been excellent for his heart and lungs, unfortunately not so great for his bones and joints. For the past twelve months, his hip joints started to let him down. Right now he felt stabbing pains in both of his legs even though he had only shuffled around the archives rooms all day.

His doctor kept babbling about arthrosis and hip replacement surgery, but Frank truly couldn't be bothered. Herr Kaiser, the evil head of personnel whom Frank frequently and vociferously exposed as an idiot and a liar, had been trying to get rid of him ever since Frank turned sixty last year, and Frank didn't want to give the bastard any ammunition to shoot him down with.

Frank simply enjoyed blurting out unwelcome truths when people started lying. He knew where all the bodies were buried and how to annoy people with loud, inconvenient revelations. It wasn't, perhaps, always tactically shrewd, especially in a bureaucracy, but it amused him.

As diocesan archivist, he knew too much, or more precisely, knew everything. Only he and the archbishop had access to the secret files; as diocesan archivist, he naturally had access to all the files. He had mentioned this to the newly elected archbishop a few years ago and offered to bring him any personnel files he might want. But Archbishop Schlosser said he was only interested in how people did their jobs now, not what they had done in the past.

Frank had liked this naïve, young archbishop immediately. Archbishop Schlosser was intelligent, hard working, and easy-going, a man in his mid-forties with curly, blond hair and more kilos than absolutely necessary. This archbishop genuinely wanted to know how his employees were doing and how he himself could do a better job.

Frank and the archbishop indulged in frequent, politically incorrect conversations. After most of the employees had left the building the archbishop often came to the archives to let off steam and complain about the idiocy he was surrounded by. He appreciated Frank as his most discrete listener.

Archbishop Schlosser was also a frequent and enthusiastic customer in the employee cafeteria where he ate lunch when he was in town. Every now and then, he showed up at the employee coffee kitchens on each floor of the chancery office to chat with whoever was there and see what there might be to nibble on.

Frank first suspected that Herr Hoppenstedt was in serious trouble when all of a sudden last month the archbishop wanted to see his personnel file. Herr Hoppenstedt, a mediocre lawyer at best but still vastly more intelligent than the current head of personnel, had been transferred out of the personnel department into the finance department some ten years before.

Then two years ago the new archbishop, himself an expert at canon law, determined that the archdiocese lacked an official diocesan Finance Officer, as defined by canon law Can. 494, §1 "in every diocese the bishop is to appoint a finance officer who is truly expert in financial affairs and absolutely distinguished for honesty".

Unfortunately, the archbishop then chose Herr Hoppenstedt for this position. Frank could have warned the archbishop about Herr Hoppenstedt's dubious qualifications at this point, but he took the archbishop at his word, that he didn't want to know about people's pasts.

Then two months ago, the tax people, accompanied by the police, showed up at the chancery office asking about various discrepancies that the archdiocesan Finance Officer was responsible for. The errors were cumulative rather than criminal, just the result of a combined stupidity and laziness on the part of the Finance Officer. However, the money the archdiocese owed the government was considerable.

The archbishop then defined this as a grave mistake and invoked canon law Can 494 §2 "The finance officer is not to be removed while in this function except for a grave cause to be assessed by the bishop."

When Frank brought the archbishop Herr Hoppenstedt's personnel file, the archbishop grimaced and asked, "Herr Dr. Wetzel, could you perhaps use a new employee in the archives?"

Hoping that the archbishop was making a bad joke, Frank looked around the inexpensively furnished office before he sat down and answered, "I sort of hoped that those days were long gone, when the archbishop moved all his problem employees into the archives."

"Yeah," the archbishop said, folding his hands on his cluttered desk. For the first time, Frank thought the man looked older than his forty-five years. Taking off his horn-rimmed glasses, the archbishop said, "My predecessors had it easier. Don't worry; I think too much of your archives to move my mistakes into them. We'll put Herr Hoppenstedt on administrative leave, justified by grave cause."

"With pay?" Frank asked out of curiosity.

"Yeah," the archbishop answered. "In the hopes of getting him out of the way. He has permanent civil-service status with us and would be impossible to fire. Besides, he also has only four more years until he retires. Paying him his salary and telling him to stay home costs a fair amount of money, but peanuts in comparison to the damage he has already caused the archdiocese. I don't even want to think about how much more damage he would cause if I let him stay."

The archbishop looked out his window. Frank had the impression that the archbishop now wished he had never taken on this job.

In the weeks that followed, Herr Hoppenstedt complained loudly to all the other employees, gave sobbing interviews to the newspapers and television stations, begging for his job back.

Eventually the archbishop took away his keys to the chancery office building and notified the doorkeepers that Herr Hoppenstedt was forbidden to enter the building. After that, people frequently saw Herr Hoppenstedt skulking around outside.

Hmm. Bolts of pain in both hips, no difference whether he stood, walked slowly, or sat. It was definitely time for Frank to go home. A warm bath often took away the pain. He was glad he had kept his cheap efficiency apartment just down the street from the chancery office. Even limping, he could be home in ten minutes.

He cranked down the loud, metal shutters on the windows in the reading room facing the street so that no one could break in. Looking out, he saw the young auxiliary bishop walk down the Pfaffengasse. Herr Hoppenstedt sat on the wall, drenched in the rain, and watched the auxiliary bishop walk by. Once said bishop was no longer in view, Herr Hoppenstedt stood up and raced down the street.

Frank shook his head. Who was Herr Hoppenstedt stalking now?

Frank checked all the rooms in the archives, turned off the lights, and then left the building via the Pfaffengasse exit where he had fewer steps to navigate. His hips didn't like it when he walked up or down steps.

Frank pulled the hood of his coat over his head and walked slowly, hoping to appease his hips. As he walked past the auxiliary bishop's house, he saw the bishop and Herr Hoppenstedt through the bishop's dining room window.

Now that was interesting. The auxiliary bishop wasn't famous for his empathy, his hospitality, or his willingness to listen to anyone. Maybe Herr Hoppenstedt had worn him down. Frank continued on his way home.

The traffic in the Pfaffengasse hadn't decreased. One of the other Fredburg north-south streets was probably backed up. However, in the dining room Herr Hoppenstedt complained loudly enough for Bishop Tellheim-van Enz to hear him above the noise.

"Herr Bishop, don't you have anything stronger to drink?" Timo asked, nervously fooling with the cell phone in his pants pocket.

Bishop Tellheim-van Enz shook his head and spread a minimal amount of margarine over the thin slice of dark bread and poured himself a glass of mineral water. He ignored the small plate of sliced Gouda cheese next to the plate of sliced bread.

Timo, clothes still dripping with rainwater, took his hands out of his pockets, piled three slices of cheese on his bread, wolfed it down, and shivered. Bishop Tellheim-van Enz didn't heat any rooms unnecessarily not even in November. Warmth would only increase the stench from Herr Hoppenstedt's wet clothes.

"Nothing alcoholic, Herr Bishop?" Timo asked.

Bishop Tellheim-van Enz managed to suppress his snarl. That was another thing he would change once he became archbishop. He would insist on "Your Excellency" as the required form of address for bishops. Being called merely bishop was insulting for a priest of his station.

Bishop Tellheim-van Enz chewed slowly. Chewing and swallowing slowly not only made him appreciate the taste more, it gave him the illusion of fullness so that he ate less. He drank his glass of mineral water just as slowly. Control was everything. "No," Bishop Tellheim-van Enz said. "I only drink mineral water, and I prefer for you to be sober while we make our plans."

Herr Hoppenstedt glared at him and piled three more slices of cheese on a slice of bread. He poured himself a glass of mineral water and drank it in one gulp. He resembled an escaped convict. What little hair he had left on his head had been cut to a minimal length, almost shaved. The style didn't flatter him. Neither did his puffy, bloodshot eyes.

Bishop Tellheim-van Enz sighed. Again, you had to work with the material at hand. In this case, it was probably most efficient to be direct.

"Herr Hoppenstedt, I need you to kill the archbishop," Bishop Tellheim-van Enz said. "Then I can become his successor and I can fix things for you."

Timo shook his head and whined, "No, no way. I'm not a murderer. I just want my job back. I deserve my job back."

"Actually," Bishop Tellheim-van Enz interrupted him. "You don't want your job back as much as you want your high position back. You want the honor and prestige that comes with being the Finance Officer of the archdiocese, not the actual work involved."

Timo stared at him. "I deserved the high position I got," he said.

"From what I've heard," Bishop Tellheim-van Enz began. "There were many complaints about your work over the years."

"All unjustified," Timo insisted. "Some of the people I hired didn't turn out to be good enough. But how could I have known that? I thought they were fine. Then back in the 1980's, I volunteered to introduce computers into the chancery office. I already had a computer at home, so I knew what needed to be done."

Bishop Tellheim-van Enz said dryly, "But from what I've heard, the expensive mainframes with dummy keyboards and black-and-white monitors you selected never worked right and had to be replaced with networked PC's after only two years. The unique software that came with the package was incompatible with every other program and a waste of time for the secretaries who had to learn how to work with it."

"How was I to know that Microsoft software would replace Lamb?" Herr Hoppenstedt grumbled. "Back then no software was compatible with any other."

"But the point was," Bishop Tellheim-van Enz continued. "You cost the chancery office a million marks with your computer work. Later when the chancery office introduced electronic time tracking, you only let the IT people buy the cheapest hardware. The time-tracking software kept crashing until the IT people went to the vicar general who overruled you and ordered adequate devices."

"Herr Demeter in the personnel department never criticized me," Timo said.

Bishop Tellheim-van Enz didn't bother to reply that Herr Demeter's dementia had been a poorly kept secret in the archdiocese, and that his successor Herr Kaiser wasn't considered much more competent. He tried to dredge up enough patience to manipulate Herr Hoppenstedt sufficiently.

"Yes, yes," Bishop Tellheim-van Enz said. "I agree that you have been treated unfairly, and if I were archbishop, I would give you your job back immediately. But as a lowly auxiliary bishop, there is nothing I can do. You have to help me become archbishop if you want your high position back. The present archbishop won't help you. He thinks it was a mistake to have given you this high position in the first place."

"So we have to kill the archbishop?" Herr Hoppenstedt asked, piling more cheese on the next slice of bread.

"You, not we", Bishop Tellheim-van Enz thought.

Trying to appear sympathetic, he looked at Herr Hoppenstedt sadly and said, "I know it's hard. Think about how unfair Archbishop Schlosser was to you. He will never give you your job back, but I will. There is no way we can get the archbishop to step down voluntarily. I honestly don't see any other possibility than eliminating him."

Timo shook his head. "You're right, you're right," he said. "I want my job back. I want the recognition. I want the people to be in awe of me, especially the ones who gossip behind my back. But I don't know if I can kill anyone."

"I understand," Bishop Tellheim-van Enz said soothingly and took another calculated sip of mineral water. "You are a good person, but a person who is in a situation where he doesn't have a choice. You deserve your job back. The only thing between you and the job you deserve is the archbishop. And we'll be in this together. I'll help you."

Timo glared at him and stuck his hands back into his pockets.

Trying another strategy, Bishop Tellheim-van Enz said, "After all, no one lives forever in this world. The archbishop will just be on his way to heaven a little sooner than he might have thought. As Christians, we believe in eternal life. It's only a temporary change in the order of things."

"But how?" Herr Hoppenstedt said.

"Finally," Bishop Tellheim-van Enz thought. Now they could get down to discussing a practical plan.

"Accidents happen," Bishop Tellheim-van Enz began. "We all know that. And sometimes they have regrettable consequences."

"An accident," Herr Hoppenstedt's eyes lit up. "Then I wouldn't have to kill anyone. It would all just be an accident."

"Well, a planned accident," Bishop Tellheim-van Enz said. "I'll smuggle you into the chancery office at six in the morning on Friday when no one else is there. You'll have to hide in various basement rooms until evening. You are, after all, forbidden to enter the building."

"At precisely six in the evening the archbishop will get an e-mail that looks like it came from the chairman of the employees' council asking him to come up to the newest employees' smoking area on the fifth floor, an outdoor stone porch with a low wall around it. That's where you will be waiting and will make sure that the archbishop falls over the open porch wall five stories to the street."

"But if I push him, that is murder," Timo said.

"No, no," Bishop Tellheim-van Enz said soothingly. "You will be justifiably angry about your job. You try to talk to the archbishop and make sure that he stands next to the wall. Then you will shove the archbishop just because you are angry and he will happen to fall over the wall onto the street. It will be a regrettable accident and you will certainly not have to report it. It will simply be best for you to hide in the building again until I let you out on Saturday."

"And then everything will be all right. I'll become archbishop, you'll get your job back, and we will both be happy."

Frank sat at his kitchen table with his bottle of Ginter beer from the local Fredburg brewery and a sausage and fried egg sandwich. His legs and hips felt much better. The bath had helped, but unlike other days, it didn't make him sleepy, even though he had had a long, strenuous day. He couldn't get the picture of Auxiliary Bishop Tellheim-van Enz and Herr Hoppenstedt out of his mind.

What could Herr Hoppenstedt be doing in the residence of the auxiliary bishop? Herr Hoppenstedt was on paid administrative leave and forbidden to enter the chancery office. He had no work-related issues to discuss with an auxiliary bishop. More to the point, the auxiliary bishop wasn't known for suffering fools gladly and up until a month ago had never given Herr Hoppenstedt the time of day. It was very unlikely that the auxiliary bishop wanted to do Herr Hoppenstedt any favors.

Frank had a kind of pragmatic horse sense about people, partly due to his age and partly due to having worked in the chancery office for over forty years. He remembered that Agatha Christie had once let Miss Marple explain that you could learn a great deal about evil by living in a village. The same was true about working in a bureaucracy, even or especially a religion-based one.

Herr Hoppenstedt was a stupid fool, and Bishop Tellheim-van Enz was a sociopath who never wasted his precious time. Why would the two of them be dining together at the bishop's house?

The next morning Frank deliberately left his apartment later than usual, planning to say his legs were bothering him if anyone asked. He knew that the auxiliary bishop was always in his office by seven thirty. Walking slowly wasn't painful.

As luck and plan would have it, when he got to Bishop Tenheim-van Enz's house, he felt that he needed to sit down, and so he rang the bell. Cecilia Salbei opened the door almost immediately.

"Frank, I'm so glad to see you," she said. They were old friends, ever since Frank got her the housekeeper's job with the previous auxiliary bishop. She was Frank's age and just as well preserved, with medium length, thin, straight white hair, a slightly chubby physique, and sparkling blue eyes that didn't miss a trick.

"Cecilia," he said. "Thanks. Can I come in for a few minutes?"

She pointed toward the dining room. "I'm glad you stopped by," she said. Her usual cheerful face was slightly contorted by a worried frown.

"I called you in the archives, but you weren't there," she said. "I heard a troubling conversation last night, and I don't know if I should take it seriously. And if I do, I don't know what to do about it. If I go to the police, no one will believe me."

Frank walked in slowly. The house smelled like detergent, cleanser, and glass cleaner. Cecilia had always been a diligent housekeeper, first for her beloved husband and, although she didn't need the money, after he died, for the previous auxiliary bishop. As she told Frank, she needed to keep busy, and housekeeping was something she was good at.

All these chancery office houses in the Pfaffengasse had the same impractical floor plan, a huge staircase in the middle of the hall and many small rooms with thin walls branching off around it. Sounds bounced through the bare walls. He could hear the kitchen appliances clearly as he walked into the dining room on the right.

"Between Herr Hoppenstedt and your boss?" Frank asked as he sat at the long, light-brown table. "I saw the two of them through the window on my way home yesterday and wondered what on earth they would have to talk about."

"The bishop told me to take the evening off," Cecilia said as she sat down next to him. "But I had nowhere to go on such short notice, and so I stayed in my room. Around five-thirty I heard loud voices."

"You room is exactly opposite to this room, isn't it," Frank said. "So, if you wanted to, you could listen in on conversations here."

"Easily, even with my door shut, especially since the bishop didn't bother to close the dining room door," Cecilia admitted. "But I can't believe what I heard, so I'm glad I can talk to you about it. It sounded like they're planning to murder the archbishop."

Frank looked up at her. "Your hearing is excellent for your age. If that's what you heard, that's what they said. You've been working for him for a couple of years now. What do you think of this auxiliary bishop?"

Cecilia looked him in the eye. "I can't complain," she began cautiously. "As an employer he has always behaved correctly. He considers me useful and doesn't do anything that would make me want to quit. Otherwise, he has absolutely no interest in me. "

"He can control himself, and he has learned proper manners. He almost never entertains here in his house, but whenever these dubious Opus Dei people show up at the door, he takes them out to eat at the exclusive Waldseemueller Hotel."

"And?" Frank asked.

"And, he is a monster, a sociopath, completely incapable of caring what happens to other people. He thinks he is the only person in the world who matters. I've stayed with him because I felt useful here, and, as I said, he doesn't treat me badly. He never raises his voice or complains. In my opinion, though, he is more than capable of murdering someone, if he thought such a murder would be useful to him."

Frank nodded. "That's pretty much what I've always thought about him, too. How safe are you? Will the bishop suspect that you overheard the conversation?"

"No," Cecilia said firmly. "He never pays any attention to what I do. He gave me the evening off and then forgot about me. I went into my room and took a nap until the loud voices woke me up. I didn't have any lights on, and my door stayed shut. I heard the entire conversation."

"After the bishop got rid of Herr Hoppenstedt, these Opus Dei people rang the bell — I recognized their voices — and the bishop left with them. By the time the he returned, I was asleep."

"That's good," Frank said. "So, how and when are they planning to kill the archbishop?"

"Late Friday afternoon," she said. "They are going to lure the archbishop up to the fifth floor where the employees' smoking area is, that drafty open-air porch. Herr Hoppenstedt will then jump out from behind a pillar and push the archbishop over the edge so that he falls to the street and dies."

"Tell me everything you can remember," Frank said. "Then I'll talk to the archbishop. And, I have some police friends we can talk to."

Frank strolled slowly down the Pfaffengasse, partly not to call attention to himself and partly because his hip joints were starting to hurt. He used his key to enter the side door of the chancery office and went into the archives. His three archivists were all at their computers, and the reading room was already full of genealogists.

It was past nine, and so the archbishop would be in the Tuesday morning meeting with the chancery office priests and heads of departments. On Tuesdays, the archbishop's secretary Sister Gertrudis always left for her noon break early, knowing that the archbishop would rush back hungry and then immediately leave for lunch in the employees' cafeteria.

Frank would wait in the archbishop's office as soon as Sister Gertrudis was gone. As the diocesan archivist, he had a key to all the offices.

It was twelve-thirty. Frank sat on the uncomfortable, plain wooden chair in front of the archbishop's desk when the archbishop came through the door. The wooden floor shuddered a little under his weight. "Herr Dr. Wetzel," Archbishop Schlosser said. He looked surprised. "Can I help you?"

Frank stood up, though his hips rebelled a little. "Archbishop, do you have a few minutes for me?" he asked.

Archbishop Schlosser sat down behind his modest desk and ran his hands through his blond curly hair. "What's on your mind, Herr Archives Director?"

"I'm glad you're already sitting down," Frank said and looked the archbishop in the eye. "I think you need to trust me. I have reason to believe that Bishop Tellheim-van Enz and Herr Hoppenstedt plan to kill you."

"All right," Archbishop Schlosser said, obviously startled. "You have my full attention."

Frank told him everything he had observed and what he heard from Frau Salbei. When he was finished, the archbishop got up and lumbered over to the east window. "I like to look at the Burgberg mountain when things get too unpleasant in the chancery office," he said. "The view is very soothing."

"Anyone else might find your story unbelievable," the archbishop continued. "But in the short time I have been archbishop, I have learned to trust the diocesan archivist. He knows everything and has excellent judgment with regard to the other employees. So what do you advise?"

"Well, first we need to inform the police and request police protection," Frank said. "It's not enough for you to just stay in your office on Friday. Then your murderous auxiliary bishop will come up with a new plan."

"An old friend of mine from college is a police detective here in Fredburg. We should talk to him. I think it would be best if undercover police officers were here. They can decide how to protect you. If there is a way to catch Herr Hoppenstedt without endangering you, they might know it. Then we just have to find a way to prove that the auxiliary bishop was in on the plan."

Archbishop Schlosser made some phone calls and then left for the cafeteria, promising to go on to the police station after he had something to eat. Frank went back to the archives and called Cecilia. He suggested that they stroll to the police station in about an hour. By then the murderous auxiliary bishop would be back in his office. The man never changed his schedule.

Frank met Cecilia at her door after he saw the auxiliary bishop enter the chancery office. The view from the archives windows facing the street was often useful. Since his hips hurt again, they took the streetcar to the Fredburg North police station, an old red sandstone building where the archbishop was waiting at the door.

Police Commissioner Matula, a short and stocky, balding man in his sixties, immediately invited the three of them to his office. "Please sit down," he said. "Great to see you again," he said to Frank. "What can I do for you?"

"Prevent a murder," Frank said dryly.

"That fits my job description," Commissioner Matula said. "Whose?"

Frank told him everything they knew. Commissioner Matula wasn't at all skeptical, on the contrary was very helpful. He said three undercover police officers, claiming to be from the office for workplace safety, would come and examine the fifth floor porch area on Wednesday.

Three different police officers would spend Friday in the chancery office and make their way to the fifth floor in the late afternoon, making sure that Herr Hoppenstedt didn't see them. Once the archbishop got the e-mail that was to lure him to the fifth floor, he would call the police officers and not proceed until they gave him permission. The police officers would prevent the archbishop from coming to harm. That was the top priority.

Frank suggested having the police officers claim to be genealogists on Friday so that they could wait in the archives where no one would notice them. The archbishop wondered how they would then be able to prove that he was to be murdered if the police officers prevented anything from happening. Commissioner Matula asked him to trust the police to get sufficient evidence; that was their job.

"All right," Archbishop Schlosser said. "You do your job, and I'll get back to doing mine."

"Just follow our instructions," Commissioner Matula said. "We will protect you and see that those who try to harm you are prosecuted."

The three of them left. The archbishop walked back to his office, and Frank invited Cecilia to cake and coffee at a nearby café. "Do you know where the auxiliary bishop will be on Friday?" Frank asked her.

"He has a confirmation celebration in Neckarbrudersheim on Friday afternoon, and so his chauffeur will pick him up around noon. It's a three-hour drive each way. They won't return until Saturday afternoon," she said.

"Can you stand the uncertainty until Friday?" Frank asked.

"No problem," she said. "The auxiliary bishop won't pay any attention to me; he never does. And I have already told him that I'm taking the weekend off to visit my sister, so I'll be gone if and when the police talk to him."

"Don't take any risks," Frank said. "If you have any misgivings, let me know."

Frank was more worried than he wanted to let on. As an archivist, he knew better than to underestimate the evil that human beings were capable of. Friday morning he saw Herr Hoppenstedt skulking around the archives rooms in the basement but made sure that Herr Hoppenstedt didn't notice him. Herr Hoppenstedt seemed to be fairly drunk already by eight in the morning.

Late Friday afternoon the three police officers stopped peering at the church records in the archives reading room and left discretely. Frank saw them get into the elevator. Then the archbishop called him. "It's on. I got an e-mail from the employees' council asking me to come to the smoking porch on the fifth floor. I called the police officers in your archives, and I'm off," he said. "Wish us luck."

"Be careful," Frank told him. "No matter what, don't get near the porch wall." Frank put down the phone and walked around his office. Then he walked into the reading room. Then he looked out onto the Pfaffengasse. Then he limped back to his office.

Frank was worried. What if something went wrong? Something could always go wrong. Maybe it was too risky for the archbishop to be the bait. What if Herr Hoppenstedt had a weapon? Could even three police officers stop a determined killer?

Minutes later Frank saw the three police officers drag a handcuffed Herr Hoppenstedt out of the elevator. The archbishop followed them to the side door of the chancery office and then came back to the archives.

"So, what happened?" Frank asked him. "Are you okay?" Frank motioned for the archbishop to follow into Frank's office. Frank sank into his office chair to the relief of his hip joints.

"Everything went as planned," Archbishop Schlosser said, leaning on the doorframe and breathing heavily. "I went up to the employees' smoking area. Suddenly Herr Hoppenstedt lurched out of the shadows and stumbled over toward me yelling about how he wanted his job back. He tried to run into me, but fell over his own two feet. When he stood up and tried to shove me, the three policemen came out of their hiding places and grabbed him."

"Herr Hoppenstedt started crying, yelling that he wasn't a bad person, that the auxiliary bishop forced him to make the archbishop have an accident and fall to the street."

"So he admitted everything," Frank said. "With the testimony of Frau Salbei that should be enough to press charges against the auxiliary bishop, shouldn't it?"

"Even better," Archbishop Schlosser said as he sat down next to Frank's desk. "It turns out that we underestimated Herr Hoppenstedt. He may not be the brightest bulb in anyone's lamp, but he is nicely paranoid. He kept his cell phone on record while he was at the auxiliary bishop's Monday night. The police have the whole conversation. No matter what the auxiliary bishop thinks he has for an alibi, he has convicted himself with his own voice."

"And what are you going to do?" Frank asked. "Traditionally, archbishops tended to push scandals under the rug so as not to upset the faithful churchgoers."

"Well," Archbishop Schlosser began. "On the one hand, of course I am expected to forgive any trespasses against me. On the other hand, when I became archbishop, I promised complete transparency as far as the church was concerned."

"I gave the helpful police officers the telephone number of the parish priest in Neckarbrudersheim where the auxiliary bishop should have arrived by now. The police there will arrest him. I will press charges, and will make myself available to the media for any and all questions."

"Good for you," Frank said. "Can I invite you to a beer in your favorite restaurant across the street?"

"Only if you ask Frau Salbei if she would be willing to continue to take care of the house until the pope names a new auxiliary bishop. That could take over a year. Naturally the archdiocese will continue to pay her salary."

Frank cranked down the metal shutters in the reading room, and he and the archbishop left through the side entrance.

For Your Love
Denise Johnson

Hal Burton arrived on scene first. A seasoned investigator going on twenty-three years with the force, he still enjoyed working as a patrol officer. Monsoon season had ended and a chill hung in the air, despite the early evening hour.

Police tape surrounded the modest two-story stucco house, located near Old Town Scottsdale. The homes were set close together, just ten feet apart from one another. A U.S. flag hung nearly limp from the flagpole out front. Off to the right of the concrete porch, he waited for Sadie to arrive. While the fresh air was nice, the scent of a far-off wildfire was not. An unmarked SUV pulled up and he watched as she exited the vehicle.

"Hey, Hal. How are you doing?"

He enjoyed his cases with the young female detective, who was bright and not overly bubbly. "Can't complain."

Her newly cropped bob bounced as she nodded. "What do we have?"

He shook his head. "Don't know, figured I'd wait for you before heading in."

Inside, the home's décor was mid-century modern. A piano sat near the stairs and there were piles of record albums stacked alongside the couch. Perhaps, they were meant to take the place of coffee tables, Hal surmised.

Officer Long led them to the body. A white male clothed in navy blue pajamas lay splayed out on his back. A knife protruded from below his abdomen, blood pooled around him.

"Do we have a time of death yet?" Sadie crouched down, careful not to let her department issued windbreaker touch the floor.

Long shook his head. "Coroner hasn't been here yet. We interviewed a witness who heard shouting coming from this house about an hour ago. Sally Genovese. She lives across the street."

The timeline made sense to Hal since the victim's blood was beginning to coagulate.

"Did the witness say whether the voices were male or female?" Sadie asked.

"Both male, according to the witness." Long answered.

"Any insight into the vic?" Hal liked that he could ask whatever was on his mind and not have to worry that Sadie would be offended. He wasn't out to take anyone's job, but he did enjoy the thrill of a new investigation.

Long nodded. "This guy was really into music. Guess he was in a band at one time. A collector, too. That piano, over there, was owned by some famous musician."

He pointed towards a shiny, black Steinway in the corner.

"Oh, when we arrived, there was music playing on that over there," Long directed their attention toward a bookshelf next to the fireplace where a vintage, suitcase-style record player and its speakers stood.

The olive-green player was much like the one Hal had gotten at a flea market as a kid.

Sadie walked over and peered down at the record still on the player. "The Yardbirds, For Your Love." She shook her head and looked at Hal.

"Really, you've never heard that song?" Hal motioned to Long who still wore his protective gloves. "Can you play that?"

The young officer nodded and placed the needle on the record. The song came on and Hal was instantly transported back to his childhood kitchen, listening to the tune while his mother fixed dinner.

"It's a catchy tune, don't you think?" Hal mouthed the chorus. "They were a big UK band in the mid-60s."

Sadie's eyes widened in recognition. "Oh, wait. I think my parents had that album."

"Ouch. Let's keep our age difference out of it," Hal joked.

"There were a lot of bands named after bugs and animals back then," she added.

She had a point. The Animals, the Beatles, the Monkees, the Turtles. Hal didn't know why that was.

"Here's a little-known fact, Eric Clapton was a member and played guitar on that track," said Hal.

"Really?" Sadie asked.

Hank nodded, pleased he could offer a morsel of information that she hadn't known.

When the song was over Sadie stood up and glanced at him. "Let's take a look around."

They began inspecting the rooms in the home. Each one was more colorful than the next. The half bath downstairs was painted a deep maroon color and decorated with what appeared to be small, wooden hand drums and shakers. Nothing seemed out of place, so they moved on to another room on the first floor, a den. The deep blue walls, covered with album covers, made the room seem a bit claustrophobic. But then, Hal's opinion shouldn't matter much. He had no eye for home décor, instead relying on a widowed neighbor to assist him on paint and furniture decisions.

"Do you see that?" Sadie pointed to a nail protruding from the wall. "I wonder what hung there?"

They finished their cursory inspection of the den and headed down a long hallway toward the kitchen. The bright yellow walls held many framed photos of various sizes of Rock and Roll greats of the 50s and 60s, some were even signed. Sadie had already made it into the kitchen when he called out to her.

"I think I may have found the answer." The photo he stood before showed the victim smiling proudly as he pointed to a guitar that hung on his den wall. A closer look revealed the Fender guitar was signed by Clapton.

Sadie made her way back to where Hal stood. "A theft and a murder. Do you think it was worth anything?"

"Most things signed are worth something to someone." Hal noticed Officer Long and walked over to him.

"My partner has been going door to door interviewing neighbors and one interrupted him asking why the music was back on. I thought you might like to speak to him. His name is Gary Winston." He pointed toward the front door.

Sadie had made her way to the two and motioned for Hal to go ahead. "I'll take the rooms upstairs."

Hal could hear the man before he caught a glimpse of him.

"Why the heck is that music on? I had to listen to his damn music over and over some nights. I swear he was obsessed! He'd play the same albums over and over."

Hal opened the door wider to see a portly man, in his mid-forties, neatly dressed in pressed khaki pants and a blue button-down shirt.

"Good evening sir, I'm Officer Hal Burton. I understand you are a neighbor of the deceased?" Hal gestured to Officer Long to leave them alone.

"Yes, yes. I live right there." He pointed toward a virtually identical home to the deceased's, except there was a well-manicured lawn in place of river rock.

"Alright, why don't we head over there, where it's quieter." Hal gestured to the man's home.

"I can't believe how much attention this has gotten." He shook his head and quickly ran his fingers through the sides of his jet-black hair.

They walked up to Gary's bright red front door.

"Gary, would you mind if I went inside your house to view the victim's home from here?"

Gary paused. "Uh, sure."

As he opened the door, Hal cruised past him trying to get a glimpse of as much as he could. While he kept it tidy on the outside, the inside was a different story. The foyer, living room and hall were filled with boxes.

"You moving?"

"No, I'm an online e-tailer."

Hal nodded as he turned into the kitchen.

"Officer Burton, you took a wrong turn. You can see his house from the dining room."

Hal peeked out into the hall. "My bad. Too many scenes in one day." A small white lie.

Through the window in the dining room, he noticed he could see quite a bit of the home's interior. He caught a glimpse of Sadie standing near one of the victim's windows.

"So, is e-tailing a lucrative business?" Hal asked.

Gary's posture loosened. "It's tough, a lot of competitors but it's more about making your own hours and not being controlled by anyone."

Hal nodded, silent as his eyes remained affixed on Gary, who seemed to recognize he was under scrutiny and stiffened.

"Alright, Gary. Thanks for your hospitality. We're going to continue speaking to the homeowners on this block before it gets too late."

Sadie met Hal outside. "How did it go?"

"He's a nervous guy, for sure, but seems a bit meek." Hal pointed across the street. "Should we head over to the witness' home?"

Sadie nodded and as they were about to cross the mostly desolate street, Hal noticed a car without its headlights on barreling at them. "Whoa!"

It was a beater to be sure, an old 1990s maroon Honda. There was considerable rust on it, not often seen in the Southwest. Sadie rushed over to the driver's side door, where she met the female driver, a young woman in her mid-20s, just as she stepped out of the vehicle.

"Ma'am, you need to slow down," Sadie said, flashing her badge.

The girl, dressed in all black, giggled. "*Ma'am,*" she repeated in a mocking tone. "I'm a little young to be called *ma'am*, don't you think?"

Just then, Sally Genovese stepped out of her house. "Julie!" She admonished the young woman. "How many times have I told you to slow down?" Mrs. Genovese adjusted her gaze to the investigators. "You must be the two I was told to speak to by that young officer."

Hal nodded. "Yes, we're investigating the death across the street."

Mrs. Genovese moved her rotund body away from the front door to allow Hal and Sadie in. "Please come in."

Hal followed, while Sadie lingered, choosing to follow Julie inside.

Colorful, floral wallpaper lined the foyer. The house was smartly furnished, and the décor seemed to highlight the dark wood that adorned the fireplace mantel and staircase. Mrs. Genovese directed Hal and Sadie to sit in the living room.

"Julie, come and help me make some tea for our guests," she said, as she continued into the kitchen.

The young woman seemingly ignored the request and instead came into the living room. "So, you're investigating the guy's death across the street? Was it murder? Do you have any clues as to who did it?"

Sadie sat next to Hal on a hard, gold loveseat. "Did you know him?"

"Uh, no. Not really." Julie suddenly retreated from the conversation. "Sally! I'm going up to my room!" Hal and Sadie watched as she took the stairs two at a time.

Mrs. Genovese returned to the living room with a tray of china teacups and some condiments. "Where did that girl go?"

The three shared small talk for a few moments before Sadie began questioning her.

"How long did you know Tom Klein?"

The old woman paused, "I guess as long as he's owned the house. Six years, I think." She nodded, as if to confirm her answer. "He was a nice man. Kept to himself, but he sure did enjoy music."

"So, you didn't have any problems with him?" Sadie pushed for her to continue.

She shook her head, "Oh, no. I am across the street though, so it wasn't very loud to me."

Sadie glanced out the window. "What about his neighbor, Gary Winston. Did they have any problems?"

Mrs. Genovese was about to take a sip of tea when she stopped. "Oh, yes. They argued quite a bit. Gary didn't like that music. Neither did Julie," she glanced up the stairs.

"Is Julie your daughter?" Hal asked.

"Oh, no." Mrs. Genovese laughed. "She's much too young. I met her at church about a month ago. She needed a place to stay, and I have room since my husband died last year."

"We're sorry for your loss," said Sadie.

Hal realized he needed to use the restroom and that it couldn't wait. Damn prostrate, he thought to himself. "Mind if I use your bathroom?" He smiled sheepishly.

"Not at all. But you'll have to use the one upstairs, the downstairs one is in the middle of renovations." Mrs. Genovese pointed towards the second floor.

Hal nodded and made his way upstairs. While the first floor was meticulously neat, the second floor was far messier. Julie's belongings appeared to be strewn everywhere, with clothing and a blanket hanging from the stairs' railing. As he made his way to the bathroom at the end of the hall, he noticed a side table piled high with mail. He hesitated as one letter caught his eye. It was from an adoption agency, and it was addressed to Julie. He slid another piece of mail that was on top of it aside, so he could read the rest. The letter stated that Tom Klein was her biological father and he had requested that she not contact him. Hal pulled out his cell phone to get a photo of it. He finished just as Julie opened her door.

"What are you doing up here?" She appeared startled.

Hal pointed toward the bathroom, "Needed the head."

She slammed the door shut, but not before Hal caught a glimpse into her room. Suddenly, the song made sense. He quickly turned around and rushed downstairs.

"Sadie, can I talk to you?" Hal asked.

She looked surprised and nodded. "Excuse me, Mrs. Genovese."

The woman smiled as she picked up the tray of empty teacups. "I'll be in the kitchen if you have any more questions."

Hal whispered in Sadie's ear. "It was Julie."

Sadie appeared surprised but followed Hal upstairs to confront the new suspect.

"Julie, it's detective Davis and officer Burton, we'd like to ask you some questions."

The two waited for a reply, but instead heard a loud noise prompting them to barge into the room. "She went out the porch." Sadie rushed over to the window. "She's outside!"

Despite a bum knee, Hal rushed down the stairs and out the front door. "Don't let her leave!" He yelled to Officer Long, who stood outside the victim's house. Long sprinted towards Julie's car and flung the keys out of her hand.

Hal limped across the street. "Julie Hawkins, you're under arrest for the murder of Tom Klein," he stated breathlessly.

Her brooding, tough exterior melted, replaced with that of a needy child. "It's not fair. He had money, a nice house. Why didn't he want me? He spent all that money on silly music and instruments, while I had to scrape by my entire life!" She whined.

Hal motioned for Officer Long to cuff her as Sadie walked towards him. "Nice job, Hal. I noted the letter, the victim's guitar hanging on Julie's wall, and the bloody clothing piled in a corner of her bedroom when you gave chase—I think we nailed it."

Despite an urgent need to use the bathroom, Hal smiled, basking in yet another successful investigation.

"You sure you don't want detective status?" Sadie asked, offering another grin as she approached her SUV.

He shook his head, "Nah. The paperwork's a killer." Hal watched as Long nudged Klein's daughter into a waiting squad.

Angel
Christina Hoag

The funk punched me in the nose soon as I entered Angel's office. Thick, rancid grease. Like a South Los Angeles street corner. I glanced at the window. Shut. Then I spotted the source on a corner of his desk. A couple of half-eaten Whoppers and ketchup-splattered fries piled like a freeway smash up. The food looked like it'd been there for a week.

I couldn't help myself. "Shit stinks, man."

Angel was slumped in his chair, his eyes sunk in dark halos, holding an inch-thick folder. Mine, no doubt. He tossed the folder onto his desk and shoved the burger and fries into the garbage bin using his forearm like a street sweeper. "Guess I can tell you, Mags. My wife left me. For a drunk with a Harley."

Then I realized. The burgers were sitting where his wedding photo usually was. "That's heavy." Angel was *buena gente*. He was a parole officer, but he was all right. He liked me. He always said, "I hope I never see you again."

He took out a framed picture from a drawer and handed it to me. The photo was new when I started my third stint with him. He was dressed in a bowtie and tux, beaming like he was in a Colgate commercial, leaning into *la novia*. Dark curls caressing smooth shoulders, white lace and satin, sparkling tiara holding back a veil. *Una princesa latina.*

"Beautiful. Like something out of a *novela*." I handed it back. He tossed it in his drawer and shoved it closed with a bang. "You got kids with her?"

He shook his head.

"*Menos mal, entonces.*" My memory tugged. I thought he told me once that he did have kids, but I must've got it wrong.

He exhaled a gust of stale breath. "You pissed clean and I'm happy to hear you got a job. You can get outta here." His voice was flat as a bald tire.

"A'ight." I put my hands on the arms of the chair to stand.

"She'd been seeing him for close to a year."

I sat back down. "That's bad. You didn't even suspect?"

He shook his head. "I trusted her. You know, that old saying, 'love is blind.' *Bueno*, not anymore." He yanked the drawer open and flung the photo in the garbage bin with a clang. Then he took it out, dropped it on the floor and stepped on it. The glass ground beneath his heel.

I felt a hot wash of shame for him. There's something embarrassing about a man crying over a woman who done him wrong. "*Pues*, guess I'll…"

He cut me off. "You know anything 'bout that drive-by?"

The suddenness of his question sliced me. My mind zigged and zagged. What did he know? I played dumb, always the best bet. "Ah, what drive-by?"

"The one that's all over the news, the one they're protesting about, the one where the little girl got killed in the crossfire. Nine years old." His eyes had turned hard as drill bits.

"Nope. Stayin' clear a all that like I told you. I'll see you next month."

His gaze held me a moment longer then collapsed. "Next month."

I walked to the door and turned at a clinking noise. He was wiping ketchup and shards of glass off the photo with a napkin.

"I begged her not to go," he said. He looked like a puppy dog that lost its mama's teat.

"Angel, *los hombres* don't beg. They get even."

He stared at me, his eyes sparking like a lit fuse.

So when Angel called me a couple days later and wanted to meet on the other side of the city at Venice Beach, I had a notion of what it was about. The hamster in my brain got on its wheel. Maybe I could turn this to my advantage.

It was a day without even a pimple of clouds in the sky. The ocean was a ruffled skin of deep blue. The usual band of freaks roamed the asphalt strip that ran along the toast-colored sand. A *pendejo* in a turban and robe rollerbladed up and down, twanging an electric guitar; another wore nothing but a Speedo to show off his *paquete*, prolly stuffed with a sock. White kids with rat's nest dreads, bare feet crusted with filth, selling stupid woven bracelets and other useless shit.

I headed to the meet at the gondolas. "By the drum circle," he said. "Follow the beat." Or the scent of weed. You could get high just breathing around here. A gang of hippies were gathered around a grassy knoll under a palm tree banging bongos and buckets. Girls with pierced noses and lips floated with their arms wide open, eyes shut, trancing on molly or acid.

Angel sat on the back of a bench, feet on the seat. I recognized him right away even though he was wearing black Ray-Bans and an Angels cap pulled low, a jacket with the collar hiked around his neck. Like he was a tough guy in a movie, except his leg was bouncing like a jackhammer. I choked back a laugh.

Angel told me once that he grew up in a rough part of South LA. He was one of us, but he wasn't street. You could say he had a marshmallow vibe, plus he looked the part. He liked his burgers and burritos. He saw the good in people, understood why some of us who grew up in the hood stayed in the hood. So, the fact that his wife had been stepping out on him wasn't exactly a shock. Still, he didn't deserve that.

I hopped up next to him and flicked the bill of his cap. "Angels, dude? Really?"

"What? I'm a fan," he said.

I cut to the point. "So, whassup that you make me come all the way out here?"

"I was thinking 'bout what you said."

Like I figured. "Yeah?"

"I need a favor."

"Okay."

"This guy, the one I told you about, with my wife, he needs to be taught a lesson, a good one."

"Can't argue with that. Taking another man's woman…"

"I want him put out of action for a while. A long while, but not permanent."

I paused, like I was taken aback, thinking about it. "What do I get in return?"

"What do you want?"

I had my ask ready, but I spun out the moment. I dug in my jacket pocket and pulled out a Snickers. I unwrapped it, broke it in two and offered him half. We chewed, watching some Rasta fool throwing paint on burlap sacks on the pavement as he bebopped to reggae tunes blasting from a boombox. His so-called art looked like something out of a kindergarten class.

I balled up the candy wrapper and made a perfect hook shot into the garbage can. I'd had plenty of practice on the yard. "I need an alibi. For that drive-by."

"Thought you weren't involved."

"Angel, I have to protect myself. I'm on parole. The five-o don't need no excuse to sweat me. You know how it is. With my jacket, they can pin a bunch a shit on me, and I'll be going away for the long haul faster than you can fire an AR-15 clip, and they'll get a bonus for clearing cases. It's a matter of time before they bring me in. You know how it is," I said again. I was more nervous than I realized. I took a deep breath to calm myself, like they taught us inside. "You can say, that night, the drive-by, you checked up on me on a home visit, off-hours, making sure I wasn't hanging with the homeboys. You found me watching TV. Put a note in my file so it's official."

Angel finished his chunk of Snickers. "That's not gonna fly. Nobody does home visits at 9:45 at night."

He was really down on the details of this drive-by. He continued. "We could say I ran into you at the Pollo Campero. I go there a lot. You sat at my booth, and we talked for fifteen-twenty minutes as we ate."

"Yeah, that sounds good. Real good, as a matter of fact."

"We talked about you staying out of the life, your job at the salvage place. You asked me how much weed it would take to show up on a piss test. I told you 'even a toke on a blunt.' And make sure you go and take a look at the menu, so you remember what you ate."

Angel was better at this than I gave him credit for. We shook on it. His fingers were sticky with chocolate. He told me he'd call me that night from a burner phone with the 411 on the guy.

This could really work, I thought, as I walked back to my car, a pep in my step. In fact, maybe I could play this for the long run, pump a few favors out of it.

Angel called me right on time and gave me the when, where and who. He'd done his homework on the dude. I was impressed. Turned out he was harder than he looked. "The rest is up to you," he said.

That Thursday night, I got my homies together and we took a ride out to the Valley, to the strip bar where the lowlife, one Darnell Washington, hung out every week with his crew. Angel told me he got there around nine, left around midnight. He drove a lime-green Harley hog. "You can't miss it," Angel said.

The homies weren't happy about doing a mission so soon after a drive-by, especially because it brought down so much heat, but I told them, since they messed up by not following my orders, they owed me. First off, they were dumb enough that the fool made them and ran out of our turf and into Florence-Firestone. Worse, they fired anyway even though both he and them were going at speed. They missed him and capped a kid who'd run into the front yard to pick up a doll her brother had tossed out the window.

"You fools are like them Keystone Kops," I said. "It's embarrassing."

They agreed to do my mission.

Sisters was a squat box of a building with an oversized neon sign of a *jaina* that flashed one body part after another, two flashes on the all-important top and bottom anatomy. Big Harleys with saddle bags and windshields were lined up in a row in front of it like an electric rainbow—purple, yellow, orange, red, blue. And lime green. My man, Darnell, was inside.

I parked in a corner lot where we had a good view of the front and back of the building and settled into the driver's seat. I snapped a bite off an Almond Joy. Flaco was riding shotgun. Tweety, Cojo and Jackie napped in the back, smushed together like a litter of fuzzy kittens. After a while, I leaned my head back, let my mind drift off about my girl, then Flaco elbowed me.

"We got action."

I sat right up as Flaco roused the homies. A half-dozen fools were spilling out the door, talking loud like they owned the night.

"Shee-it! Fresh air's sobering me right up," one said.

They straddled their Harleys, strapped on their helmets, gunned their engines. The lime green bike stood empty.

"Where our boy at?" I muttered.

The bar door banged. The straggler came out and headed to the green bike. "Here we go," Flaco said.

I turned the key in the ignition. Darnell's crew was already pulling out onto the main boulevard. He was having trouble finding his kickstand.

"That fool's wasted," Jackie said.

"Better for us," I said.

He put on his helmet, one of them old military-style ones with no visor. His bike finally roared to life, and he wheeled out onto the boulevard. We pulled right behind him. He was driving slow, so I dropped back a ways.

"He's not gonna make us. He's putting all he got just keeping that bike upright," Flaco said.

"Yeah, like you're the expert at not getting made," I said. Flaco shut his mouth.

Darnell turned off the boulevard and wound through several side streets, just like Angel said he would. He'd given me his whole route. He must've followed him one night. Then he turned onto a dark stretch of road flanked by a golf course behind a tall chain-link fence.

"Get ready," I said.

We pulled our bandannas over our noses and tied our hoods tight under our chins. I floored it and overtook him. He turned his head and twisted the throttle. The bike zoomed ahead. Either he was that competitive road-rage type or maybe he cottoned on that something was off, but I was ready. I gassed it just enough to pull ahead of him, then I yanked the steering wheel and cut him off sharp. The bike swerved and spun out from under him. He went down.

We leapt out. Eight hundred pounds of metal was lying sideways in the street. Darnell groaned a few feet away by a ditch. We worked him over for maybe a minute or two then a dog barked. Security from the golf course, I guessed.

"*¡Ya!*" I said. We hightailed it out of there.

I called Angel on the burner with a one-word message. "Done."

*****

A couple of weeks later, I went to see Angel for my regular monthly appointment. We'd had no contact since the mission like we agreed. I'd kept up with the newspaper to see if anything came up about Darnell. If it did, I didn't see it. The job had rolled out nice and smooth. Because I didn't leave it to the homies.

Angel looked like a new man. Hair slicked back and shiny, mustache trimmed in a neat edge above his upper lip. He was even wearing a tie, which he kept smoothing. He smiled at me.

"Everything work out, huh, bro?" I said.

He gave me a thumbs-up. Why wasn't he saying anything? An AC window unit clattered like a ball on a roulette wheel. His office was freezing, but a drop of sweat rolled down his temple. My spidey sense tingled. I wanted to bolt, but I couldn't.

"Hey, I gotta make this short, get back to work," I said, still standing. "I pissed clean, right? We good?"

"Sit down for a minute, Mags," Angel said.

"The shop's real busy. I told *el jefe* I'd be right back."

"This'll just be a sec. Gotta go through the motions." He stuck out his hand at the chair in front of the desk. I sat. He shuffled through some papers. Dabbed his forehead. The vibe was off, I could feel it. I drumrolled my fingers on my knee.

The door opened. I turned. A man and woman in cheap suits entered. My eyes went straight to their waistbands and caught the telltale glint of gold. I slid a look at Angel. His eyes were burning holes in his desk. That's why he was edgy. I took a deep breath. I was cool. I had a solid alibi.

The detectives introduced themselves. LAPD Homicide. They started asking me about the drive-by, if I knew about it, what I knew. Then they got to the point.

"Where were you on the twelfth at 9:45 p.m., Magdaleno?" the woman said.

"Uh, the twelfth? What day was that?"

"Wednesday."

I rubbed the cleft in my chin, pretending to ponder. "I think that was the night I went to the Pollo Campero. Yeah, in fact, I ran into Angel here. He can tell you."

We all turned to Angel. He looked up at me, new steel in his eyes. "Nope. Couldn't have been me. I never go to that place."

I felt like I'd stuck a wet finger into an outlet. Son of a bitch. He'd set me up, but ... Darnell Washington. No, that was real. Then something clicked in my brain. Angel never told me what part of South LA he was from. Suddenly I knew.

"You from Florence-Firestone?"

He nodded. "The little girl killed in the drive-by? She was my daughter," he said. "Like you said, Mags, *los hombres,* they get even." He leaned forward and lowered his voice. "And the smart ones, they get others to do their dirty work, and the real smart ones, they get both done in one fell swoop."

The world dropped away like I was in a tunnel. All I felt was the cold steel of cuffs around my wrists.

Dandelion Heads
Marie Anderson

Cigarette smoke fogs the bingo parlor. Scattered throughout the room, thick steel support beams rise from floor to ceiling, interfering with Kenny's sightline. He'll have to scout the whole room. Every seat he can see at every long table is occupied. A few old men, a few women probably under 60, but mostly old ladies like Mother. And mostly, like Mother, their hair is white and puffy and wispy, like dandelions gone to seed.

Kenny stands in the doorway and pats the gun hidden inside his coat pocket. He scans the crowded bingo parlor. Mother couldn't have hidden herself any better if she'd tried.

The gun is heavier than usual because of the special silencer he'd added. He'd used a whole paycheck to buy the silencer from a tall twitchy figure in a ski mask in the parking lot of an abandoned motel. Normally he wears the gun holstered around his waist as he patrols the warehouse at night. But he couldn't stroll into The Pink Palace Bingo Hall with a 7.65 mm Vzor 70 blue-steel semiautomatic belted around his stomach, not even wearing his work jacket with SEYMOUR-DVORAK SECURITY printed on its back.

He steps away from the entrance into the room. A crepe-necked old gent behind the drink table is squinting at him again. No matter. Not even Mother would recognize him under his new brown wig. But he isn't relying only on the wig. He'd crayoned on thick brown eyebrows, glued on a lush brown beard and mustache. Itchy but way cool. Staring at himself in the cloudy bathroom mirror before he'd left his apartment, he'd been stunned by his transformation. He looked strong, manly, like a Biblical Samson. The contact lenses are probably a mistake though.

His eyeballs feel scratchy and dry, as though Saran-wrapped. He blinks and pops wide, blinks and pops wide. Maybe he should find the little boys room and peel them off. Like he really needed to disguise his eyes, make them brown. Like Mother's. Like Mother would even remember his eyes are gray. Gray flecked with green. His father's eyes, probably, despite the variety of descriptions of his father's eyes she'd given Kenny over the years. Cross-eyed. Blood-shot. Rheumy and pus-rimmed.

Yeah, find the little boys room. But first, find Mother.

He shoves his hand inside his coat pocket, grips the gun's butt, and casually switchbacks his way up and down the narrow aisles between tables. Some players had pushed their metal folding chairs out while they screech conversation with other players. Kenny's progress is slow. He mumbles "scuze mes" and smiles apologetically when scowling players clatter their chairs out of his way.

Bingo hasn't started. The players' heads bob over their cards. Some have several cards masking-taped to the table. Shrill voices cluck and caw.

He can't resist. As he passes the heads of puffy white hair, he blows out his breath long and hard, turning his head left and right. No one notices. He smiles, imagines puffs of hair exploding off heads and drifting away like dandelion seeds.

*****

"Kenny! Blow hard and make a wish!"

Mama pushed a wormy green stem into Kenny's face, shoved the dandelion head to his lips. He took a deep breath, wished for Mama to never leave him, but before he could blow, his nose tickled and his gahdamn pie hole sneezed all over her hand. She screeched and flung the dandelion away. She raked her long red nails across his bare arm.

"Sorry, Mama! Sorry, Mama!"

"Keep your sorries in your gahdamn pie hole! You're such a nastly little boy, you. Nastly! Nastly!"

She hauled herself up from the scratchy blanket, ran jiggly to the water fountain behind the swings, leaving him alone on the blanket that itched his legs. He watched her far away by the water fountain, scrubbing her hand under the stream of water. He looked at the scratches on his arm. They oozed blood and burned, but he bit his lip to keep from crying, because if he cried she would go back to their apartment again without him, and he was afraid to cross the busy street that separated the park from their apartment building all by himself.

Drivers couldn't be expected to see little boys. Their cars and trucks would smack him high into the air and he'd crash down onto the asphalt and their big tires would roll right over his broken-up bones and squash out his guts and brains. Little boys always need to hold their mama's hand when they cross the street.

He was supposed to be her little girl, she said to the other mothers in the park, she said to ladies waiting behind her at the grocery store, she said to the various tall hairy men that snorted and spit and drank and burped their way through the apartment at night, and then counted wrinkly green bills into her outstretched palm. She said to them all how she'd had to give away the pink sleepers, the colorful little dresses, the soft pink blankets and floppy dolls. She'd had to paint over the little blonde ballerinas leaping across the pink walls of what was supposed to be her beautiful baby girl's sweet little bedroom. "And birthing this kid wrecked my insides," she'd say. "No more babies. I'll never have my little girl."

*****

Aha! There she is! A steel beam had hidden her from him.

Until now.

He stands across from her, watches her plump scarlet lips flap and squawk out conversation into the ear of a white-haired old lady to her right. She stops talking only to suck on her cigarette. Still Merits, he can see. She blows out a stream of smoke and lifts her head. Their eyes meet. She smiles. Purses her blubbery red lips and air-smacks a kiss.

Oh dear Lord. Could she really be smooching a kiss at him? He shudders. She winks a long-lashed eye, the lashes still as black and stiff as how he'd always known them, black and stiff as a dead spider's legs.

*****

The spider lashes brushed his cheek. Mama oozed over him. He shrank back into his bed. Held his breath against the smells. Cigarettes, wine, lilac perfume.

"Kissy, kissy, Kenny."

Her real lips had disappeared. Now she wore her sausage ones, shiny and bright red. He turned his head, escaped the sausage lips and landed instead on a plump, powdery cheek. His hands under the blanket clenched so they wouldn't fly to his lips to scrub away the taste.

"You be a good little boy for, uh...that nice lady over there. She gonna babysit you." Mama heaved herself off his bed and looked at the strange lady standing in the doorway to his room. The lady was very pink and very thin and had a faint mustache. She was chewing on an unlit cigarette. The lady nodded at him. Winked.

Mama tottered on purple high heels to the lady in the doorway. "He's an angel," she said to the lady. "Be no trouble for you at all. Feel free to have at it all. Refrigerator. TV. Phone. Well, no phone. A little problem with the mails. Payment sent. Payment lost. Damn post office, right? So, anyways. Everything else, feel free. Mi casa, su casa, right?"

Kenny didn't see Mama again for three weeks. The pink lady slept and smoked and watched TV. He got himself off to school. Drank Diet Coke and ate cookies, crackers, and dry, stale Cheerios.

*****

He emerges from the little boys room, cold water still beading his face. He'd peeled the contacts off, but he'd left his glasses at home, so things are fuzzy. No matter. He knows where she is.

He's almost always known where she is. But he's never had the balls to right the wrongs she caused. It's her fault he's unlovable. Unwanted. He didn't need the therapists to tell him that. What he needs is payback. His new job as a security guard has given him the tool. He's going to use the tool before he loses the job, which he knows will happen sooner rather than later. History always repeats itself for The Unlovables. The Unwanteds.

A loudspeaker voice calls numbers. B7, O64, O75, N32.

Cigarette smoke fogs the room. Old bodies and old breath heat the air. Again he grips the gun in his coat pocket and strides through all the bobbing dandelion heads to the one that belongs to Mother.

Again he stands across from her, behind a wheelchair occupied by another dandelion head. Hearing aids plug Wheelchair's ears. Wheelchair tilts her head back, eyeballs him with watery blue eyes. "Do ya mind?" she croaks.

He blows on Wheelchair's dandelion head. She grunts and looks back down at her bingo cards. He grips his gun. Clenches his jaw.

Mother's head is lowered over her three cards. Her blue-veined hands flash over the cards. Her red claws pounce upon each number hit, slide shut the little plastic door over the called number.

He raises the pocket of his coat. Points the gun inside the pocket. Points it right at Mother.

O72.

"Bingo!" Mother lifts her arms. She's wearing a sleeveless pink sweater, so when she raises her arms, he sees she still doesn't shave, though now the hair curling from her armpits is wispy and gray instead of prickly and black. She shakes her arms, screeches "Bingo!" again and again. He watches her arm flesh jiggle, loose, pink, freckled.

Freckles infect his arms. He hates freckles.

She looks his way. Their eyes lock.

His finger touches the trigger. She cries out. "Kenny! Hey, my Kenny! My boy! You grew a beard!"

And shock that she recognizes him causes his hand to throb up just before the bullet flies out. Despite the silencer on his gun, Kenny hears not the soft pop he expected, like in the movies, but the bark of a loud firecracker.

Is it because the room is so loud, and the bingo players are mostly so old and hard of hearing that no one screams or gets up from their chairs in fright?

No one pays any attention to him, the righteous assassin in the bingo parlor.

Kenny watches something hiss through the bubble of dandelion seeds on Mother's head. He sees something ping into the steel support beam behind her chair. He watches a few cottony white tufts of Mother's hair float gently to the floor.

He sees it all, slow motion, everything moving slow and drifty, until Mother claps her hands and he blinks.

"Bingo, Kenny! I got me a Bingo! Oooh we gonna party tonight! Woohoo! Hey, you lookin' good, my main man. Been a while! You finally grew yourself some hair." She squints, shakes her head. "That beard's a little crooked though."

A voice on the loudspeaker warns players to preserve their covered numbers until the bingo can be verified.

Mother's fat red lips split into a smile. He sees that her teeth are new. Very white, oversized, like a horsey's.

"I got me the first Bingo of the night, Kenny! $250! Ya finally brung me *good* luck, kid. About time, right?"

He smiles back at her. He continues smiling at Mama even as the crepey-necked old gent stumbles toward her with a leering smile.

"You're welcome," Kenny manages to say. But now she is hugging the crepey-necked old gent who is verifying her win. Now she is no longer looking at her little boy, though he continues smiling so hard his face hurts.

He smiles and smiles, even as he backs down narrow aisles, his shins hitting chairs, his backside bumping tables. He smiles and squints to see better the crepey-necked old gent plop green bill after green bill into Mama's outstretched palm. He blows his breath out hard, one last time, but no dandelion seeds explode off heads. No wishes will come true. Not this time. Not this night.

But there'll be other nights.

The Harbert Curse
Heather C. Morris

Cybersecurity expert Vera Dawes inhaled the tang of her artisan pizza and the doughy richness of the ale plunked onto her corner table by a long-suffering waitress. She lifted the glass, taking a satisfying swig of her Friday night ritual. Around her, the basement dive pulsed and hummed, conversation echoing off crumbly brick walls. The background buzz helped banish all thoughts of malware and data mining. Old acquaintances and hundred-year-old curses were absolutely the farthest thing from her mind.

"Vera? Vera Dawes? 'S that you?"

A tall man trying to hide his advancing age strode toward her. She hunted through her memories till she found a match. *There it is*, she thought.

"Eric Williams? What're you doing here?"

When she was a brand-new analyst, Vera and Eric sat in neighboring cubicles. He'd helped her complete a top-notch security coding project. But after she'd left years ago for a more intriguing position, she hadn't seen a physical or computational trace of him.

"Nice to see you too."

Vera took a bite of pizza. The cheese tasted stringier than she remembered. Perhaps because of the unwelcome intrusion.

"Well, umm," he shifted, clearing his throat. "…I work for Harbert Enterprises now." Eric motioned to the men who'd appeared behind him, "These are the owners—John and Kyle Harbert. We heard this place has the best pizza and beer in town." He nodded at her dinner. "Guys, this is Vera Dawes, one of the best computer hackers I know."

The two men—one young and sullen, the other middle-aged and

weary—said nothing and kept their hands in their pockets. Vera nodded. She took another long swig, glancing around the bar. She didn't remember Eric being this dense.

"John here," Eric motioned to the older man, "is Kyle's uncle. The family business runs the gamut from investments to shares of local companies. They needed an IT guy, so they hired me a few years back."

Vera stared at him, hoping the conversation was over, but Eric shifted from one foot to another. He appeared desperate to engage with anyone else, even a former colleague whom he hadn't seen in ages. Vera sighed and waved one hand toward an empty seat. Eric smiled, plunked down his beer, and dropped into a chair.

The Harbert men hesitated. The elder shifted uncomfortably; the younger glared at Eric. Finally, both sat. The older one perched on the edge of his chair with a ramrod-straight back. The younger man tapped his cell phone and glared at the screen.

"What about you? What have you been doing?"

"Same ole, same old."

Eric laughed and turned to the younger man—*Kyle, wasn't it?* Vera thought—saying, "Just like the Vera Dawes I remember. A woman of few words."

"Something I appreciate in a female," Kyle Harbert said, his lips lifting in a sneer, his eyes never leaving his phone.

Vera's eyes hardened and her hand tightened around her glass. But she said nothing.

After a stiff pause, Eric switched the subject to cryptocurrency, excluding the Harbert men. Vera nodded, shrugged, and sometimes uttered a monosyllabic answer. It was all the encouragement the loquacious Eric Williams needed. After a few minutes, their conversation was interrupted by an expletive from Kyle Harbert. The surrounding conversations hushed, and all eyes turned to the red mop of curly hair still bent over his cellphone. His uncle glowered.

"Is such language necessary, Kyle?"

Vera noted the venom-laced look Kyle threw at his uncle. "It's my father. He's had a heart attack." John Harbert's face turned pale, even in the low light of the bar. "What do you think, *Uncle*? Your own *brother's* dying. That a good enough reason for my 'language'?"

The young man stood and walked a few steps into the crowded room, tapping his phone then raising it to his ear. Vera eyed the reticent uncle seated across from her. His face was a mixture of confusion, humiliation, and something else she couldn't quite place.

Within moments, Kyle had returned, issuing a curt, "C'mon." He turned away suddenly, not waiting to see who followed. John Harbert hurried after his nephew, who had stormed through the bar's whispering patrons and scaled the steps. The hum of conversation resumed.

Vera looked at Eric, who had been stunned into silence by the manner and speed of his employers' departure.

He took a deep breath. "Whoa. Sorry about that."

Vera shrugged. She had encountered worse.

"Should you follow him?"

"Me? Nah." Eric slowly rotated his almost empty beer glass. After a pause, he continued, "Did you see Kyle's face? And John's. It's like they had seen a ghost. And, in a way, they had. You see, the Harbert family is old money here in town, and with old families come old curses!" He looked up from the table, his blue eyes gleaming, "Want to hear about it?"

"Nothing like a good curse to pique a girl's interest."

Eric laughed.

"Again—the Vera I remember. Cutting through deception. Seeing clearly. Ok, a curse may not be the best conversation topic, but," he shrugged, "It's all I've got."

Vera's eyes sparkled. She may have resented the intrusion moments ago, but Eric Williams was growing on her. She motioned for a waiter and they each ordered another glass. Once they were sipping their second round, Eric began.

"The Harberts are an old, old family. More than a hundred years ago, they owned the largest estate around. About that time, a Harbert—named Mitchell, maybe…oh, well—began to suspect that his wife was not faithful. He found her in a 'compromising situation,' let's say. She swore that she was innocent, but her husband, Master Harbert, wouldn't listen. Later, she had one child—a son—and he vowed that the boy was not his child and would never inherit any of his money. I forget what he did—something misogynistic and brutal like beating her and sending them both away penniless and on foot; anyway, he as good as killed them. She told everyone she met that she was innocent…until the day she died. And with her last breath, she cursed the Harbert family forever. No first-born son of a Harbert will ever inherit—that's the curse.

"Well, time passed, and the lady's innocence was proven beyond a doubt. The story goes that old Harbert killed himself in despair. But the amazing thing is that from then until now, no first-born son has ever inherited the family fortune. It's gone to younger brothers, or nephews, and such—but never the oldest. Kyle's father is the second of four sons—would you believe the oldest died in a freak car accident many years ago? And you know what? Since I've started working at their company, I've heard Kyle say that he's secretly worried something tragic would happen to him."

Weird story, Vera thought, then said, "Well, now his father is dying, and Kyle appears fine, relatively…so, an oldest son will inherit?"

"Yep. So much for the family curse. Just an old bedtime story, designed to scare the oldest kids into obedience. Can't stand up to the strain of the digital age."

Vera didn't reply. Eric glanced at his phone and stood.

"John Harbert just texted. He wants me to pick him up at the hospital." He looked at her closely,

"Bye, Vera Dawes."

She took a sip of beer, nodded goodbye, and settled back into blissful anonymity.

*****

When Vera pulled up her news feed the next day at work, she learned the sequel to last night's events. A headline announced the tragic deaths of both Kyle Harbert *and* his father.

Vera was not often surprised. She allowed herself a moment to analyze the sensation.

The article described how David Harbert had died at midnight at St. Luke's Hospital from heart attack complications. But Kyle had been found dead of a drug overdose early that morning by his friend, Eric Williams. 'I just can't believe Kyle would do this,' Eric was quoted. 'Maybe he was in shock cause his dad just died. But OD? Kyle was a health nut. He wouldn't touch drugs.' The article included a statement from the lead investigator who confirmed probable suicide, citing depression. His father's recent death combined with a decline in his company's stock prices had driven Kyle Harbert to take his life. Vera's eyes narrowed when she read the news article's mention of the curious Harbert family superstition. The article concluded with a statement that Kyle had left no will and David's will still named his brother Warren as the beneficiary.

Kyle strikes me as the kind of guy who has a lot of enemies, Vera paused, *The police are going to investigate Eric for sure.*

She surprised herself when she found Eric Williams' number buried in her contacts. She tapped out a text and hit the green arrow:

Heard about the Harberts. You ok?

A few minutes elapsed before her phone dinged –

The police think I did it. This whole thing's a nightmare.

Oof. Keep me posted.

I have an alibi.

"That's what they all say," Vera muttered out loud to the darkness of her server-closet-turned-office. Many people would have pitied her, relegated to a windowless room full of flashing lights and humming machines. But she relished the quiet, the focus, the isolation, and the speed of setting up shop in the middle of her company's server farm.

"But could he…?" she didn't finish her thought. She had

encountered plenty of criminals in her line of work. From what she remembered, Eric Williams was the kind of guy who drank a little too much or gambled more than he could afford. But she preferred to not think him capable of anything more than that.

However, her chance meeting with Eric and the Harberts piqued Vera's interest in anything related to that family. She set a Google alert, which funneled an article to her inbox two days later. It labeled Kyle Harbert's death a suicide and confirmed Eric's innocence.

A few months later, she received the death notice for a man named Warren Harbert. She took a break from her latest project to read his obituary.

The brief article detailed how Warren's death had not been wholly unexpected, on account of his ongoing battle with colon cancer. He was married but the couple had no children. His brother—the John Harbert that she met at the pub—took over as manager of the family assets and estate.

This whole Harbert situation is like something out of a bad novel. I sure hope Eric's not still mixed up with that family.

Vera closed the web browser and typed out more lines of code.

*****

Vera studied the cryptic text message she'd received from an unknown number. The sender identified herself at the end of the text as 'Mrs. Harbert—John's wife,' and she requested that they arrange a time to meet in person.

I don't have time for this, Vera thought. Her finger hovered over the trash can icon, but all the Harbert deaths came to mind…and she couldn't help herself. She was intrigued. She sent a reply.

Mrs. Harbert turned out to be a tall, middle-aged woman—active and fit—with a decisive demeanor. She burst into Vera's shadowed office as she finished the final line of code for a malware tracking app.

When Mrs. Harbert spoke, her voice carried the broad tones of the Western states.

"Ms. Dawes? Finally. Helen Harbert, John's wife. You're a difficult woman to track down. No one in this company has any idea where to find you! Eric Williams suggested I talk to you. He said you see things differently than most people." Her voice held hope and concern. When Vera didn't respond, she asked, "Do you remember my husband, John?"

"Sure. I remember. We met a few months ago at the Brewhouse. Eric introduced me to him and his nephew, Kyle."

"How amazing that you recall so much about a random meeting?"

"Well, it *was* the same night that Kyle *and* his father both died."

For three heartbeats, no one spoke, then Helen cleared her throat.

"Actually…that's why I'm here, Ms. Dawes. It's just, well, I'm worried."

"What about?"

"About my husband, John…and…maybe…myself."

Vera yawned. *Please tell me she didn't pop in for marital advice!* She glanced at her phone. *Good. The code for my new app's working. At least the day isn't a total loss.* She looked up when Mrs. Harbert spoke.

"You see, John's convinced he's going to die. Soon."

Vera's silence and her expression must have conveyed exactly what she thought. Mrs. Harbert sniffed, "Maybe this isn't serious enough for you?"

"Mrs. Harbert, I'm not sure how I can help. I work with computers. I'm not a doctor or a psychiatrist or a detective. Have you been to see one of them?"

"John's in the best of health—he walks three miles every day. As far as mentally…well, you probably think he's suicidal at best and delusional at worst," Mrs. Harbert stood, "I have wasted your time and mine. I didn't want the police involved, but I guess it's unavoidable…"

Vera leaned back in her desk chair and gestured for Mrs. Harbert to sit back down.

"What would you tell them? The police, I mean. That your husband—an older man—*thinks* he's going to die soon?"

The visitor sighed and dropped back into the chair opposite Vera.

"You're right. I don't have anything to go on, and I have nowhere to go," she raised her eyes to Vera's, "But I have this horrible feeling that something is going to happen…"

Vera waited. She knew there was more.

"…and the strange thing is, John won't do anything about it."

There it is, Vera thought.

"So, you've discussed his…mood? What did he say?"

Anger flashed in Mrs. Harbert's eyes, "It's no use talking to John about it—he's obsessed with this family curse. He's completely wrapped up in the Harbert history and genealogies, heirlooms and portraits. Since he took over the family business, its holdings, and the estate, he has become superstitious to a degree that I never knew possible. I'm from out West, Ms. Dawes, there's no such thing as old money there—not really. Oh, we have plenty of ghost towns and ghost stories, but nothing like these family curses. It was alright when we were first married—gave John's relations a bit of glamor— but now most of them are dead and gone. No one thinks anything is amiss. And none of them, Ms. Dawes, but especially not my husband, will do anything about it."

"So, he doesn't seem to care?"

"No! 'He's resigned himself to his fate,' he says. It's ridiculous!" Ms. Harbert slammed her fist into the arm of the chair.

After a moment, she added, "You asked about his mental state, Ms. Dawes. It's not good. John's had a series of bad investments, and he has fallen into a depression I've never seen."

Vera picked at a hangnail, "But you don't believe in this curse?"

"No! It's nonsense. And anyway, can a curse poison someone?"

"What?" Vera leaned forward.

"I said—could a legend or a curse poison someone? I don't know what to think about John's morose outlook. Could be depression, could be some weird obsession with family history. But last week, he passed out after dinner. When I couldn't get him to respond, I rushed him to the emergency room. They ran tests, found he had been drugged, and pumped his stomach. A few days later, I found this…"

She placed an empty prescription painkiller bottle on the end table between them.

Vera studied the label.

"It says 'John Harbert'?"

"Yes, but he filled that prescription after his knee replacement surgery almost a year ago. He never used it."

Vera thought for a moment, then said, "Mrs. Harbert, what you are telling me could be completely circumstantial. However, he could also be in danger. Who is regularly at your house?"

"Amy Phillips, my husband's assistant and Eric. John works mostly from our estate in the country. He spends hours in meetings with Eric and Amy. Oh, and Kyle's sister, Kelly Harbert, and Warren's former wife, Mary also stay with us for weeks at a time." She lowered her eyes, "My heart hurts for them, Ms. Dawes. They have no one else."

"Warren Harbert? John's other brother who died?"

"Exactly. John had to watch his brother, David—Kyle and Kelly's father—and another brother, Warren, both die. And all this after his oldest brother was killed in a car crash." She looked away, and when she met Vera's eyes again, they held a deep fatigue, "It wears on him. He is not the man I married."

"Sorry for making you feel bad for coming, Mrs. Harbert. I might be able to help, but it would be easiest if I could stay with you."

"Of course. John won't mind. He doesn't seem to care about much of anything these days. Except the family history, of course. It infuriates me the way he seems to welcome misfortune."

After she walked Helen Harbert to the door and verified the address of the family estate, Vera hoped she hadn't welcomed her own misfortune by agreeing to investigate.

*****

Twenty-four hours later, Vera found herself speeding down two-lane roads through small towns with names like Pikesburg and Starling. She allowed her mind to wander—arranging and rearranging facts like Tetris blocks. She spoke infrequently, talking above the purring engine,

"...Kyle dying so soon after his father. On that night so long ago. I wish..."

But she never finished her wish.

Instead, she returned to what she knew about the facts of the cases— <u>all</u> the Harbert cases. She began to dissect the circumstances surrounding the deaths of each Harbert heir.

There was Kyle's father, David. She only knew what Kyle spewed on that fateful night: that his father had suffered a heart attack. But what was the official diagnosis? Had an autopsy been performed? And then Kyle himself had died later that night. An overdose by a young man with no drug record? A few months later, another brother, Warren, was dead. From colon cancer...or was he "helped along"?

Yep, every death could have been arranged, she thought.

And now John. Suppose he had died in the ER. Who would benefit? He had no children. It was all so strange. Could the police really have overlooked three *murders*? In one family?

Vera rolled her eyes, tightened her grip on the wheel, and hoped she hadn't become mixed up in some middle-aged woman's odd ideas.

The Harbert's country estate consisted of a two-story, sprawling, white mansion with wrap-around porches. The house was surrounded by gardens bursting with hydrangeas and roses in the peak of summer bloom. Vera swung her Prius around the circle drive, unsurprised when a valet greeted her, asking for her key fob. As she watched her car glide toward the garages, Helen Harbert burst from the house, welcoming Vera warmly.

Helen showed Vera to her husband's study, introduced her, and left her with John Harbert. Vera noted that he had greatly changed in the intervening months. His shoulders hunched, his eyes were dim, his hair was tinged with more gray. A flicker, almost of pain, passed over his face periodically. He listened while Vera explained why she had come to stay for a time.

"How very practical. But completely unnecessary. Just like Helen. Of course, you may stay, Ms. Dawes; I thank you for coming. Even in the face of the inevitable. See, we Harberts *know*—none of us can escape the curse."

Vera reminded John Harbert of the empty prescription bottle that his wife found, but he seemed unimpressed.

"Maybe I took them all and don't remember? That is quite possible."

"Surely you would *remember* something like that?" Vera studied John Harbert closely. He didn't look at her and didn't respond, "You're not even willing to concede that your wife's idea of attempted murder is possible?"

"Maybe. Probable? No. The curse will get me in the end."

"You're willing to believe in some curse, but cannot imagine a real-life threat?"

"Because there is no threat. Who could possibly want to kill me? But the curse—it took all three of my brothers. My nephew, Kyle. Everyone before them."

Vera held John Harbert's gaze, "But this curse—Eric told me the story that night we first met, in the bar—it's only supposed to affect the oldest son?"

He shrugged. Vera tried a different tactic.

"*If* something were to happen to you, who would this estate pass to?"

"Kelly would manage the family business and this estate."

"Your own wife won't inherit any of the Harbert money?"

"She will have our townhouse in the city and my own personal money—a very large sum. Investments were my strong suit in former years. But the current documents state that the Harbert family assets—the company and the estate—will pass to Kelly."

They were interrupted by a sharp tap on the door. A tall, trim, athletic woman with wavy brown hair and intelligent eyes strode in, carrying a stack of papers.

"Not now, Amy. I'm tired," John Harbert passed a hand over his eyes, then waved it between Vera and the newcomer, "Amy, this is Ms. Dawes. She'll be staying with us for a while, at my wife's request."

"Oh," Amy said stiffly—not looking directly at Vera—before turning back to her employer, "You can't put off signing these documents forever, sir. I'll come back tonight." She shut the door behind her.

"She's been after me for weeks to sign them," John Harbert sighed. "If you'll excuse me, Ms. Dawes? I need to lie down."

Wonder what his secretary so desperately needs him to sign, Vera mused. She showed herself out, easily finding the front door and a path to the gardens.

Vera ambled around the side of the house to the backyard, where she found Mrs. Harbert lounging near the pool with two other women.

Helen introduced the younger, a lovely woman with piercing green eyes, as Kelly Harbert. The older woman had gray hair and rested one hand on Kelly's arm. Vera learned that Warren Harbert's widow, Mary, and Kelly were almost inseparable, and that Kelly had studied to be a nurse, before devoting herself to Mary and the rest of her family.

After an interminable period of small talk, Vera excused herself to roam once more—her feet taking her in wandering circles, her mind meticulously sorting facts.

*****

Vera's stay at the Harbert's country home was pleasant and relaxing—though what some might consider idleness resolved itself into vigilance upon closer inspection. She spent her days probing the Harbert's wireless network and observing all comings and goings at the house. Eric Williams visited most evenings, either stopping by for a chat with the ladies or a drink with John.

"Had to stop by to share a beer with my partner," he would grin.

Kelly and Mary maintained an unofficial residence at the house during the summer, spending their days lounging poolside or driving into town. Nothing disturbed the idyllic nature of the estate. After a few days, Amy Phillips asked John to sign a stack of more documents. "You must, sir. The company shareholders are expecting them," Vera heard her say as she watched them from a distance.

*****

The next day, the Harberts and Amy Phillips decided they would meet

Eric for dinner at a café in a nearby town and invited Vera to join them. She could tell they were relieved when she refused, citing work.

Finally, she was alone with the sprawling house and the housekeeper, Sadie, who came once a week.

Vera went straight to work. She had been slowly gathering information—from unguarded electronic and physical files. But there was still one device that she hadn't been able to access. Its owner never set it down. Today, it had been left charging on the docking station; she moved swiftly and precisely, without leaving any electronic "fingerprints."

Bingo.

With a satisfied smile, Vera fixed a sandwich and strolled to the porch where Sadie was sweeping.

"I'm glad they's all gone out," Sadie fussed, "So hard to clean with the Harberts and all their people around."

Vera dropped into a lounge chair, taking a bite of roast beef and swiss.

"They's rarely goes out no more. I hope's they's enjoying themselves. You know, order drinks and such. That restaurant has marvelous mixed drinks—"

Vera paused in the middle of a second bite.

"Drinks? Alcoholic?"

"Yep, some of the best in the county. And the buffalo dip…I wish they'd asked what I—"

Sadie stopped suddenly as Vera launched out of her chair, sandwich dropped and forgotten, and paced the patio. They both turned toward the sound of tires on the drive.

"Why's they back so early?" Sadie asked.

"Something's happened," Vera whispered.

Sure enough, they heard Helen Harbert's worried cry from the circle drive, "Help! John's passed out again."

"But we shook him awake," Eric said, as he rounded the corner of the house, supporting John on one side, while Helen propped him up on the other.

Mary, Kelly, and Amy Phillips trailed solemnly behind.

"It's nothing," John's faint voice slurred.

"Last time you landed in the ER," Helen retorted, "Now, you are going to lie down. No work for him tonight, Miss Phillips."

Amy Phillips opened her mouth to speak, then stopped and pursed her lips. Helen bustled John through to a nearby sofa, where she ordered Kelly to fetch him a pillow and Mary to fill up a glass of water.

The mood in the living room was somber. Sadie disappeared into the kitchen. Vera watched Amy Phillips closely—she kept twisting one strand of hair. Mary couldn't settle, repeating, "He passed out. He looked horrible. White as a sheet. Just like Warren. And he's so young." Helen's face was resolute, but Kelly had fixed Eric with a hard stare. He couldn't meet her eyes, instead chatting with Vera and the other ladies briefly. He finally departed with a harried look.

Vera watched him leave—*Was he "enjoying a beer with his partner"? One too many?*

Amy Phillips fidgeted and fussed, eventually leaving for home a few minutes after Eric.

Sadie finished her cleaning with a pinched face and fearful eyes. Vera helped her carry her cleaning supplies to her car around 9:00 pm.

"Do you always stay so late?" she asked the compact woman.

Sadie nodded. "To watch over Mr. John and Ms. Helen, Ms. Dawes. Ms. Helen told me about you. She said you's here to help. So help." She jammed her finger into Vera's arm, punctuating the last two words, folded herself into her car, and slammed the door.

Vera watched her disappear down the winding driveway, her face thoughtful.

Never fear, Sadie. Tonight's the night.

When she made her way back inside, she made sure to bid Kelly, Mary, and Helen good night before slipping off to her guest room. Kelly had fixed her with a sullen gaze, Mary would not meet her eyes. Helen sat erect and determined, informing Vera that John had retired to bed early.

Vera settled into bed with a manual on Javascript coding and waited.

In the small hours of the morning, she grabbed her black backpack and walked purposefully to the Harberts' bedroom. John was asleep alone in the large bed. Helen had insisted that he be able to rest undisturbed, but she was sleeping in an adjoining room where she could monitor him. Vera took up position in a far corner, with a clear view of the door and the room. She could hear deep, regular breathing coming from the bed.

Just as I thought—he's drugged. So that he won't struggle—

Setting down the backpack, she pulled out her phone, night time video equipment, and a small pistol, which she tucked into her waistband.

She had barely finished setting up the equipment when the door softly opened, and someone entered the room. Vera punched record, capturing a moving shadow and the sound of quick, hurried breaths. Footsteps crossed the floor to stand beside the bed. The light from a cell phone fell across John's sleeping form, but the person holding it was still in shadow. The figure propped the light on the bedside table. With one hand, it tipped over an empty prescription bottle next to the cell phone light…and with the other, the shadow gripped a syringe!

Vera tapped the SOS button on her phone and sprang forward. Silently, she turned the light from the intruder's phone onto the face of the one in the act of murder.

The face of Kelly Harbert, John's own niece.

She lunged at Vera, her eyes full of madness and fury, the syringe pointed like a dart. Vera sidestepped, tripping Kelly. She fell, howling.

"Dispatch…" came a voice from Vera's phone.

Vera kicked the syringe into a far corner and pulled the pistol from her belt, pointing it at the malevolent murderer, "This is Vera Dawes. Reporting an attempted murder at the Harbert estate…"

*****

Police officers escorted Kelly, handcuffed and spewing expletives, out of the house. Vera calmly packed her equipment, then made her way downstairs to where Helen and Mary Harbert huddled in the living room. Both women raised shocked faces to meet hers.

"Kelly did this?" Helen breathed, "I just can't believe it."

"I thought you suspected someone?" Vera cocked her head quizzically.

"Yes, but…I mean…not Kelly! How? Why?"

"She's been untraceable up to this point. And she almost finished her plan."

"What plan?"

"I suspect it began as a niggle in her mind as her father lay dying: *Who will inherit his money?* I found the text messages to prove she thought that she and Kyle would inherit. Must have caught her off guard to find out she'd killed her own brother for nothing."

"Kelly *killed* Kyle?"

"Someone who was not suicidal and is a health fanatic dies from a suicidal drug overdose? And there was no note?"

Mary Harbert gasped, "But Warren inherited the estate, the company, the money…" She trailed off.

Vera shrugged. "Yep. And who was right by your side nursing her poor, ailing uncle?"

Mary's eyes flashed, "No! How dare you insinuate…Kelly is kind and caring—she's a nurse!"

Vera remained silent and watched understanding slide across the faces of both Harbert women.

After an interval, Helen choked out, "She knew about medicines…doses…how to administer them…"

Vera pulled out her phone, "Exactly. Her attempt on John's life tonight was almost a copy of Kyle's 'suicide.' Between the video from tonight, her text message transcripts, and dosage spreadsheets I found on her computer, well, let's just say, it's pretty incriminating stuff."

Mary sobbed quietly. Helen looked away.

Vera watched the patrol car cruise down the long estate drive. She turned to go, but stopped when Helen's soft voice said,

"And all this time I suspected Amy!" She shook her head, "Poor girl! Thank you, Vera Dawes."

Vera nodded and walked to her car. Time to return to the comfort of the humming servers in her basement office.

*****

Vera monitored her news feed for articles about the attempted murder or Kelly's arrest. Nothing.

Good. No need for that family to suffer anymore.

Kelly Harbert was booked into a mental health facility where she awaited her trial. John appointed Eric to be his full partner; and, with Eric's expertise, the estate and investments, as well as his friend's morose outlook, improved.

A few weeks later, Vera's phone pinged when Eric texted.

Thanks again for all your help.

Sure. You ok? Vera replied.

Thumbs up

And John? Still going on about the Harbert family curse?

Nah. He's good. Distracted by my news.

What news?

You'll find out soon. Hope you can come.

??

A fat envelope stuffed with thick cardstock arrived in her mailbox a week later. A wedding invitation. Eric Williams and John Harbert's attractive assistant, Amy Phillips, were to be married in the summer.

Vera chuckled.

"So...*that's* why he spent so many evenings with the Harberts. 'Having a beer with his partner.' Sure. He probably used the crazy Harbert curse story as his conversation starter."

My Hand to God
Wendy Harrison

I was watching Milton Berle on our little black and white TV, but even Uncle Miltie couldn't keep me from dozing. I jerked awake and looked at the empty armchair next to me. Pat should've been home by now, him and Molly. That's what he named our German Shepherd, after his mother, may she rest in peace. The real Molly would'a been pissed off if she was still around to hear he gave her name to a dog.

I pushed my 62-year-old self out of the chair and headed downstairs, then through the grocery and out the door.

The city streets were as quiet as Newark streets ever got. Pat always said it was the best time of day. I felt safe walking alone after dark. It was 1952, and our neighborhood was under the protection of Mr. Zwillman, Longie Zwillman. I didn't care what the papers said. He was always good to us. Me and Pat made a good team, and Mr. Z appreciated us. I took care of Bridget's, the little grocery store we started, and Pat ran the numbers from the back room for Mr. Z.

In case you don't know, people around here loved playing the numbers each day. They'd bet on a three-digit number, and when *The Star Ledger* reported the attendance at the Atlantic City race track for that day, the ones who picked the last three digits won the bet, and boy, were they always happy.

Pat always walked the same route with Molly, so I headed up the block, figuring I'd run into him. I started to see flashing red lights, and then I heard a sound I knew I'd never forget. Molly, howling like her heart was breaking. I started to run, best I could. As I turned the corner, I saw the black and whites, their lights flashing, blocking traffic to let an ambulance through.

I pushed my way through the crowd of lookie loos coming out of nowhere. "Molly," I shouted, and the howling stopped.

"Don't hurt her." I screamed at the cop pointing a gun at Molly, who was protecting my Pat. He was face down across the sidewalk, the back of his head all bloody. So much blood, shining in the light from the street lamp.

I ran past the cops and grabbed Molly's leash. "Good girl," I said through the tears that I couldn't stop.

They kept me there for a while, taking down Pat's information and listening to me tell them over and over that I couldn't think of anyone who would want to hurt my husband. It was the truth. Pat was no angel, but he had a code, my husband did, and never cheated no one. Finally, they let me take Molly and leave.

She stayed with me on Pat's side of the bed. If it hadn't been for her, I don't think I would've made it through the night.

In the morning, I tried to find the strength to do what had to be done. Call O'Malley's Funeral Parlor. Hide Pat's paperwork, in case the cops decided to look around. And especially make sure people got paid or I'd be in for a world of even more hurt than I was already.

Someone knocked on the glass door of the store. I made my way through the narrow aisle between the canned goods and the cereal and breads.

"Bridget, how're you doing?" Sergeant Mikey Walsh grabbed me in a big hug. I held him tight for a minute and then stepped back.

"Come in." We walked to the back counter where I'd been sitting.

"I heard about Pat on the morning report." Mikey shook his head. "I can't believe it."

I described what I saw. "I couldn't tell for sure. He was shot, wasn't he?"

Mikey hesitated.

"I need to know."

"Yeah, he was shot, one in the head. They're thinkin' it was a robbery gone bad, but he still had a roll in his pocket." Pat always carried a roll of bills so he could pay when someone hit the number.

Mikey and Pat grew up together, with Pat becoming what some would call a criminal and Mikey what some would call a dirty cop. Not much difference between them. I was hoping he might know something about Pat I didn't, something to explain why someone would kill him.

"Who would want to hurt Pat?" I waited, hoping he would have answers.

"I got nothin'. You?"

I shook my head, and Mikey patted my hand. "Mr. Z is going to look into it. He said to tell you you're gonna be okay. Anything you need, you let me know and I'll pass it along. In the meantime, he'll take care of the arrangements with O'Malley's. Collum will be calling you soon."

Mikey stood. "Like I said, whatever you need."

I walked him to the door and decided to leave it open, let in the fresh spring air. I had the usual morning customers, picking up groceries and playing their number. The ones who heard the news were real nice, telling me what a good guy Pat was.

When it got quiet, I sat behind the cash register, just sitting. I was trying not to think at all. It hurt too much. Sounds from the street floated into the store, but I wasn't paying much attention until I noticed two kids go past. One of them was doing most of the talking. He sounded upset.

"I was tryin' to save him. He damn well died right in front of me. If I hadn't bent down to pet his dog, I would'a been dead myself. It messed with my head, I swear."

I couldn't believe what I was hearing. Maybe it was some weird coincidence. But maybe it wasn't.

When they passed the door, I ran to it. I remembered to turn the sign to CLOSED and stepped outside, looking down the street so I wouldn't lose them. My hand to God, I didn't mean them any harm. If what I thought I heard was right, one of those boys saw my Pat get shot.

It was easy to follow them. They were too busy talking to pay attention to a gray-haired old lady in sneakers back behind them a ways.

They stopped at an apartment building on the same block where Pat died. When the talker turned to say goodbye to his friend, I recognized him. He came into the store every couple of days for a few groceries at a time. Liam, his name was, Liam Byrne. A sad case. Father doing a ten-year stretch for armed robbery and mother working the streets. He was always polite so I usually slipped something extra in the bag for him. Liam was a good kid in spite of what he had to work with.

His friend went on down the street, but that was okay with me. It was Liam I wanted. I held back until he went into the building. I walked into the lobby and waited, listening to his footsteps going up the stairs. He only went up to the second floor. I followed and saw a door closing at the end of the hall. I moved as fast as I could and made it before it shut all the way. Liam turned.

"Mrs. Ryan. What're you doin' here?" He looked younger than his 17 years, until you looked into his eyes.

"I need to talk to you, Liam." I kept my voice soft. I didn't want to spook him.

"What's this about?" He kept his hand on the door, ready to push it closed.

"It's about the man you watched die. It's about Pat."

He wasn't much of a poker player. I could see the thoughts making his face twitch. Tell me I was nuts and to leave? Tell me it was none of my business? Threaten to call the cops? "I don't know what you're talking about."

I moved past him into the apartment. "Close the door. I just want to talk. I heard you and your friend when you passed the store." I sat on a small worn couch. There wasn't much furniture in the room. There was no sign of his mother, and I didn't ask.

"What do you want?"

"I need to know what happened." We stared at each other, and then he gave in.

He said how he went downstairs to have a smoke and enjoy the weather. Then Pat came along with Molly, and they talked for a bit.

"He was getting ready to move on, and I bent over to pet Molly. That's when I heard the shot." He stopped and swiped at the tears on his face. "It came from across the street."

"Did you see who it was?"

Liam shook his head. "I only saw his shoes. Shiny black Florsheims. I could see them in the streetlight when I hit the ground myself. I grabbed Molly's leash. Didn't want her to run away. By the time I got up, the guy was gone. I looked at Mr. Ryan. I knew he was gone too."

His sorrow was real, I had no doubt.

"Then what did you do?"

"I wrapped the leash around Mr. Ryan's hand so Molly would stay." I knew Molly never would've left Pat there alone, but he didn't need to hear that. "Then I went inside. I was so scared. I called the cops, but I didn't say who I was." He looked at me. "I should'a stayed with him."

I felt for the kid. His life was hard enough without that load of guilt he was taking on. "You did the right thing. You made sure Molly was okay. You called for help. There wasn't nothing you could've done for Pat more than that."

I was thinking about the shoes. You didn't see a lot of black Florsheims in this neighborhood. Too expensive. Maybe that would get me somewhere, but I didn't see how.

When I got back to the store, Molly was happy to see me. She was gonna miss Pat almost as much as I was. The phone rang in the back room.

"Mrs. Ryan? It's Collum, over to O'Malley's?"

The funeral arrangements. I had forgotten about them. Collum took over from his dad a few years back. He insisted on calling me Mrs. Ryan, instead of Bridget like I told him to. He was following in his daddy's footsteps, always bein' a professional, even though I knew him since he was in diapers.

"I was going to call you."

"No need. Sergeant Walsh told me about Mr. Zwillman takin' care of everything, but I need to ask you somethin'. Can you come in and pick out a casket?"

It made me sick, thinking about Pat being put in a box. "Could you do it for me?" I was holding back tears. "Something nice. Not too fancy. Pat would hate that."

"Don't you worry. I promise, I'll do him proud." He hesitated. "About the wake."

I knew what he was thinking. "No wake. No open casket." I remembered what Pat looked like, the back of his head messed up. I didn't want to imagine how his face looked. He wouldn't want anyone to see him that way, even if they could pretty him up. "How about if we have the funeral at your place and then go on to the cemetery? We bought plots in St. Barnabas years ago. Pat wasn't much of a church goer, but maybe Father Jack would say a few words."

His voice was gentle. "I'll see to it. I'll let you know when the medical examiner releases him to me."

I thanked him and hung up. I felt weary to my bones. It was time to close up the store and go upstairs to lay down for a while. I knew I wouldn't be able to sleep, but I was having trouble just staying up on my feet.

Next thing I knew, Molly was barking her head off and the bell downstairs was ringing. I stumbled out of bed and saw I had fallen asleep in my clothes on top of the coverlet. "I'm comin'. Hold your horses," I yelled down the stairs and made a quick trip to the bathroom.

When I got out, I saw a cop standing at the foot of the stairs and realized it was Mikey.

"How'd you get in?"

"The store wasn't locked up. I was getting' worried about you."

I explained how I had fallen asleep. I couldn't believe I had forgotten to lock the door. "I guess it all caught up with me." Molly started to pace and whine. "Quiet, girl. I'll take you out. Just hang on." I looked at Mikey. "I'm sorry. It's time for her walk. Pat usually took her around now."

"It's okay. Do you need anything?"

"The only thing I need is to find out who killed my Pat."

Mikey shook his head. "It's gonna be hard. There's no witnesses. No evidence to work with."

"And they're not going to care much about some numbers runner, are they?"

"Now don't talk that way. Pat was a good guy. You and I both know that. But I'll stay on top of it, I promise." As Molly began to bark, Mikey stopped trying to be heard over her. "I'll see you, Bridget."

I thought maybe I should tell him about Liam, but I didn't. The kid didn't need the cops busting his chops. I was sure he would've said if he knew anything else. After he told me how he made sure Molly didn't run away, I knew he had nothing to do with it.

The next morning, Liam came into the store.

"How're you doing?" He spoke softly, and I had to lean a little toward him to hear. His face was pale, and he looked more tired than I was.

"I'm okay. But you don't look so good."

"I keep seeing it. Over and over."

I sat him down at the counter. "Coffee?" He nodded, and I picked up the pot keeping warm on the hot plate. I filled a mug and put it in front of him as I pointed to the sugar bowl and creamer. "Help yourself."

I freshened my own cup. "Sometimes, it helps to talk about what's eatin' at you. Could you tell me again how it happened?" He was starting to refuse when I stopped him. "It would help me. I can take it, and maybe you'll think of something, anything, that would help find out who did this."

He told me the story again, stroking Molly's head. She had come from the back when she heard his voice and settled against his leg. Liam kept his eyes on her, telling her about it. Easier that way.

When he was done, there was nothing different from the first time, but I thought about something he said. "Liam, tell me again the part when you heard the shot. Where were you standing?"

"I was on the curb, facing Pat and Molly on the sidewalk. I bent down to pet her." He stopped. He had the same idea I did. I could see it on his face.

"So the shot came when you bent down?" He nodded. "Could he have been aiming at you, not Pat?" It was hard for me to even say the words. He was just a kid. But kids around the neighborhood grew up fast and got into trouble just as quick.

His hand shook as he tried to take a sip of his coffee. I could see the thinking going on in his head. No poker face, I remembered. He dropped the cup, which broke as it hit the floor. Before I could stop him, Liam ran out of the store.

*****

We had to wait a week for Collum to get Pat's body released, but the funeral was just like Pat would'a wanted it. I couldn't believe how many people turned out. I saw faces I hadn't seen in years. People who moved out of the neighborhood but still remembered the good times, stopping by the store for groceries and shooting the breeze in the back room with friends.

I noticed there was a big wreath of flowers with a ribbon with Pat's name on it next to the coffin. I walked to it.

"Least I could do." I knew that voice. It was Mr. Z. I never expected to see him there. He was like a god to Pat, the reason we survived all these years, what with the grocery store not makin' enough for us to live on.

He patted my shoulder. "I wanted to pay my respects. He was a good man, Bridget. He'll be missed."

"He thought the world of you." I paused, debating whether to go on. "This probably isn't the right time, but I wanted you to know I'm going to keep up with the back room."

I was relieved when he smiled. "Pat always said you were the brains behind the business. We can talk about it later, but I'm sure we can work it out." He handed me a card. "Call me anytime."

I looked down. It was a business card. I didn't see many of those. The raised letters spelled out "Z&Z Enterprises, Inc." There was a phone number under the name.

"That's my personal number," he said. "Don't give it out, but use it if you need to. I want you to know, I'm looking into this. Pat was like family."

He said goodbye and moved toward the door. I hoped he would find whoever did this. Didn't bother me a bit, knowing what he would do to the low life who took my husband from me. I wished I could be there to watch.

Father Jack said some words about Pat, even makin' a joke about how he only saw him on Easter and Christmas. Then Mikey went to stand up front by the coffin. When I'd told him I was worried I'd break down if I talked, he said he would do it. I noticed he wasn't wearing his uniform. I guessed he didn't want any trouble with his bosses, knowing Pat wasn't exactly on the up and up and him being a cop. It was one thing being a dirty cop when most everyone was on the take, but no one would've appreciated him advertising he was friends with a known criminal, even though I never thought of Pat that way.

Mikey talked about how he and Pat had each other's back growing up and even started to tear up, like I was afraid I would do. Molly started to growl. I tried to hush her, but she wasn't used to crowds like this, and I couldn't get her to stop. "What's wrong with you? That's Mikey." I yanked at her collar. Mikey looked over at us and finished up fast. I appreciated him not being mad at how I couldn't calm her, but I didn't have a chance to thank him before Father Jack ended the services with the Lord's Prayer.

Collum came over and told me it was time to head to the cemetery. The car with the coffin went first, followed by the one with Collum driving me, Molly and Father Jack. Mikey's car fell in behind us. I had asked that it only be family, which meant me and Molly, but I knew Pat would appreciate him being there.

Standing by the grave, Father Jack said a few more words and finished with the "ashes to ashes" part. Molly was still acting up, and I bent over to get her quiet. Mikey came closer to say his goodbyes. His feet moved next to Molly. From where I was leaning over her, I saw he wasn't wearing his usual scuffed uniform shoes. To go with the suit he wore for the funeral, he was wearing glossy black Florsheims.

I stayed bent over, petting Molly, trying to hide what I was thinking, and then I stood up. Mikey was looking at Molly who was showing her teeth. "I'm sorry about that," I said. "She's been really upset about all this. She misses Pat."

Mikey didn't meet my eyes. "Don't worry about it." He took a step toward me, to give me a hug, but changed his mind. I didn't blame him. Molly was a sweetheart most of the time, but right now, she was lookin' like she might go for his throat.

"I'll check in with you," he said and turned and left.

I thanked Father Jack and said my goodbye to Pat. I had a lot of thinking to do.

When Molly and I got back to the store, I left the CLOSED sign showing and went upstairs. I wrote a list of questions on a piece of paper. It all came back to Liam. Did someone want to kill him? Why? Could it possibly have been Mikey? I wouldn't put it past him. From what Pat had told me over the years, his friend had done some pretty bad things, like beating up people for Mr. Z. I always knew there was more stuff he wasn't saying, stuff that was even worse. He probably was afraid I'd let it slip.

I couldn't shake the sight of those Florsheims. It didn't surprise me, Mikey wearing expensive shoes. He always had way more money than a cop should have. If he had been aiming at Liam but killed Pat by mistake, he'd be furious, no doubt blaming Liam instead of himself. But what kind of beef would he have with the kid? I had to find Liam.

When it got dark, I took Molly for her walk. I stopped at Liam's building and went up to his apartment, Molly going ahead of me on the stairs. I knocked on his door. No answer. I knew he was probably scared. "Liam? It's Bridget Ryan. And Molly." I gave the dog the hand signal to bark. "Please let us in."

I heard the lock turn. Liam peeked around the door, making sure it really was just us. Inside the apartment, we sat across from each other, me on the couch and him on a chair. Molly looked at each of us and chose to lie down at Liam's feet. It was a good choice. He looked sad and very frightened.

"Did you figure out who might want to hurt you?" I kept my voice soft and calm. Molly's tail thumped on the floor.

Liam reached over to pet her. "I think so. But I don't know how he found out."

"Who found out?"

"The one whose book it was." He started talking faster. "I didn't steal it. I found it in the alley, behind McDougal's Bar."

"Slow down. What kind of book?"

"A notebook. With spirals holding it together. It fell during the fight."

"What fight?" I tried to unravel what he was saying. "Start from the beginning."

"I do some work for Mr. McDougal, washing glasses and cleaning up. When I took the trash out to the cans in the alley, I saw two guys fighting. Wasn't much of a fight. The big guy was pounding the other one, sayin' things like, don't short me again. That kind of thing."

"Then what happened?"

"I stayed back where they couldn't see me until the big guy finally stopped. He looked around and then walked away down the alley. The other guy stayed still at first. I thought he might be dead, but he got up and left going the other way."

"Did you recognize them?"

"Not the little one. But the big one's a cop. I've seen him around. And he was wearing Florsheims. That's probably why I noticed the shoes that night. When, you know."

"Where's the notebook now?"

"I was afraid someone might be comin' to look for it, so I hid it real good. So good, he didn't find it." He explained that the day before Pat was killed, someone had been in his apartment and tore it apart looking for something.

Liam got up and went into the bedroom. He came back with a small spiral-bound pad and handed it to me. "I put it inside the radiator. They stopped running the heat in March, even though we could'a used it." As I opened the cardboard cover, he added, "It's got lots of numbers. I didn't know what to do with it."

He was right. It had lots of numbers and names, too. I needed time to look at it, see if I could figure out what was worth killing for, but I had my suspicions. Mikey was the bagman for Mr. Z, collecting his protection money from all the stores. Even I made a payoff for the grocery store. Didn't matter we were already giving Mr. Z a share from the numbers. That's just the way it was.

I flipped through the pages. This must be Mikey's way of keepin' track. No doubt in my mind he was the one who broke into Liam's apartment. I guessed he decided if he couldn't find the notebook, no one else would, so killing Liam would put an end to it. He didn't figure on the kid bending over to pet Molly. Cost my Pat his life. But the fault was all with Mikey, and I had to figure out what to do about that.

I asked the boy if he had somewhere else to stay. He said he had an aunt in Irvington, the next town over. She would take him in. I slipped him a few bucks to take the bus in the morning. I felt better, knowing he'd be okay.

Back home, I put on a fresh pot of coffee and looked through the notebook. There were four columns. Date. Name. Dollar amount. Another, smaller, dollar amount. It didn't take a genius to put it together. The names were familiar, the owners of the stores all through the neighborhood. Even me. The first amount was what was paid. It was easy to figure out because I knew how much I paid each week. The second amount must be what Mikey turned over to Mr. Z. He was skimming. A very dangerous game. No wonder he took a chance shooting at Liam.

But how did he know Liam had it? I knew where I might find out.

The next morning, I waited until ten, when Danny McDougal's bar opened. Danny and Pat had been friends, and I had seen him at the funeral. When I walked through the door, the place was dark and smelled like spilled beer. The only decoration was a neon sign flashing "Budweiser" once in a while, when it worked up the energy. The regulars were already there, on their favorite stools, starting the day with the hair of the dog.

"Hi, Danny." I sat on an available stool, and Molly flopped down on the floor next to me, looking up at him behind the bar.

"Hey, Bridget. How're you doin'? It was a good send-off for Pat. Terrible thing." He looked over the bar at Molly. "Hey, girl. Want your treat?" Her ears perked up as he reached into a jar of pretzels and tossed one to her. "Good catch." He smiled at me. "She always got her treat when she came in with Pat."

"You were a good friend to him. Can I talk to you, Danny? Somewhere quiet?"

The bar was already quiet, but he got the message. "Sure. Come on back."

Molly and I followed him to a small office tucked near the exit to the alley. "What's going on?"

"It's about Liam and something that happened here before Pat was killed."

"Liam? He didn't have nothin' to do with it, did he?"

"No, not like that."

"Glad to hear it. He's a good kid."

I told him I was aware. "Can you tell me if something happened in the alley a couple nights before Pat was shot?"

Danny took time to think. "You mean the beatin'?"

I nodded. "I know Mikey beat the crap outta someone."

"The guy wasn't paying, and Mikey was giving him a lesson. He walked away, so it wasn't serious."

Now for the most important part. "Did Mikey come into the bar later, looking for something, or someone?"

He thought again. "Yeah, he did. He wanted to know if anyone was out in the alley after he left. He dropped something, and it was gone. I told him Liam took out the trash that night." He must've seen something in my face. "Was that the wrong thing? I didn't mean no harm."

I told him it was nothing, I was just curious. I stood and headed to the door with Molly. "Thanks. Don't give it another thought." I left before he had a chance to ask me anything else.

I had solved Pat's murder but now what? I couldn't go to the cops. What would I tell them? What would Pat want me to do? I know what he wouldn't want. Me taking the gun he kept in the back room and blowing Mikey's head off, just like he did to Pat. I played it out in my head. How it would sound. How it would feel. But there was a better way, one I knew I could live with.

I sat at the kitchen table with the phone in front of me. I had to make sure I did it right. I took out the business card and dialed the number. "Mr. Zwillman? This is Bridget Ryan. I have something I need to tell you."

Discord
Ruth Morgan

'Mum, are you comfortable?' Lenny Tallis asked.

'Yes Lenore,' a blue veined hand reached out.

Senior Constable Lenore Tallis sounded to her ears awkward and posh. She preferred Lenny, her mother dismissing it as 'blokey' in the same way she dismissed Lenny's decision to become an accountant. And then join the police force. 'It's such a waste of your beautiful soprano voice.'

The name was typical of her mother, selecting a name from opera to remind everyone who she was and the path she'd expected her daughter to follow.

'I'll see if the nurses have a vase for the roses, back in a minute.' Lenny left the room, her work boots beating out a tattoo on the polished floors. She returned with a vase wrestling the blooms into the semblance of an arrangement.

In the other bed, lay an elderly woman, the gentle rise and fall of her chest the only signs of life. Her white hair was cut short, and her shoulders were covered by a pale blue silk nightdress. The voices had woken her and she opened her eyes to discover the cause of the disturbance.

'I'm Elisaveta Shillingsworth. And you are?' she demanded.

'I'm Lenny,' she heard her mother wince. 'My mother is Lucia.'

'I was promised a single room,' Elisaveta's voice was scornful. 'I don't want to share with some ignorant old woman.'

'It's only for a couple of days. We're short of beds at the moment,' said a nurse checking on her patients.

Elisaveta snorted.

'I've got to go back to work,' said Lenny. 'I'll come and see you later.' And leaning over she gave her mother a kiss on the cheek her nostrils filled with the smell Dior face powder. It was something that took her instantly back to childhood.

As she walked across the carpark, Tony Shillingsworth came towards her. Lenny stopped, opened her mouth to speak, then squaring her shoulders kept walking. There was nothing left to be said.

*****

Ignorant old woman indeed, Lucia smiled to herself. Facing death hadn't changed Elisaveta. She was still the prima donna, an OBE, a soprano who'd graced the opera stages of the world. She'd returned to Whitworth, the town of her birth, to spend her last days in familiar surroundings according to news reports. Nonsense. The Elisaveta she'd known was as hard as nails, without a single sentimental bone in her body. So why was she really here?

She may not remember Lucia—yet.

Lucia dozed off, to be woken by the lyrical opening notes of Casta Diva from the first act of Norma. It had been Elisaveta's signature aria from the opera she'd made her own. Considered one of the most demanding soprano roles written it highlighted her almost limitless breath control. The irony was now she struggled to breathe despite the oxygen mask.

Elisaveta moved restlessly, the bed squeaking. 'I demand a replacement bed that does not squeak.' Her voice was a whisper. 'They need to listen.'

Her imperious tone wiped away the years, taking Lucia back to childhood.

Lucia was the quieter one, a foil for Elisaveta's boisterous personality. As class began, Lucia had put her hand up, a request to be excused so she could visit the draughty long drop toilet. Had the teacher heard, or chosen to ignore the child from the wrong side of the tracks? Then it was too late and she was the child made to clean up the pool with a mop. She'd been ashamed, hurt, her legs wet and uncomfortable.

'You didn't listen,' said Elisaveta, when the class resumed. 'This is your fault.' She stood upright, addressing the teacher without fear.

'The headmaster's office, now, both of you,' snapped the teacher, holding the door open. Lucia walked outside, mortified by the squelching sound from her panties.

'Here,' Elisaveta said, pulling her behind the toilets and helping her clean up. 'You'll just have to put on your sports bloomers,' she said throwing the wet underwear into a bin. 'Let me do the talking,' as she knocked on the headmaster's door.

Lucia was a tentative child, afraid of her own shadow.

Elisaveta never backed down, afraid of nothing.

Lucia wondered if she was afraid now. Did she see death sitting in the corner of the room deciding who to take first? Or would she stand her ground and defeat even him.

'It is my favourite opera, my favourite aria,' Elisaveta said when the music finished. The last demanding phrase filled the air competing with the rattling sounds of trolleys, the clattering of saucepans in the kitchens and the faint sounds of sobbing from a distant corridor.

'Do you like music?' she asked.

What a question? The high notes soaring out into the world, the glorious compositions of Mozart, Puccini, Beethoven. Music still made Lucia's soul sing even if her body and mind were failing.

'I like music,' Lucia's cautious reply.

'And sang like an angel according to my mother,' said a nurse bustling into the room to dispense good cheer and medication.

'You sang?' asked Elisaveta, a pause. 'Professionally?'

'Yes.'

'Your debut was in Milan wasn't it?' asked the nurse. 'My mother collected all your records.'

'Lucia Tallis.' Elisaveta stated, without waiting for confirmation. 'Pull the curtains nurse please. I'm very tired.'

The nurse shrugged. Everyone had always done as Elisaveta asked, except Lucia. Elisaveta had neither forgotten, nor forgiven.

*****

Lenny sat in the driver's seat, hands clenched on the steering wheel. Tony was the last person she wanted to see. She didn't even know he was back in Whitworth. Seeing him again was as unlikely as Lucia and Elisaveta sharing a room. No doubt, that's where he was going—to see his mother.

Tony. She sighed, switched on the ignition and headed back to work.

There was no point thinking about things that couldn't be changed.

Lenny settled behind the computer to resume work. The case involved embezzlement, money laundering and the murder of George West at nearby Milford. Her role was to collate the evidence for the prosecution case against Mackenzie Holten, ex police officer charged with corruption and murder. She enjoyed the methodical nature of the work and the challenges of being a copper in a rural city. The case enabled her to use her accounting background.

She'd been content, looking after her mother at home with nursing support until her condition deteriorated and the moment came they'd both feared.

The River Hospice was attached to Whitworth Base hospital. A small unit with six beds, the big picture windows overlooked the gardens, and the rose beds. Her mother had always adored roses, and already the bare stalks were covered in green shoots. It was unlikely that Lucia would live long enough to see the buds open. Each time she went to visit, she took a bunch of roses. The flowers were lovely but lacked the intense perfume of the roses covering the arbour in the back garden.

Of all the people in the world she anticipated would share her mother's last days—top of the list had to be Elisaveta Shillingsworth. The last person she wanted to see again was Tony.

She closed her eyes for a moment, driving the memories back into the past where they belonged.

A moment's peace was shattered by the ringing telephone.

Lenny shook her head. 'Tallis.'

*****

The music of Lakmé soothed Lucia's tired mind as she remembered the first time she'd sung the Flower Duet with Elisaveta. The harmonies and soaring notes still filled her eyes with tears.

She'd fought hard for her career, working in supermarkets and cafes to pay for tuition, struggling on the pittance from scholarships. The music made the battles worthwhile.

They'd competed against each other at eisteddfods since they were seven and until their teens, their rivalry was friendly. Then, everything changed.

Lucia had made a casual comment to a fellow music student about Elisaveta's ambition to make her debut at Covent Garden. An innocent enough remark twisted into something different. When her former friend challenged her about breaking confidence, Lucia remarked that it was something everyone wanted to do, and what everyone in their class was aiming for.

'But,' Elisaveta spat angrily 'not everyone is planning to sleep their way to the top because they don't have the talent.'

'I didn't say that,' Lucia protested loudly. She could see from Elisaveta's tight-lipped expression she wasn't believed.

Before the end of the day, the tables had been turned and Elisaveta had told classmates Lucia's darkest, deepest secret. The thing she'd confided in a moment of despair to someone she thought she could trust.

Lucia knew something had happened when she was called into the principal's office, and asked to sit down. The school chaplain was also present. 'Lucia,' she began. 'I wonder if there is something going on at school, or at home you may want to discuss.'

A cold sweat broke out over Lucia's skin. 'I know I haven't been getting assignments in on time…' she began, knowing in her gut what they wanted but determined to remain silent.

The two adults glanced at each other. 'There are some rumours circulating…' they began, 'disturbing rumours about your family life.'

'I know,' said Lucia, her voice unsteady.

'Is there any truth in them?' the principal asked. That was typical thought Lucia, more interested in the reputation of the school than in the welfare of her students.

'They're lies,' Lucia stated. 'It's unwise,' she said. 'To listen to gossip and foul rumours spread by girls who ought to know better. Is there anything else, I don't want to be late for another class.' Her head held high, her gaze holding firm.

*****

Lucia's singing and confidence suffered and she missed the opportunity to sing The Flower Duet at a concert on the Sydney Opera House stage.

She continued to study at the Conservatorium.

Elisaveta landed a place at the Juilliard School of Music in New York and it was three years before they met again.

*****

Lenny returned from lunch, humming softly and planning to untangle another section of West's complicated ledgers. As she walked into the office, she stopped suddenly.

'What the hell are you doing here? I thought I made it clear…' she asked the man sitting at the other desk in her office.

'Ah Senior Constable,' said Inspector Mark Findlay. 'We have the services of Tony Shillingsworth, a forensic accountant … you know each other?'

'Yes,' they said at the same time.

'Then I hope your relationship can remain professional? Constable? Mr Shillingsworth?'

'If you will excuse me for a moment Inspector, I'm going to get a coffee from downstairs. It will give Lenny a chance to tell you why she won't work with me.'

He was gone from the office almost before she could protest.

'Is that what you're going to do Lenny?' asked Inspector Findlay.

'I can't work with him,' she stopped, and took a deep breath. 'Isn't there someone else?'

Findlay shook his head. 'He's been working with the Fraud Squad in

Sydney. With your combined expertise we have an opportunity to link laundered funds to local criminal activity.'

'Can I clarify who is in charge?'

'Mr Shillingsworth is a civilian. It's a police operation.'

'So, if it came to the crunch, I have the authority?'

'He's only in Whitworth for two months, so make the most of his skills.' He looked steadily at her. 'I know it's a difficult time Lenny, for both of you. There is professional support available if either of you need it.'

'I'll let him know. You can't change the past. It's time to move on.'

*****

The office door opened bringing with it the smell of fresh coffee.

'I wasn't sure you still took sugar,' said Tony, putting a cup on her desk along with two sugar sachets.

'Thanks.'

'Can we work together?' he asked sitting opposite.

'Yes.'

'So bring me up to speed.'

*****

After work, Lenny returned to the hospice. She wanted to make the most of the time left. As she walked down the hospital corridor, the soaring sounds of opera reached out to greet her.

'Lenore,' her mother asked, 'would you put on another CD, that one's just about to finish.'

'Which one?'

'Merry Window,' said a voice from the bed alongside.

'La Traviata,' argued Lucia

'Well, which one?' asked Lenny.

'It's my CD player, my choice,' said Lucia.

'I've never liked La Traviata, too soppy,' muttered Lenny. 'Can we have something else?'

'Cosi fan tutti, I've always loved Mozart,' said a male voice from behind her.

'I have to put up with you at work, and now you follow me here.' The snap of anger was clear in her voice.

'Tony has good taste. He got that from me.' Elisaveta championed her flesh and blood.

'A debateable point,' muttered Lenny. 'He has good taste in music.' Cosi was one of her favourite operas, and he knew it. 'I'll see you tomorrow, mum.' Lenny turned to leave.

'Don't go, just because Tony is here,' said Elisaveta. 'Such a shame you let him go.'

'I'm going because it's been a long day, nothing to do with Tony,' Lenny lied. 'Good night mum.'

Leaning over, she kissed her mother on the cheek. The skin was already cool, and she knew time was running out.

She turned and walked quickly from the room, determined to hide the tears streaming down her cheeks. They'd had a troubled relationship, regardless, she loved the difficult old woman, and there would be a huge hole left in her life when she died.

Behind her she could hear hurrying footsteps on the gravel. 'Lenny, I'm sorry you're upset, my mother doesn't always think about what she says.'

'She knew exactly what she was saying.'

'That's unfair. She's very frail.'

'Stop making excuses for her,' tears rolling down her cheeks. He reached out, and she pushed his arm away. 'It's over. I can work with you, if I have no choice. But there's nothing between us now. Your actions made sure of that.'

'And you don't forgive. Do you? Just like your mother.' And he walked away.

Lenny drove from the carpark sobbing.

*****

After five years away, Elisaveta had returned to Australia and joined the chorus of Opera Australia with Lucia, the two singing alongside. As two young singers at the start of their professional careers, both born in the same town, it was natural they resumed their friendship and soon they became inseparable.

Then Lucia fell in love. Antonio Campaggio was the middle son of a musical family, making his way through the ranks of the company already singing solos. She asked her good friend Elisaveta to sing at the wedding and watched her steal the man she loved. At the reception as the time came for speeches, Lucia had gone into the warm summer evening to look for her husband. She'd found him, in the arms of Elisaveta.

'He loves me,' she said, her arms around his neck. 'You made a mistake, let him go, he's mine.'

'No. Leave now.'

A flash of anger crossed Elisaveta's beautiful face, her lips tightened. She dropped her arms and walked away.

Even now, forty years later, Lucia remembered the pain, and the struggle to stop the tears ruining her makeup and dripping mascara onto the white silk gown.

Guests cheered when the couple walked into the hall. On what ought to have been the happiest day of her life, Lucia painted a smile on her face that didn't waiver. She began her marriage with the agony of a broken heart knowing the man she loved, loved another.

Instead of a night of passion, it had been a night of arguments ending with torrents of tears. Even as her new husband made love to her, she knew he was imagining she was someone else.

Lucia told herself over and over that she was happy. It was a lie to ease the pain.

Now, in the other bed, was the woman who'd taken the love of her life. As the last notes of Merry Widow Waltz faded, beauty was replaced by the sounds of the hospital, the living and the dying, the rattling of trolleys and voices fighting for supremacy.

*****

Lenny poured herself a second glass of wine, a Led Zeppelin CD on the stereo. Was it an act of rebellion against a childhood diet of opera? She loved music, in all its forms. She listened to two tracks and then swapped it to Classic FM.

How was she going to manage to work with Tony? The history between them intruded at every moment, and yesterday had been hard enough.

Tony had been in her first class on her first day of university. She still remembered her mother's shock when she announced she'd applied and been accepted to study accountancy.

'But your beautiful voice, what about that? And to choose such a colourless profession, all that gray.' It was Lenny's first overt act of rebellion against her strong willed mother, and not the last. Her choice to be called Lenny rather than Lenore was the second.

While Lucia's career was played out on the international stage, Lenny soared among her classmates graduating with honours and starting work at one of the big accounting firms in Sydney. Tony, followed suit, and they moved in together.

Being in the wrong place at the wrong time changed their lives.

Lenny had gone to the bank, a quick trip on her way back from a lunch that ended up lasting twelve hours.

A bank robbery gone wrong, turned into a siege, and Lenny and three other women were held hostage. She emerged shell-shocked and traumatised, running across the street straight into Tony's arms. As a witness, she gave evidence in the trial that sent the robbers, to jail for long sentences. Apart from the mastermind who vanished.

Unsettled Lenny struggled at work, deciding to take time off and she returned to her home town of Whitworth. A chance meeting with a friend who'd joined the police force, a long discussion, a bottle of wine and a decision was made.

She returned to Sydney a couple of days later.

As she drove towards their unit, she saw Tony open the door for a woman—someone she'd worked with. She pulled into the carpark and caught the lift upstairs, without advance warning of her arrival, and let herself in. He was surprised to see her back and instead of a loving return, their meeting turned into a no holds barred argument with hurt and anger on both sides. Things were said impossible to take back.

Lenny knew he'd betrayed her trust, sleeping with a friend. She didn't give him the opportunity to explain. All men were the same, her mother had taught her that and now Lenny knew she was right.

She stormed out, slamming the door and stayed a motel. Going into work the following day, she quit, arranged for her possessions to be shipped into storage in Whitworth and went to Goulburn to begin her new career leaving the past behind her.

It was five years since she'd seen Tony. And now she was working with him every day and the past was a constant presence in the room like an unwelcome and persistent ghost.

Lenny cleaned her teeth, locked up, turned out the lights and went to bed. Tomorrow she'd work out a way to exorcise the ghost.

*****

In an increasingly unhappy marriage, Lucia came home to discover Antonio had left and moved in with Elisaveta. Lucia fled to Italy. There were lovers, classes with well-respected teachers, then on her 27th birthday, her solo operatic debut at La Scala.

The following year, came the request for a divorce. The papers were full of the news—baritone Antonio Campaggio marries Elisaveta Shillingsworth after their shared debut in *The Merry Widow* at Covent Garden.

Elisaveta had never forgiven Lucia for refusing to give up Antonio. And Lucia had never forgiven Elisaveta for ruining her marriage. Neither woman had learned to forgive, a trait they'd passed onto their children.

And now, nearly forty years later, they were side by side in a hospice.

When Antonio was killed in a car accident in the Swiss Alps, she'd had his body embalmed and shipped back to Australia. He was buried in an ornate black marble crypt in the cemetery overlooking the river. The woman in the car was buried in Switzerland. Lucia remembered the newspaper speculation about the nature of their relationship. He'd always been a womaniser. And for the first time she could see Elisaveta had suffered too. Getting out of the marriage freed Lucia to meet the real love of her life, Lenore's father. The man who'd died five years ago from cancer. And now, very soon, she sensed, she would join him.

For the last year, she'd lived with Lenore, and with increasing medical assistance she'd been able to stay at home. To some extent the two women had rebuilt their relationship. Lenore would be alone with Lucia died. Approaching forty with no love in her life, work was no substitute for a satisfying relationship. And the only man Lenore had ever really loved was Tony.

Lucia hit replay on the CD player and the glorious sounds of Handel's Messiah filled the room.

If Leonore wouldn't make a move, then Lucia would. But first there needed to be a conversation with her roommate. Something they'd avoided for a lifetime.

She had to start somewhere. And time was running out.

'Lisaveta, are you awake?'

*****

Lenny loved Thursday evenings. This was the time when she set aside her work, to devote to her other love. Music. She'd sung all her life and had recently joined an A cappella group that sang at local nursing homes and hospitals around Whitworth. Lenny with her clear soprano had been a welcome addition. She'd arrived, the music of the songs they were rehearsing running through her mind.

She heard the doors open, but didn't open her eyes, swept away on the music. At the completion of the song, she opened her eyes to see Tony Shillingsworth, sitting opposite, smiling gently.

'We have a new member joining our group, a reasonable baritone he tells me,' announced the choir master.

Lenny could feel the heat rising in her face.

'Lenny I believe you know Tony? Would you introduce him to the group?'

Reluctantly she walked to the front of the stage and made a reasonable fist of it. What did she add? That he couldn't be trusted?

He was a handsome man, silver strands through the dark hair, highlighted at the temples. She could see other members of the group casting admiring glances in his direction. For the first time in years, she looked at him through other eyes. He caught her glance and smiled. She realised music, the connection they'd always had may just be the bridge that would enable them to cross the past. It was a way of laying the ghosts to rest.

The rehearsals went well, and his voice fitted in beautifully. Afterwards he walked her to her car, as he'd always done. 'See you in the morning,' she said.

'Before you go, can we talk? There's a bench overlooking the river.'

They walked side by side in silence.

'The night you came back from Whitworth…'

She stood. 'There's nothing to talk about.'

'Lenny. Please.' There was something in his voice she hadn't heard before.

'Please sit, and listen?'

She shrugged, not promising anything.

'What you thought you saw isn't what happened.'

'I know what I saw. There's no point to this conversation.'

'Lenny, please, just let me finish. You wouldn't let me explain then. Please let me explain now. I was tempted. I was alone. I was convinced you wouldn't come back to me, that I'd lost you forever.'

'I was always coming back.'

He reached over and kissing the tip of his finger, put it on her lips. He'd always done that when she was angry or upset about something. He'd remove it, then take her in his arms and kiss her gently. She realised, to her surprise, that's exactly what she wanted him to do now

'Cass came to the flat to drop off some files for a meeting the following morning. She was always flirty and kissed me.'

'And it went no further? I don't believe that.'

'I was tempted, I admit that. With her it would have been just sex. With you, it was love. And,' he paused, his voice unsteady, 'I didn't want to be like my father. It's always been you, the only one I ever loved.'

She leant over and whispered in his ear, and he burst out laughing.

'It's a deal and I believe you're a good shot!'

'It's been a long day. We'll talk more tomorrow.'

They walked back to the carpark, hands touching.

As she reached into her bag for the car keys, she glanced at the phone. 'Something's happening,' she said, playing the first of the messages.

'This is Sister Williams from River Hospice. Please ring me urgently.'

Tony wrapped an arm around her shoulders as she dialled the number, putting it on speaker.

'Lenny, your mother has taken a turn for the worse. I think you'd better come now.'

'I'm on my way Sister.'

'Lenny, I'll drive.' Tony held out his hand. 'We don't have time to argue.'

She handed him the keys and got into the passenger seat.

*****

'Lenny …' said Lucia softly, struggling to breathe. 'Together?' she looked at Tony. A tear trickled from one corner of her eye. 'He's a good man.'

From the other side of the room came Elisaveta's voice. 'Tony, push my bed closer please.'

A nurse appeared and helped push the beds together. 'It won't be long,' she said.

Lenny nodded.

Elisaveta laid her hand on Lucia's. Lucia's hand turned, and took it. Her other hand was holding Lenny's.

Tony slid his arm around Lenny's waist.

In a faint voice, Elisaveta began to sing the first words to Ave Maria. Tony followed with his baritone, and Lenny joined in, her soprano voice soaring to fill the room.

Three voices sang as one.

A gentle smile moved over Lucia's lips, the lines from her face faded, and she sighed softly, and lay still.

Nothing but the Sleuth
Diane Arrelle

Gretchen glared at the headline with disbelief. *How'd that no-talent cow do it again?*, she wondered for probably the fiftieth time.

"Will ya look at that," she shrieked at Bill.

Bill looked up from the computer and glanced at the newspaper Gretchen was holding in a white knuckled grasp, wrinkling the text into illegible creases.

"I presume you are not ranting about the sports scores or last night's Borough meeting?" He asked with a sigh.

"I'm talking about April Later. She supposedly solved another murder for the police. I swear that woman has no writing ability and that our police force must be a bunch of morons who could be replaced by a bag of potato chips and still be as effective if not a tad more compassionate to a person going just a few miles over the speed limit while rushing to get to work on time."

Bill shot Gretchen a cruel smile and said, "Gosh, Dear, could that be sour grapes I'm hearing, and perhaps one of the worst sentences ever uttered by a writer?"

Gretchen glared at her husband. "Leave my writing out of this. I'm a damned good reporter and I know I'm a better author than April Later. I just need a good break."

"Like your neck," Bill muttered.

"I heard that! But I'm serious, I write damn good mysteries and I could solve crimes just like her, if you'd only give me a chance to do some investigative journalism."

Bill swiveled in his office chair and faced his wife. "Gretchen, I know we are married but I am still the editor here and I'll have to say it again, you are a good correspondent, one of the best I have at covering town events, but you are not logical enough nor talented enough to be an investigative reporter. April Later may be lucky with her mysteries but as our village's only amateur sleuth, she is a living, breathing wonder. Face it, she's damned good and we, in this burg, appreciate it."

Gretchen glared at Bill a moment and then turned and walked over to the filing cabinet. Yanking open a drawer, she pulled out a fat file and started waving it at him. "Look at this, Later April, her file is so full it frightens me. Don't you think that it is strange that there are so many murders in such a small town? Don't you think it's strange that everywhere this woman visits somebody dies?

Bill just shook his head and went back to his computer. "Why don't you go home, dear, and work on your newest attempt at a mystery."

"That's just what I'm going to do," Gretchen muttered storming from the office. "I'm going to solve myself a little mystery. Yeah, I'm going to find out why April Later is always around to solve the crime."

Getting into her car Gretchen dialed her cell phone. "April? Gretchen Harris here. Say, are you busy? I was wondering if you'd meet me for lunch. I'd love to do a feature on you."

Fifteen minutes later Gretchen was seated at the local bistro. Sipping a Vodka Collins, she waited for April to come. "I need a way to trip her up," she mumbled and signaled for another drink. She just finished that drink when April entered the dark restaurant. She stood silhouetted in the doorway for a minute until she moved into the room and joined Gretchen. She fluffed her perfectly coifed silver hair and smiled her million-dollar greeting letting her deep wrinkles turn up into smile lines."

"Gretchen, dearheart. So good of you to call. I just can't believe that you'd want to do a story on me, your paper has always been so kind. And I have another novel coming out so the publicity will be great."

Gretchen signaled for another drink stared into April's deep-set blue eyes and got to the point. "April, I want to do an article on your superb deductive skills. There are so very, very many of us who want to know how you do it, solve vicious crime after violent crime. Why, you've probably solve more real murders than fictional ones."

April smiled, and slowly sipped her sherry. "I guess I just have to say it is my writer's natural curiosity. Must have been a cat in a past life."

She laughed and Gretchen gulped down her drink and waved for another. *More like a dog*, she thought with a smirk. *A great big silver bitch, one that kills just for the fun of it, maybe even a wild dingo.*

"I just have a knack for finding clues and once I uncover one clue, I'm hooked until I can solve the case. I know I'm just an old busybody, but if I can help this community, if I can pay back my public by putting criminals where they belong, then I feel like my life has been worthwhile. After all, I feel that we are all put on this good, dear, earth for a reason and I know my reason has to be more important than writing silly old books. I mean, Gretchen Dear, you are a fine newspaper writer, don't you feel like you should have a bigger purpose?"

"Uh…sure," Gretchen said trying to concentrate on making the room stop spinning. She took another sip and tried to sit up straighter. "I want to right society's wrongs too, and I plan to start by proving that someone in this area is a serial killer!"

There, she nodded to herself, *I've put all the cards on the table, exposed my hand, let the cat out of the bag. Now the ball's in her court. Oh my God, I'm thinking in stale cliches, I need another drink.* Gretchen waved a limp hand to the waiter for another round.

April was smiling, her bright blue eyes sent the message that she seemed to be enjoying herself immensely. "A serial killer? A mystery that needs to be solved and I've missed it. Well, good luck Dear. Now, if you will just excuse me for a moment I must go powder my nose."

Gretchen thought about getting up, but decided to wait for the restaurant to come to a complete stop.

April was back in no time at all, as far as Gretchen was concerned, but perhaps she had just grabbed a little nap while the older woman was gone.

"So, Gretchen, how is your writing going? Still trying to sell a mystery?"

Gretchen groaned as she tried to hold onto the edge of the table before it threw her to the ground.

"I take that as no luck yet. Tell you what, Dear, why don't you send me one of your manuscripts and I'll ask my publisher to critique it for you."

Struggling to find the words, to force her tongue to respond, Gretchen spat out a slurred tirade. "Critique my ass, send it to him and he'd buy it. You're just scared that I'm onto you. So you want to buy my cooperation. Well, just you wait and see, I'll get the goods on you lady. I'll prove that you aren't solving murders, you're doing 'em. I just can't figure out how you've bamboozled everyone else in this dump of a—"

"GRETCHEN!"

Gretchen stopped yelling and turned to see Bill behind her.

"Gretchen, I could just kill you for this." He bent down and helped her rise to wobbly feet. "April, thanks for calling me. I'm truly sorry for my wife. She didn't mean it, it's the jealously speaking."

April smiled at them. "No harm done, a little controversy never hurts book sales you know and I know she has a good heart. It was the alcohol mixed with the green-eyed monster speaking, not dear, sweet, Gretchen. I'm sure that someday she'll make it as a writer."

"If she lives that long," Bill said and half-walked half-carried Gretchen to his car.

That evening when Gretchen woke, the house was dark.

"Bill?" she called. "Bill are you home?"

She got up on unsteady legs and staggered to the bathroom and threw up. After a shower, two cups of black coffee and a handful of pain killers, Gretchen called Bill at the office. No answer. "Must be out on business," she said knowing that he probably wasn't. This was one avenue she didn't want to investigate at all.

Investigate! That's right, she remembered. She wasn't finished yet, in fact now that she had blown her real intentions toward April, she really had to act fast. Throwing on her coat she walked the half mile to April's ivy covered gingerbread cottage. "Too damned cute for words," Gretchen said eyeing the dark domicile. "I bet she's got plenty of ugly evidence hidden inside."

She tried the knob and was surprised to find the door unlocked. "Some mystery writer. Trusts people just because small towns are supposed to be so safe." She went inside and took a mini-flashlight from her coat pocket. She searched the entire house then noticed the basement door. She went down and turned on the light. The entire back wall was lined with filing cabinets. She opened the first five and found them filled with manuscripts, contracts and newsclippings. But the last two were it. "Aha the evidence is down there!" she whispered with triumph. "I just need to make copies of this and I'll have the news story of my life." She rifled through the folders, one for every person in town. Each was full of gossip and facts, each held the life story of a real person. Gretchen was so involved that she didn't hear the sound behind until it was too late.

She felt the cold steel against the back of her head.

"Yes, Gretchen Dear, it is a gun and if I shot you dead right now, it would be an open and shut case of breaking and entering and the unfortunate aftermath of self defense against a robber. But I'd like to avoid that."

"So would I, April," Gretchen said with a shaky voice.

"Gretchen why don't you take out your folder and tell me if my facts are correct."

Gretchen read through tears of fear and tears of humiliated anger. Yes, all the facts were there. Single until she was 40 when she met and married Bill five years ago. A borderline alcoholic, a so-so reporter, a failed mystery writer, a bitter and burnt out human.

"Now dear, take out Bill's."

Gretchen read on with a sinking feeling as all her fears were realized. She'd trapped Bill with a false pregnancy and he'd stopped being faithful about three years ago. An unhappy man in an unhappy marriage.

"See Dear, you really are pathetic, not only ruining your own existence but poor Bill's as well. Such a shame, such a waste of a nice man."

Gretchen turned slowly and looked at April, "You going to kill me?

April shook her head no.

"Why all the files?" Gretchen asked. "You really are the killer aren't you? I just don't understand how you did it and got all those innocent people to confess?"

April laughed, her voice sounding like happy jingle bells. "Let's go upstairs and sit down, I'm too old to be standing around in damp basements."

She waved the gun, motioning for Gretchen to go first and followed a safe distance behind.

Once in the living room, Gretchen was shocked to see Bill sitting on the couch apparently asleep. "Is…is he…dead? Did you poison him? Are you planning to pin this on me? It won't work you know. I won't confess."

Motioning Gretchen to sit in the armchair across from her husband, April giggled, sounding like a schoolgirl. "Dear me, he's quite all right, just in a deep hypnotic state. I'm a licensed hypnotist you know. Did that for a living before I started writing. Anyway dear, Bill is all right for now and I promise you that I won't hurt either one of you."

Gretchen stared at her nemesis and shuddered. *What was going on? What was this woman planning?* Gretchen knew she was right, that April Later was a cold blooded killer, so why was she lying to her?

"What now?" Gretchen asked. "Why have you done this to my husband?"

"To set up the scenario. Dear girl, you were almost on the money. I've caused every crime since I've moved here and decided to become a writer. You see, I'm not very imaginative, a fatal flaw for a novelist. I needed the crimes to be carried out before I could write about them. I needed to see it, to write it. I was good enough to set the scene to provide the motivation. I was just not good enough at the description. So I had others do the crimes for me."

"But how?" Gretchen asked, interested in spite of her fear.

"You know that old saying that you can't hypnotize someone to do something that they are morally incapable of doing?"

Gretchen nodded, looking at Bill with a chill of fear.

"Well, I got around that by studying people and finding out what they would do. That is how I got them to commit the crimes. I hypnotized them to do what they secretly wanted to do. And then I pretended to solve the murders. It was easy and the police here really aren't very sophisticated. The murders helped me with my writing the books, and this amateur sleuth business helped sell them."

Gretchen looked at Bill slumped over and shuddered at all the grief she'd caused him. "And now?"

"Well, Gretchen, because you were so clever, I'm now afraid that I'll have to cause another crime. If you started asking too many questions others might follow suit. Right now, I'm just a beloved and sacred celebrity here. No one suspects me of any of the coincidences because fame makes the masses blind. Nobody wants a hero to be mortal."

Gretchen sat in silence, finally wordless.

"So here's the plot. I've hypnotized your husband and he's now going to take you home. Everyone heard him threaten you this afternoon and nobody will really blame him, actually they'll feel sorry for him. Poor, poor Bill, turning to other women for comfort and love. Poor Bill, humiliated at work as well as and all over town by that alcoholic shrew. I won't even have to solve this one. Even the police will be able to see Bill did it and with good cause.

Gretchen found her voice. "Bill won't do it."

April laughed. "This time you are dead wrong. Now I really must leave." April went out the back door and called into the room, "Bill, you will awaken now and respond when you hear the command. Gretchen you'll really like this. Bill, the word is Sleuth."

Gretchen shivered with horror as Bill snapped awake and stared at her with the most malevolence she had ever seen.

She started to call to April.

To stop him.

But he was already dragging her out the door and toward home, using a tight two handed grip to the throat.

Two Peas in a Pod
Issy Jinarmo

Barry Smart, a tall, slim-built man with a receding hairline, looked at his reflection in the bathroom mirror. He gave his chin a rub and ran his fingers over his top lip. For 32 years he had sported a moustache. He was now 62, on holiday at a NSW resort with his wife Brenda who was still asleep. "It's time for change," he said to the bathroom mirror.

Twenty minutes later he was in the kitchen preparing eggs and bacon for his wife and himself. Every few seconds he rubbed his hairless upper lip and smiled.

"Bren, breakfast," he called, wondering what Brenda would say when she saw her 'moustache-less' husband.

Brenda joined Barry on the verandah of their suite overlooking the shining waters of the Barrington Coast and quickly devoured her breakfast. She made no mention of Barry's changed appearance. He was amazed.

"Let's go for a walk before the heat of the day," she suggested.

"Good idea," commented Barry, looking intently at his wife. Still no reaction!

Half an hour later the couple were window-shopping in town. Brenda stopped outside the jewellers. She grabbed Barry's hand. "Look, Bazza, look at that stunning sapphire ring. What a perfect anniversary gift," she cooed, her gaze intently focused on the ring.

"Whoa up, Bren," Barry said, "not so fast, there's no price tag."

"Come on, let's enquire," Brenda suggested, pulling her husband through the shop door.

'Still no comment about my moustache,' thought Barry, miffed his changed appearance had gone unnoticed by his wife.

"May we be of assistance?" enquired the jeweller.

"My wife would love to look at the sapphire ring you have in your window, the one with no price tag!" Barry said, emphasising the word 'no.'

"It has a very unique setting. It's $15,500," the jeweller replied, as he removed the ring from the window and placed it on a velvet pad in front of the Smarts.

"That much!" exclaimed Barry.

Suddenly, Brenda gasped. "Oh, my goodness Barry, where the hell has your moustache gone?"

"You've actually—" The rest of Barry's sentence was cut short.

Through the door burst two men pushing Barry and Brenda aside. The taller man removed the ring from the counter, placing it in a small bag while the other man turned the 'Open' door sign to 'Closed' and began feverishly throwing jewellery from display cabinets into a beach bag.

The jeweller attempted to hit the alarm bell. The tall man noticed his movement, viciously hitting him to the ground. He did not move!

Brenda looked intently at the tall man. He was the same height as Barry, his hair more plentiful, but, amazingly, he had a moustache making him look like Barry's twin! Well, as he had looked prior to his shave!

Barry, too, was aghast. Firstly, because the robbery was happening before his very eyes but, secondly, at the appearance of the tall man. It was as if he was looking at himself in a mirror. It was him earlier, before he shaved off his moustache!

The tall man stepped over the unconscious jeweller, and pushed Brenda and Barry into the strong room at the rear of the shop.

"That's amazing," he said, staring intently at Barry, "you could be my twin brother except for my moustache. Hey, Alan," he called.

His accomplice joined him in the strong room. "Good Lord, you're a dead ringer for him," he exclaimed, pointing at Barry.

"Exactly the reaction I wanted, thanks mate. I'm removing my mo.

If the police check any CCTV around here they will be totally confused and we will be long gone."

"Not so fast," yelled Barry, pulling his mobile from his trouser pocket.

The tall man knocked Barry to the ground. Brenda screamed in horror.

"Come on Jimbo, stop admiring yer twin and get outta here, we got a good haul," Alan pushed the door open and ran to the car parked a few yards down the road.

Jimbo wasn't the brightest card in the pack, although he'd have argued the toss with anyone who said that within earshot. He grabbed the mobile from Barry's hand and put it inside his jacket. "Don't want you calling the cops do we, Buddy? Give me yours too," he yelled at Brenda.

Shaking so much she could hardly open her bag, Brenda shoved her phone into his hand and dropped to her knees beside Barry, begging him to talk to her. He lay still.

Jimbo ran to the car and jumped into the passenger's seat as Alan hit the accelerator and sped off down the road. They took a quick turn not far out of town down a dirt track that led to the river where their rowboat was moored.

"With a few more hauls like this one we'll be able to upgrade to a speedboat no time at all," Alan had the dollar signs shining in his eyes. "These country bumpkins ain't no match for city slickers like us, Jimbo."

"I hope no one got a good look at us. Did ya see any CCTV around?"

"Nope. Wouldn't matter too much anyway. No one knows us, we're a long way from Melbourne, Buddy. This car won't even be missed by that shopper yet, she paid two hours in the meter, nice one fer us,"

Meanwhile the jeweller was coming round and groaned as he reached out and touched the alarm bell. An ear splitting siren rang out, further adding to his spinning head, and it was through a blur that he saw Brenda trying to help Barry to his feet. In his daze he thought she was wrestling with him and when two uniformed policemen burst through the door, he yelled, "Officers, Officers, help her. Grab him. He just tried to rob me, him and another bloke."

The cops grabbed Barry by the arms and flung him against the wall, one pulling handcuffs from his belt and expertly applying them to Barry's wrists within seconds. It was all too much for Brenda she screamed and fainted.

Meanwhile Alan and Jimbo rowed happily down the river, pleased with their morning's work and anxious to get to their tent in the dense bushland to count the spoils. Alan was still unaware that Jimbo had the two phones in his jacket.

They were quite expert rowers and it took them no time to follow a hidden estuary along a heavily wooded area. They slipped in the mud as they pushed the rowboat up and out of sight not far from where they had set up camp. Alan broke some branches and covered the slip marks.

"Okay, Jimbo, I think we have that well hidden." Alan looked at his watch. "I'd reckon they may have found the stolen car by now and they'll realise we escaped by boat. I'm sure they'll assume it was by motorboat so look further afield. We need to lay low for a few days then head off back to Melbourne where we can find buyers for this loot, should make a pretty penny, I reckon. No one will even know we were here."

"Yes Alan, but what about me, they will recognise me, they have a true identity. It was a nasty co-incidence, that guy looking like me."

Alan didn't reply. He had planned to get rid of Jimbo somewhere along the way anyway, he had coerced him into helping; he knew Jimbo was a bit scatty and in dire need of money.

As Brenda came around, she yelled hysterically, "No, no. He is my husband. We came in to look at a ring when the robbers burst in. We were shocked as the tall man was the spitting image of my husband, Barry. He knocked the jeweller out as he was trying to push the alarm, leaving him unconscious, then he hit Barry. I was trying to get Barry to his feet as the jeweller woke up and thought the worse. Please believe me." The jeweller scratched his head, "Yes, well… oh, my head hurts."

The police officers looked at each other, realising they had been heavy-handed and removed the handcuffs off Barry

"Call an ambulance, Officer Browning, they all need to be checked over."

Sirens shrieked almost immediately. The jeweller held his head. Barry didn't look well either.

"Give me your names," instructed the officer-in-charge. The rest will have to wait until you are able to be interviewed. Do you have CCTV installed?"

Two hours later the jeweller Mark and Barry were given the 'all clear' at the hospital to return home. The police had their contact details telling both men they would be further questioned.

Brenda arranged a taxi to take her and Barry back to their suite at the resort.

"Take care, Mark. We'll call in and see you when Barry is feeling more up to it."

Mark nodded. "I apologise again for confusing Barry with the tall robber. It's uncanny how they resemble each other. I'm glad you are both okay. Let's hope the police track the thugs down."

Alan told Jimbo they should lay low at their campsite for a couple of days before heading back to Melbourne. Alan's mind was fully occupied with getting rid of Jimbo. He was a liability!

Jimbo was restless. "Oh, come on, mate, we can slip into town again and have a few beers."

"Are you totally crazy?" Alan punched Jimbo in the chest. "We're not going anywhere …yet."

Jimbo's shoulders slouched. "It's okay for you, mate. But that fella in the jewellers he could be my twin. I need to find out where he lives and silence him – permanently! It may as well be me walking around town while he's out there."

Alan grabbed Jimbo by the shoulders. "Don't you understand me, we ain't going anywhere yet. You daft bastard, the police will be looking for you because of your uncanny resemblance. I think…" Alan's sentence was cut short by the sound of a mobile ringing.

Jimbo groaned. He was too late grabbing the phone from his trouser pocket. Alan pushed him down onto the tent floor. The phone continued ringing. Alan knocked Jimbo unconscious then pressed the phone. "Hello," he said softly.

"Dad, Dad, what's wrong with your voice?" enquired a young girl's voice. "Dad, say something. I've just seen you on TV. They are saying you and Mum have been involved in a robbery at a…"

Alan pulled the Sim card from the mobile. "You bloody idiot," he said, looking down at Jimbo who was groaning as he slowly regained consciousness. "Your double's probably reported his phone missing. The police will be keeping tabs on it and will know exactly where we are."

Jimbo held his head and tried to stand up. Alan pushed him back to the ground and searched his pockets, pulling out another mobile phone. "Who the hell does this phone belong to?"

Jimbo shook his head. "Can't remember, Mate," he replied. His head was swimming. Nevertheless, he was mad with himself for not concealing Barry and Brenda's phones. He didn't trust Alan and those two phones were his 'planned' extra protection should Alan lose his temper and bash him again. It wasn't the first time he had knocked him out. He was too far in on this 'get rich quick' scheme and he had his own plans about what was going to happen to their haul from the jeweller's and any other robbery they committed.

Barry and Brenda reported the loss of their mobiles to the police when they called at the resort to check on the couple.

"We'll keep tabs on those phone numbers," advised DI Mathews, the office-in-charge of the investigation. "We've also released CCTV footage of the men involved in the robbery to the TV channels. You don't have a twin brother, do you Barry?"

Barry shook his head. "No, certainly not as far as I know. I have a sister and we have two daughters."

"Please contact our daughters," pleaded Brenda, a worried look on her face. "If they've watched the news and seen the CCTV footage they will be so, so worried. We haven't been able to speak to either of them."

"We'll take care of everything, Brenda," assured DI Mathews. "We'd like you both to stay here in the resort for now. This is for your own safety. With the two suspects still on the loose, one of whom could be your twin, Barry, we need to keep you both safely out of the equation and concentrate on finding them as quickly as possible."

"We understand," replied Barry. "I'm really…"

DI Mathews' phone ringing cut short the rest of Barry's sentence. "Repeat that again," DI Mathews' voice was sharp. "He's where? Right. Keep me informed."

"Sorry folks," he told the Smarts, "your 'twin' has been spotted on CCTV heading towards this resort."

Jimbo had shaved his moustache after he 'took care of business' with Alan.

"Arrogant twit," he muttered to himself as he strode along the footpath towards the Resort. He felt little remorse for the surprise blow he had delivered to Alan's nether regions as he had regained consciousness, nor for the karate chop to his neck that he'd followed up with as Alan groaned and doubled over in pain. "Teach him a lesson that will, don't mess with Jimbo…wonder if I killed 'im, he looked pretty crook." A vague feeling of concern washed over him as he thought of the possible consequences if he had killed him.

He walked with confidence through the front door of the resort hotel. He figured if he was on CCTV they would just think he was Barry. His plan was to surprise Barry and Brenda with a visit, take care of Barry, and walk out with Brenda and make a get away in their car. He figured by the time anyone realised the deception he would be on the plane to Jakarta and his new life of comfort with the handy little package of jewels in his pocket. What he was going to do with Brenda he hadn't decided yet. As we have already established he wasn't the brightest card in the pack, although he would have disputed that fact.

"Barry Smart," he announced to the girl behind the concierge's desk. Could I have a spare key to my room please? My wife wasn't feeling well and I don't want to wake her by knocking on the door." He was pleased with his explanation.

Not suspecting anything the girl handed him the key to room 401.

"I am sorry to hear she's unwell Mr Smart. Let me know if we can do anything for you."

Jimbo nodded his thanks and hurried to the lift. He found room 401 without difficulty and knocked on the door calling "Room Service."

Caught unawares Brenda opened the door without thinking and was stunned when Jimbo shoved the door open roughly and lurched inside before she or Barry could do anything. He then stood aggressively facing them with his hand in his jacket pocket.

"I've got a gun Folks, one wrong move and I'll use it."

Brenda and Barry were not fully convinced but not confident enough to risk trying to do anything other than what he said.

"What do you want with us? We haven't got anything of value. You're mad."

"You've got something very valuable Mate…me ticket outta here and far away." He grabbed Brenda and put his hand over her mouth to stifle her scream. "We're going on a little trip Lovie."

Just then there was a loud bang on the door.

"Police. Open up."

The three occupants froze.

Receiving no response to their knock, the police broke into the room. Jimbo changed his pose to one of protection and hugged Brenda to him.

"Officers, arrest that man, he tried to break in and kidnap my Bren."

"Don't listen to him, I'm Barry," Barry shouted.

"I'm Barry, I'm the one she was huggin', you saw that," Jimbo retaliated.

Brenda stood shaking and paralysed with shock.

The police grabbed both men and pushed them roughly against the wall expertly handcuffing both.

Brenda tried to speak but the shock overcame her and she fainted.

Officer Browning rushed to Brenda, guiding her to a nearby armchair. It took little time for DI Mathews to frisk the two handcuffed men. Barry carried a wallet and his identity was quickly confirmed, while Jimbo's pocket contained the stolen bag of jewellery. He released Barry.

"I took that off him, he's the real thief." Blurted Jimbo, in a last desperate attempt to convince the police he was the real Barry. It had become clear he was lying and Brenda confirmed as she came around. "I'd know my Barry anywhere." She cooed sweetly.

The next moment Alan pushed through the already broken door, eyeing Jimbo angrily then realising the police officers were there. He turned quickly to retreat but his injuries slowed him down and made him easy to apprehend.

"Well, that's a bonus." Officer Browning whispered, "saved us searching for him."

"Charge that bastard with attempted murder. He attacked me and left me for dead. I struggled to follow him here to get revenge," yelled Alan. Jimbo scoffed and spat at Alan who lunged at him.

The officers pulled them apart. Officer Browning pushed them toward the door.

"We'll get them to the station and interview them." Reported DI Mathews, "I'm sure they will turn on each other and that will make our job easy." He grinned.

Jimbo hesitated, looking back at Barry. "Out of curiosity, where were you born?"

"McLaren Vale, South Australia," replied Barry hesitantly. "Why?"

"Me too." He laughed as Officer Browning pushed him out the door.

Murder in the Round
Lyn Fraser

What I need is a good defense attorney, and she's dead. I could never have imagined ending up here, unable to see clearly. My ears weren't affected, but I have no sense of smell, and my lips tingle continuously.

I remember going through some trial notes and hearing a knock on my hotel room door, grateful that my room service order was arriving. But when I opened the door, a woman wearing a full body hotel apron and a mask said she needed to spray my room. "Just a deodorizer as someone is burning trash illegally on the lot next door to the hotel," she said. "We don't want anyone to be bothered by the smell."

"I don't need the spray," I told her.

She came in anyway and starting spraying the room, then turned toward me and sprayed right into my face.

Detective Tucom continues to investigate the capsaicin attack on me, which should be all he needs to clear me. Capsaicin is the alkaloid responsible for heat in chilis, and it is also used in pepper spray, which some people carry as a protection. That's what was in the alleged deodorizer spray can used on me. Large doses on the skin or in any amount within eyes, nostrils or other bodily openings can render results that are quite unpleasant to the recipient thereof. I am exhibit A. The empty can was found in my trash container. No fingerprints, of course.

It was only five days ago that we began, although it feels like months. Along with the rest of the group, I signed on for this grand adventure to have some time in the Land of Enchantment, but also to solve a major mystery ourselves about the spectacular ruins of the ancestral Puebloan cliff dwellers at Chaco Canyon, Canyon de Chelly, and Mesa Verde. These sites, spread many miles apart in the Four Corners region, were abandoned almost simultaneously in the 14th century. Advanced civilizations just up and left their architecturally dazzling homesteads.

But why? That's the mystery we were assigned to solve, as if countless researchers before us haven't already tried. The objective was for each of us to develop our own theory, based on personal observations as we visited each site, as well as drawing on any information we chose from reams of studies that offered intriguing possibilities such as prolonged drought, violent marauders, cultural stress, and my personal favorite: the landing of UFO's.

I recognized that ours would be something of a superficial investigation, but the unique tool I brought that no amount of academic research, on-site studies, sci-fi speculation, or conspiracy theories have offered is the same one that draws me to my profession as a forensic accountant: hyperventilated intuition.

The group's opening session in the Kiva Room of our hotel in Santa Fe began with such promise when we met our tour leader, a short, dark-haired woman who clapped her hands together and beckoned for us to join her at a round table. We sat together, an olio of half a dozen.

"Yá át ééh, hello in Navajo," she began. "I am Shauna Soland and introduce myself by way of my mother's people, the Red Running Water Clan." Shauna explained that she worked for the tourism commission in Farmington, New Mexico, and had been engaged by Austin Travel Designers, our tour packager, to serve as guide and driver.

"I've always wondered about the massive migration from our pueblos, and I've never been fully satisfied by any of the explanations," Shauna said. "As a Diné, a Navajo, we believe our people emerged from Mother Earth, each born into our mother's clan. In matriarchal cultures, it is the women who nurture life and who create bodies and homes. So who could be better to conduct our search than a group of intelligent, sensitive women?"

Who indeed? One of the reasons I'd signed on for this tour was that I knew we'd be getting a Native leader, and it looked to me as if we'd hit the Mother Earth jackpot.

Awkwardly, most of us tried unsuccessfully to say Shauna's greeting back to her. She smiled at our efforts, then asked us to go around the table and introduce ourselves—and since we were here to solve a mystery, she suggested sharing a favorite crime fiction writer or genre.

Darlene Dillon began the intros, "sad to say," by telling us she was grieving the death of her husband of forty-one years. After trying a couple of bereavement support groups that weren't helpful, she'd turned to Scandinavian Noir for support. "Those writers offer just what I need right now—dark characters with regular doses of instability and alienation." Her remarks were met with a mixture of light applause and puzzled expressions.

I took a deep breath and went next. Grace Edna Edge. My mostly brunette hair, cut in a bob and intended to plop softly over my ears, was in its usual state of disarray, not unlike my personal life, which I did not discuss in the introductory remarks. In the spirit of group conviviality, I did mention that I'd recently attended a classic western film festival and looked forward to traveling through this area with other passengers in a coach, but not one involving whips, horses, rifles, or dangling ropes. Chuckles in response were my signal to finish, so I quickly disclosed my reading preferences: "Contemporary thrillers with unreliable narrators, untidy detectives, and chaos in the courtroom."

Meghan Zelder told us she preferred the nickname 'Zinger.' Youngest member of the group, African American, she talked about her work on the staff of South by Southwest Festival in Austin and her ongoing interest in the representation of indigenous people in film and on television. "I'm searching for a deeper truth than what classic movies and pop culture often convey about Native Americans as racy savages or as pathetically in need or as noble sufferers with magical cures."

So much for my whips and ropes.

Zinger said she was into page-turning horror mysteries, her favorite being Stephen Graham Jones, a Blackfeet. "He writes about revenge, cultural identity, and the cost of breaking tradition—which seems to fit what we're about here." She'd nodded to Shauna, who nodded back.

Next up, Marietta Palmer announced without preamble, "I'm a defense attorney, but don't hold that against me. "Everyone at the table laughed, except me. Marietta and I had a long history of opposing each other in the courtroom, to mixed results. Medium height, medium build, steely eyes, steely hair, she bent slightly forward when she spoke as if always pressing her point. "I look forward to our group mystery objective for the same reason I like to read Golden Age mysteries. It's clear in those who the good guys are, and they ultimately win."

Not always in your court appearances, I didn't point out.

Alice Fitzgerald completed the opening round. Wiry thin with curly grey hair, she appeared to be wearing her day's shopping, attired in a paisley tiered skirt with an embroidered blouse and shiny jewelry on her neck, ears, arms, and fingers. Alice said she volunteered at one of the Austin public library branches and claimed insider knowledge of reader preferences, which she'd be willing to share. As to her own, she liked a good cozy mystery. "They're character-driven with low violence, clean language, and sex off screen. That way I can imagine it for myself." She'd winked.

Alice in Wonderland.

Shauna thanked us for our thoughtful contributions and said that her own favorite mystery was *The Little Prince* by Saint-Exupery, which had just been translated for the first time into an indigenous language.

Alice raised her hand and said, "That book is not housed in the mystery section of a library. My son had to read it for school and it was in children's fiction."

Zinger said, "It's about looking under the surfaces to find the meaning, which applies to any good mystery novel."

Shauna suggested tactfully that we obviously had much to discuss, but for now would go over the plans for the next day's trip to Chaco Canyon. She gave us details on the schedule, responded to questions, and finished with a recommendation. "Before you go to bed tonight, step outside on the hotel's rooftop and look at the night sky," Shauna said. "You'll have the same vision as that seen by our ancients. The structures at Chaco are aligned with solar and lunar cycles, based on generations of astronomical observances."

With that benediction, we left the Kiva in relative silence. Later, I did as Shauna had suggested. Venus joined me along with the crescent moon and a brilliant array that included Hydra, Ursa Major, Marietta, and Zinger.

The night sky together with a bedtime shot of scotch yielded a surprisingly good night's sleep. After all the research and speculation, we were finally our way early the next morning to experiencing the haunting beauty of this landscape and what we might learn from its early inhabitants. Apparently, we were all so exhausted from planning, traveling here, posturing for the group, and getting up early for the breakfast buffet, there was little conversation on our deluxe motor coach. Shauna offered occasional commentary over a microphone as she drove, but not much.

No question about the remoteness of Chaco Canyon National Historical Park, and the last few miles of the three-hour journey were washboard rough. But after all the study and reflection, I was astonished when we pulled into the parking lot and found ourselves up close to this ancient Pueblo culture, considered the largest, best preserved, and most architecturally advanced of all ancient Southwest villages.

Shauna gave us a few minutes in the Visitor Center to view exhibits and read history, and it was evident to me as we separated that we each had a particular theory to explore. I was fascinated by the architectural brilliance on display here and the evidence of an advanced civilization, but I was also searching for something in the daily lives of the inhabitants, a dramatic occurrence or cataclysmic combination, virulent enough to cause them to flee.

We took a nine-mile loop drive that accessed six of the major sites and stopped at the largest, Pueblo Bonito, a 600-room architecturally sophisticated structure that had towered as high as four or five stories in its prime, large portions of the highest walls still standing after more than a thousand years. I could imagine the residents gathering here in this congenial space to meet with friends, argue politics, trade turquoise and squash, and participate in rituals.

Within the site, I recognized the kivas, round rooms created by the Pueblos for religious rituals and ceremonies. As I saw the others returning to the coach, I stayed back for a few moments, just standing in one of the large kivas. When Shauna came over to join me, I expected she wanted to get me moving, but instead she said, "When you live in a circular home, there is no beginning and no end. To live well, we must understand that."

"So they did everything here—cooked over a fire, made political decisions, did their church worshipping, talked about stuff, all in the same round place?" I asked her.

"With no sharp corners," she said, and we walked quietly back to the coach.

On the drive to Farmington there was, again, mostly exhausted silence as we traveled. Since no alcohol is served on Navajo reservation, we'd set up a plan in a group e-mail prior to the trip to have a social gathering before dinner each evening in someone's room for optional imbibement. Even though Farmington's not on the reservation, we went ahead with that plan, and Marietta had offered to host the first night, advising us in advance she'd be tee-totaling for health reasons.

Everyone showed up for the social except Shauna, apparently opting to reflect on the sunset. For the trip I'd brought mini bottles of wine for cocktail time and a side flask of scotch for emergencies. Zinger had beer, Darlene gin and tonic, Alice a wine spritzer, and Marietta a bottle of ginger ale.

There was lots of buzz about the day, and we shared photos from our phones. Marietta had brought each of us copies of a brochure with information on Chaco's night sky program, offered evenings during the summer, and she handed those around. She suggested we should start planning our next trip. Shauna stuck her head in the door and let us know it was almost time to leave for dinner.

After a pit stop in my room, I headed back along the hallway to meet the others downstairs and noticed that Marietta's door was open a crack. I knocked and called to her, asking if she was ready to go. When she didn't respond, I walked in to ask again and saw her on the floor near her bathroom, not moving. I rushed over, bent down, and was relieved that she was breathing. But barely. I grabbed my phone and called 911, describing her condition as best I could, responding to questions and following instructions. Once I knew an ambulance was on the way, I called the number Shana had given us to reach her in an emergency. She was inside Marietta's room quickly, taking necessary steps to support Marietta as we waited. She instructed me to call the hotel desk to let them know what was happening. An assistant manager, Julian Reyes, arrived simultaneously with the EMTs.

After checking Marietta's symptoms—that included low blood pressure and heartbeat, dangerously slow breathing, blue tint to nails and lips—the EMTs loaded her on to a stretcher for transport to the San Juan Regional Medical Center. The unanimous conclusion by everyone who knew what they were doing, which did not include me, was that Marietta had overdosed on a narcotic. An EMT administered Naloxone before they left for the hospital.

Still in the room, Shauna called Marietta's emergency contact, her grown daughter Rosemary in Austin. They discussed the situation extensively. Rosemary would make plans to come to Farmington as soon as possible, and Shauna would keep her informed.

"She said Marietta had intestinal surgery three months ago, and she's taken a prescription for pain control," Shauna told me. "She insisted her mother had been cleared for this trip. She wasn't depressed, was really looking forward to the adventure, had returned to work full steam. The med is effective and the dosage rigorously controlled. She was quite specific and helped Marietta prepare her meds for the trip. She was down to one 10 mg. Oxycontin dose each evening, and they had counted them out. Seven tablets, one for each night of the trip, and two extra tablets in case there were travel delays at either end. Nine tablets total.

Shauna and I had already found the Oxy prescription in Marietta's travel bag on the bathroom tablet for the EMTs. There were seven tablets in the bottle, suggesting she had taken the appropriate two, and there were no other narcotics in her kit.

"Something's badly off here. She could not have OD'd on her own meds. She's gotten the stuff another way," Shauna speculated. "What did she have at the social?"

"Just some ginger ale. From a bottle she opened as we were gathering."

Shauna decided to call the Farmington Police Department and consult with a detective she knew. By the time we got back downstairs, a Detective Tucom had arrived in the hotel lobby.

While Shauna spoke with him, I rejoined our group and brought them as up to date as well as I could, although they'd already had a report from Julian that it was a suspected overdose rather than a cardiac event or some other major issue, though extensive tests were underway.

"Was it fentanyl?" Zinger asked.

"She wasn't taking fentanyl," I said.

"My husband took fentanyl," Darlene said, "but he switched to tequila."

"Suicide is a suspicious death. Is that why the police are here?" Alice asked.

"There's no suggestion of suicide," I said.

Detective Tucom and Shauna joined our grouping. Detective Tucom conveyed the news that Marietta had been taken to the San Juan Regional Medical Center and was in critical condition. "She has had an incident related to the over-ingestion of an opioid medication. Appropriate medications have been administered, and her daughter is on the way from Austin. We don't know how Marietta is going to respond to the episode."

"Episode of what?" Zinger asked.

"Coma," Detective Tucom said. "She's in a coma."

No one responded to that information. Detective Tucom explained that a team was clearing Marietta's room of 'relevant materials' for analysis and sealed off the area.

Shauna told us she would stay in touch with the hospital and keep us apprised of any change. "We will all need to be available in the morning," she said, "to converse with law enforcement."

Detective Tucom said that an officer from the Farmington Police Department would meet with each of us separately the next morning after breakfast to obtain more information on the incident, especially about the social gathering.

"After we each meet with the officers tomorrow, we will see where we are about the trip. If you want to continue, that is," Shauna added. "I'll check with Travel Designers about refunds."

Julian offered us a meal in the hotel dining room.

Zinger and I, opting out of the food offer, walked back toward our rooms together and passed the entry to Marietta's, covered in yellow police tape.

"What the hell?" Zinger said.

"No kidding. But all we know is she has symptoms of overdose," I said.

"She didn't have any alcohol, which can trigger an interaction, unless she had some before or after our gathering," Zinger said.

"Or stress from the traveling," I said, interested in Zinger's knowledge of opioid-alcohol interaction. Or the scary thing, I didn't say: Someone else gave her the overdose.

In my room, I poured myself a shot of scotch. No question it was an emergency situation. If Marietta was murdered, I suspected it had to do with one of her cases. I mean, for godsake, I'd felt like murdering her.

I knew a little about the other participants from the trip bios and my own research. Zinger was active in Black Lives Matter, likely knocking heads with the Texas Republican establishment, which was Marietta's orbit. Darlene's late husband had been a major Austin property developer, ran his own company, Dillbo Enterprises, now in Chapter 11. Alice's husband was an orthopedic surgeon, could have been involved in some medical malpractice somewhere along the way. Marietta worked both sides of the fence in court, a potential adversary to any of us. Assuming that Shauna had nothing to do with Marietta's overdose since she was nowhere near the social gathering and wouldn't want to wipe out one of the paying customers, I concluded that all the rest of us were suspects.

And we were treated as such the next morning. Marietta survived the night, but there were 'complications,' undefined. We had our individual grillings by the Farmington P.D., led by Detective Tucom, and I knew from mine they were looking at three possibilities:

(1) accidental, self-inflicted overdose from an unknown source:

(2) intentional self-inflicted overdose from a source which she'd hidden; or

(3) an overdose inflicted by someone other than Marietta, such as a liquid opioid added to her ginger ale.

Shauna offered us all trip cancellation with a full refund, and a flight home from Durango. Or we could wait and see, taking a day-trip from Farmington to Chinle and back, about two hours each way with an afternoon drive across the South Rim of Canyon de Chelly. Then we would spend another night in Farmington and see where were. Or weren't.

The Chinle alternative could mean riding in the coach and standing at overlooks with an attempted murderer, but Detective Tucom offered to send an Officer Tafoya from the Farmington P.D. with us. To observe and protect. All of us chose the day-trip option. No one sat with Officer

Tafoya on the coach. I hope his feelings weren't hurt.

After leaving Farmington mid-morning, we traveled along a highway that felt like the beginning of an entirely new landscape, wide desert plains interrupted by red mesas and intriguing rock formations that stood like knolls. We passed through small villages, more like wide spots in the road, with names like Rough Rock and Rock Point that describe themselves, and another small community called Many Farms that Shauna told us is surrounded by 700 small farms run by Diné families.

When we drove through the town of Chinle, Shauna pointed out a small grocery store and told us that students at Diné College in Chinle did a project to label all grocery store items in the Navajo language but for some foods, the translation can be quite difficult. "Like deciding whether watermelon should be called *T'eehiyaan*, the word for 'raw food' or *Ch'eehiyaan* that means 'to eat in vain.'"

I laughed for the first time in twenty-four hours.

A series of overlooks provided stunning afternoon views of Canyon de Chelly's dramatic sandstone cliffs, with farms below and the ancient ruins in the distance. One of our stops, the White House Ruins Overlook, had a trail leading all the way down into the canyon to the ruins, but we didn't have the two hours required for hiking it. The next best choice became Shauna's binoculars, which she generously shared for a remarkably clear view of the ruins, thought to have been abandoned about the same time as Chaco's.

What I could see from there—which were the white, brilliantly constructed dwellings tucked into the steep, streaked cliffs—confirmed my working theory for solving the abandonment mystery, though I was still missing a key piece.

We had a short break for refreshments in Chinle, and when Shauna rejoined us she had bad news by phone from Farmington. Marietta had lost ground. "Naloxone effectively stemmed the overdose, but she's developed a respiratory infection."

Attempting to take our collective minds temporarily off the crisis,

Shauna told us more about Diné College as we rode.

"Diné's the first Navajo controlled college in the country, small but essential to our Nation," she said. "The philosophy of the college is the Navajo philosophy of life, placing all human beings in harmony with the earth. The entire campus is laid out in a round, like a hogan, reflecting our belief that education is essential to the cultural whole."

There was that round concept again.

"I'm working with the college to set up some internships for students to create Navajo owned and operated solar energy companies," Shauna said. "We want to help our students develop for the future, but there are all sorts of factors, quite honestly, that Westerners don't understand."

"Like what?" Darlene asked.

"Towers and windmills impact the landscape, so the placement is critical," Shauna said. "We don't want to interfere with a person's farm or sheep production just to get the solar power installed."

"And from what I've read, Diné businesses aren't driven by immediate profits," I said. "You look generations into the future, not just at the next quarter's earnings."

"Exactly right," Shauna confirmed, "and in case you're interested, Grace Edna, Diné's looking to hire a new business prof."

I shook my head, so aware of being a white woman, living for just a brief period as an outsider in someone else's land, someone else's culture, trying to understand even superficially what I was experiencing. Encountering concepts like holistic and harmonious, relationship of earth to sky, spiritual beliefs fundamental to every thought and movement.

Tangled up with these fresh perspectives and contradictions as we drove was the concrete reality that someone a few feet from me could be a killer.

Which seemed even more likely, back in Farmington, when I saw Shauna in the hotel conference room that had been allotted to the investigation, and she confirmed that Marietta was now on a respirator.

No one else from our tour was in the room, and Shauna shared the lab results provided by Detective Tucom. Oxy-contaminated ginger ale.

No question at that point. It was a pre-meditated murder attempt, for now. I asked Shauna how anyone currently on the trip could have known in advance Marietta had signed on, and she explained that because the number of participants was strictly limited, the list was available in the Austin Travel Designers' office. Plus Marietta had been quoted in a newspaper article about local attorneys that she was looking forward to a trip exploring ancient Pueblos.

And the group had shared the email about setting up the socials.

Shauna said that our interactions at the social would be a primary focus for the next morning's round of interrogations by Detective Tucom and his team, as well as information on any of Marietta's cases that might be relevant to motive.

"She's certainly defended some sleazebags," I offered, then said I would like to research some of her cases that might be relevant. I asked Shauna for permission to use the computer that the team had set up in the conference room, as I had far more research than my I-Pad could manage. She cleared my request with Tucom and left me to it.

Given my long experience as an adversary, I was knowledgeable about Marietta's case history and had professional access to case records. Methodically, I went through those that had significant settlements. After an hour or so, I settled on the case I thought might be most relevant to our group because it involved multiple plaintiffs with mega millions of losses.

For the case, Marietta had represented the pastor of one of Austin's mega-box evangelical churches. It received national media attention. This pastor started an investment fund with partners. The fund promised high returns, based on the pastor himself choosing, *with divine guidance*, investment opportunities in Nigeria that would help the poor. Congregants would come to him for prayer and counseling and leave with a slick folder on the fund, guaranteeing high returns, little or no risk. Money flowed in, posted returns escalated, but ultimately investors new and old were not able to cash out. Marietta defended the pastor, who was convicted of a multi-million dollar Ponzi scheme, but sentenced to only two years, and that was almost immediately reduced to community service after he agreed to lead a prison ministry. The victims had expected at least some recovery, but no funds had ever been made available or even found.

Through my access to court records, I was able to identify the plaintiffs who had lost money in the scheme and began printing out the list so I could go back to my room for emergency 'rations' and to make a follow-up plan. As the printer was running, I turned around to see Zinger coming into the room to set up equipment for a film she was going to show, and Darlene almost leaning over my shoulder.

"Whatcha doing, Grace Edna?" Darlene asked.

"Nothing. Just catching up, for my clients at home."

Darlene looked at the pages coming off the printer.

I snatched them quickly out of the printer tray, stuffed them into my backpack, and started walking toward the door.

"Aren't you staying for the movie?" Darlene asked.

"No, I need to finish this work in my room," I said, walking away.

Once back in my room, I surveyed the list of names and sure enough, found what I thought could be a connection, a man named Sidney Bonner, as a plaintiff in the Ponzi scheme. I recognized him from my research on the bankrupt company of Darlene's husband Rayford Dillon. Sidney Bonner was the Chief Financial Officer of Dilbo Enterprises. Dillon and Bonner. Dillbo Enterprises. He'd represented the company as a plaintiff.

While sipping scotch, making notes, and waiting for my room service, I tried unsuccessfully to reach Shauna by phone and left a message. That's when I heard the knock on the door and met up with the can of pepper spray in my face.

What I know so far is that I'm in a room at the San Juan Regional Medical Center, where Marietta died. So very, very sad.

Shauna hovers. Zinger has been asked not to leave the county. Darlene and Alice are in protective custody.

As soon as I was conscious, I communicated my findings on the Pastor Ponzi case to Shauna and then to Detective Tucom. They had found out much of that themselves, by then.

Darlene's husband was wiped out in the financial scheme, along with his company. He never recovered financially, physically, or otherwise, according to reports from multiple sources and threatened reprisals. Since the pastor left the Austin area, Marietta apparently became the best target for revenge. Sidney Bonner has been picked up for questioning by the Austin P.D.

Darlene scoffs at the connection.

Zinger and I have confirmed to Detective Tucom and his team that Marietta set her open bottle of ginger ale down on a counter outside the bathroom to pass out the brochures on the night program at Chaco as we all milled around, reading our phones and chatting during the social. She'd set out an ice bucket and cups that we all used for our drinks.

Darlene may have had access to a liquid opioid from medications left over from her husband's illness. Austin P.D. is searching medical records and history. Alice would also have had a medical pipeline through her husband's work and knowledge of its administration as she trained as an RN prior to their marriage. And almost any substance is available on the streets with proper connections.

The conjecture which is under review is that Darlene and Alice planned and executed the attack with the objective of killing Marietta but in a scheme so cleverly designed no one would recognize it as murder. Alice would have injected the opioid during the social with Darlene distracting the rest of us. Although no charges have been brought yet, they have retained local counsel and have reserves on the way from Albuquerque.

And I haven't been cleared. We were adversaries, Marietta and I, and Detective Tucom is still digging through our cases, some of which certainly had detrimental outcomes for my own clients, but not for me personally. Marietta could have cleared this up for me in a heartbeat if only she were available.

I am sure it was Alice at the door, based on what I can remember from height and build. And those corkscrew curls. Under the mask, I'm almost positive. And as I was printing in conference room, Darlene saw the list of plaintiffs. She knew I knew or soon would, prompting Alice to help sow confusion and delay by attacking me.

But everyone had an alibi for the time the incident in my room occurred, all watching the PBS film "Miss Navajo," shown by Zinger in the conference room. Darlene and Alice both managed to pass a detailed test on the movie, responding to spontaneous questions about descriptive scenes. Darlene and Alice got it chapter and verse. But they also could have watched the film online. The room was dark, people were sleepy, other residents from the hotel came in to watch it. Alice could have slipped out and back, unnoticed.

If Alice herself didn't attack me, they might have paid someone else to do it. The murder of Marietta shows extensive premeditation and planning. Whatever or whomever, the lack of resolution leaves me unsettled, to say the least.

Shauna's here in my hospital room now to hear my solution to the other mystery: why I think the ancient Puebloans abandoned their homes. She asks if I'm all right with her making some notes, and I nod my agreement.

"Drought." I begin. "I agree with the many studies documenting extreme drought as a primary factor for the abandonments, but there is no consensus on the specific elements associated with drought that caused the movement. In the reams of recorded documents, very little study relates to rodents."

Shauna shakes her head, I think in agreement.

"The Ancient Puebloans had covers for their food storage vessels to protect against rodents and insects," I continue. "I saw those in the Visitor Center at Chaco and in photographs from Canyon de Chelly,

Mesa Verde, and other sites. I believe that the threat of contamination by rodents would have increased exponentially as dry conditions propelled the vermin to seek alternate sources of food as the landscape dried up. We saw those smaller kivas at Chaco which could have been used for storage."

"Perhaps so," Shauna says, "But why were they so threatening that the ancient Puebloans left their homes? It had likely happened before, many times, in extremely dry conditions."

"That's where my colleague Marietta Palmer comes in to the story," I say. "She gave me my missing piece. Marietta contracted a respiratory virus in the hospital. Although the overdose weakened her condition, it was the virus that killed her, not the overdose."

"You are probably right about that," Shauna says, writing on her table. "Go on."

"I believe that's exactly what occurred across the Four Corners region. A virus from rodents developed and became virulent throughout the ancient Puebloan sites, something of an early form of the deadly hantavirus from deer mice that infected the population in 1990's."

"It was scary," Shauna says. "Many deaths, many ill. And it happened in this very area, like you're suggesting, from so many mice."

"You have taught us so much, Shauna, about a matriarchal culture. It is my theory that the result for the Ancient Puebloans was that the women in the culture were the ultimate saviors. They recognized the danger from the mice and developing disease. They joined together, not in denial or political upheaval, but in collective support. They persuaded the entire culture to leave their homes and material possessions, ultimately creating entirely new and different living spaces. It is the Puebloan women, as nurturers, who were the driving force for the abandonments."

"If I understand your solution to the mystery, you are linking drought to disease to the leadership of women in the Puebloan homes across the region, who persuaded the Puebloan culture to sacrifice materiality for the spirituality of the whole."

Shauna astounds me. Once again.

"This country and the entire world, for that matter," I said, "have much to learn from the Puebloans about dealing with pandemic."

"Thank you for your insights, Grace Edna. I've made notes and will compile the responses, at least yours and Zinger's. Not sure what to expect from Darlene and Alice."

"Regardless of where we go from here," I say, "I would like to set up a memorial fund for Marietta with contributions supporting book donations to Diné schools."

Shauna nods quietly, folds her tablet and says she will take necessary steps to help establish and promote the memorial.

As she is packing up her materials, Shauna tells me that she is not going to lead any more tours for Austin Travel Designers once she ties off the loose ends from this trip. She plans to continue to support area tourism but wants to expand her work for Diné College students.

Shauna asks if I'd like to consider taking the teaching job at Diné and tells me that most of the classes are now available online. She would be willing to share her apartment in Farmington when I need to be on site.

I'm reminded about something the brochure offered, that opening night of our trip, what was it? Something about a mythic landscape opening the window to personal transformation.

Clumsy
Kimberly Scott

Cortlandt Manor was only an hour drive North from the city; it was Upstate New York if you ask someone from one of the boroughs, but it was close enough to make me feel like I was lucky for being born there. The three of us were dependent on each other as kids. Allison was born three years after I was and I was born three years after Ben. As the middle child, I was usually the one to resolve any issues that crept into the family. Erin to the rescue—some things never change.

We shared a long driveway with the chief of police, who had a son, Alex, just a year older than I was. He didn't know it at the time, but Alex taught me what having a crush meant. Our house sat at the very end of the driveway and rumor has it the man who designed our home used to build lighthouses. There was a certain drama to it; five floors and even more staircases, one of which led to absolutely nowhere, just a door in the wall that wouldn't open—and even if it had, the other side was a seating area that was not part of the dining room but sat between that and the stairs to the foyer. It counted as a den, I suppose. We watched TV there. The reality is, we came up pretty normal as far as kids in the nineties go. In the spring and summer, we rode our bikes and went hunting for frogs. In the fall we jumped into piles of leaves and went door to door on Halloween, sans parents. We went creeping in the local cemetery and, until too many headstones went up, it had an ideal hill for sledding in the winter.

With our parents each working full time and having social lives of their own, the three of us were free to roam, and it wasn't uncommon for Alex to tag along. While Ben helped raise me, he and I both helped raise Allison. She was the baby…she felt like *our* baby, our little Allie.

She even had a locket with a photo of each of us inside, as if we were her parents. After Ben had moved into his own place and I was getting ready to join him and leap into adulthood, I made sure that she knew she would always be our baby. We both vowed to protect her, no matter how much that annoyed her.

We both failed her and, as it turns out, not even sharing property lines with the chief of police could protect her. It seems there are some horrors in this world that even a middle child can't mitigate, like why valuable sledding space is now occupied by the headstone of my forever 17-year-old baby sister and why her murder remained unsolved for 20 years.

*****

The number of times they asked me the same questions over and over again, it seemed like the detectives got paid by the punctuation and question marks were high commissions. In the days after they found Allie's body I practically lived at the station. They kept telling me to go home, especially Alex, who surprised no one when he became Officer Lucano, Jr. But even his big, brown eyes, the eyes I looked into before my first kiss, even those eyes couldn't convince me to leave. Besides, he was barely out of the academy when dispatch sent Officer Alex Lucano Jr. to respond to a call from a man claiming there was a body in a treehouse in Lander's Woods. What did he know? He only ever tagged along with us, but he wasn't one of us. Allie wasn't *his* baby sister.

The days kept adding up and I, eventually, did go home. Well, I went back to Cortlandt Manor to check on mom and dad, who seemed to turn Allie's death into a blame-game of who was the more absentee parent—they were both winning. Frankly, I think they were relieved to have something they could point to as a reason for divorce instead of just staying bored together for the rest of their lives or, God forbid, having an actual conversation. While I made it to nearly 21 before they split, it felt good to join the kids I knew who were already children of divorce. I would finally be able to relate.

Truth is I didn't want to go home because Ben was not handling any of this well and I didn't know how to help him. At least with my parents, I was used to them disappointing me and I had plenty of experience as their mediator. But even before all of this happened, Ben wasn't doing life well. I thought moving in with him would be good—for both of us. I would get a taste of grown up life and he would have an easier time making friends with his cool sister around. We would motivate each other. I could help him land a girlfriend and he could help me walk into job interviews with the unearned confidence of an average man. We could have parties on the weekends, and Alex would come over when he was off-duty and in an inebriated state I would find the guts to tell him… even though I hated cops, something about him in that uniform made me want to comply.

But none of that happened. Ben did land a girlfriend, but I won't take any credit for that. And before she left him, she left him with a nastier habit than he managed on his own. As much as I wanted him to quit, I was pissed at him, because his addiction kept him from being there for Allie as it had kept him from being there for anything or anyone. It kept him from being there for me…

I asked the cops if I could have the locket, whenever they were done processing it. After they shuffled around for what felt like hours, they said there was no locket. There wasn't anything, aside from the clothes she had on, to be processed. Thankfully, this didn't appear to be a sexually motivated homicide. Unfortunately, that also meant it didn't receive the same scrutiny as more sensational murders; the kind that can be blamed on Satan worship, the occult, and black-haired singers. Allie's murder was lacking in the stuff that made juicy, three-part documentaries or blockbuster movies.

I got very tired. I got tired of being my parents' therapist and Ben's sponsor and Allie's only real advocate. Eventually the case, along with my heart, went cold.

*****

Ben had just gotten his 7-year chip when we got the call that dad's cancer was back. This time, treatment seemed futile.

"I just hope we can get some answers before-" We all knew what mom was going to say. Over the last year or so, the two of them managed to find their way back to a friendship and she was on the call with us when we found out. We all wanted what she wanted—we wanted to know what happened to Allie before it was time for dad to join her.

Ben and I sat in silence for a moment after getting off the phone with them. When I looked up at him, he was smiling at me.

"I'm really glad you're here." His words wrapped me up in a hug.

"Me too. I'm sorry it's been as long as it has."

"Er, you have all the time you need. Seriously, you know that."

I did know that. I also knew that he had a new list of priorities; sobriety, his tiny collages and the art-therapy he had come to rely on, a loving girlfriend, and the secret recipe for the fluffiest pancakes in New York State. I, on the other hand, had a broken engagement, an anxious rescue puppy, and no apartment.

"Hey I'm supposed to see Alex after my meeting tonight. Do you want to join us?"

I could tell he was cringing at his own question, even if his back was to me.

"Why? It's not like he has any updates for us."

The last time I had heard from Alex was when he received a save-the-date and texted me to tell me he wouldn't be able to make it to my wedding. Aside from that, with no updates on the case, it seemed we didn't have anything to say to each other.

"Oh, shit. Erin. Does Alex still think you're getting married?"

"I don't know what he knows."

Ben just looked at me. He didn't need to tell me how childish and stubborn I was being. He did not need to say, out loud, that I should have joined them, that it would be good for me. There was no need for him to tell me how worried he was about his little sister closing herself off in a shield of protective armor. He didn't need to say any of that; his disapproving look did that for both of us.

Michelle got home about an hour after he left. I liked her for Ben. She was so kind and warm and, most importantly, she suffered none of his bullshit. She called him out when he needed it and I admired that. I had made a habit of protecting people or making excuses for them. Michelle and Ben were good to each other and they were both so good to me. I think having me there made them think about their own future as potential parents, and it was shortly after that realization that I decided I should be on my way.

So I packed up my less-broken heart and my few belongings and found my own place—just not before we committed to Sunday morning breakfasts. I wasn't about to give up those pancakes.

*****

Allie had a fever and Ben was spending a lot of time in his room. I know this isn't uncommon for teen boys, but Ben's solitude felt less innocent. I basically knocked my knuckles bloody on his door begging him to come with me before he finally screamed at me to go away.

"Fine!" and I stormed down the stairs.

"You sure you'll be okay?" I asked Allie as I tied the hoodie around my waist.

"Yeah. I'm really tired."

"Okay. I'll bring home some soup and I'll warm that up for you when I get back. It'll be just a little while. Don't bother Ben, ok?"

"Thanks, mom. I mean, Er." she whispered, as if she was talking in her sleep.

I was only 13 but I could already relate to neglected wives and overworked mothers. I needed to blow off some steam. I hopped on my Cannondale and flew through the neighborhood. I pedaled so hard, I fully expected my lungs would burst into flames. I almost welcomed it. Up the steepest hill of Willis Rush Road and hands in the air all the way to the bottom, wind in my hair and no one slowing me down. This feeling… it had only felt like loneliness before, but this was different. This was freedom.

I rode all around the neighborhood until I came to the field that led to Lander's Woods. The weeds were always so thick and high, we would have no choice but to walk our bikes in. I dropped mine right there and made my way through the clearing between the trees. It was the first day I could tell fall was on its way and I was wise to bring a hoodie. After sunset, it would get cold in the treehouse.

It felt foreign being there without the other two. It was almost wrong to be climbing up the ladder without Ben leading and Allie behind me, pretending she's keeping watch. I reached the top and heard music coming from the treehouse. Without recognizing the sound, I panicked for a moment. Thoughts raced through my brain; Did someone find our spot? Am I in danger? Should I just turn around and make a run for it? The one time Allie isn't keeping watch and Ben isn't here to save me if some creep found our hideaway and wants to hurt me. If I make it out alive, I'm really going to let Ben have it. I don't care what he's doing in his room—nothing is more important than the safety of his sister! How dare he? He's been brooding for what seems like months. Get over it, whatever it is, grow up!

My heart raced but my curiosity wouldn't let me back down. If I died up here, imagine how bad Ben would have felt. It would have forced him to come out of his room and engage with Allie. And Allie, waiting for her soup, would come to know how capable and amazing she already was. She would step into her power more and speak up for herself. Imagine how my parents would have had to be around more for the two of them once they realized this was all their fault for treating us like inconveniences instead of the choices they made together. Wow, maybe this was a good thing. Maybe me getting brutally murdered in this treehouse by some serial killer would change the dynamic in this family for the better.

So I took a deep breath and placed a hand on my heart, measuring the pace as it slowed to a normal beat. I paused just one more moment before I popped my head in and there he was. No escaped convict, no vicious serial killer; Alex, in his slim, green thermal, sitting in the corner with his back to me. The music continued—he had no idea he wasn't alone anymore.

"What's that song?"

His entire body jumped as my question startled him. As he turned his head, his face was immediately washed in a smile when he saw me. Even his eyes smiled.

"Er! What the hell? You scared me," he laughed.

"That's a weird name for a song," I chuckled. I made my way all the way up the ladder and waited patiently for him to appreciate how clever I was.

"Oh, yeah, it's called Clumsy. Do you know it? By Our Lady Peace?"

I didn't know it. I didn't really know any music unless my parents or Ben were playing it, but even those songs, I wasn't sure if I liked them or if I just knew them.

"No—but I like it."

"Cool, yeah. They're from Canada. I have been listening to this album a lot. It's kind of sad but I dunno, I like it, ya know?"

I didn't know about that either. But I knew that he was sharing something with me. He was telling me about this band and where they're from and, more importantly, he was telling me how he was feeling. That felt like something I ought to pay attention to.

"Yeah...hey, so Ben told me your parents are splitting up. I'm really sorry."

He looked at the boombox for a moment and nodded. Then his brown eyes shifted up to mine and I saw the tears welling up.

"Thanks," he muttered. His eyes shifted back to the speakers.

"I mean. I don't know. My parents aren't really around a lot but yours are. And they are always so nice. I'm sure they're still gonna be nice..."

I didn't know what to tell him. I didn't know what it was like to have my parents split. I just knew I wanted him to feel okay. I wanted to do the impossible and take this sad boy and make him happy. I wanted to make his heavy thoughts vanish and see him smile the way he smiled when he saw me... forever. At that moment, I knew what I said was silly, but I wanted to do anything to make him feel okay, happy, safe. He shifted his eyes back to mine before he spoke again.

"I guess I just thought they loved each other—like in fairy tales. I guess I thought that about all parents. But that's dumb, right? Fairy tales aren't real—"

And before I even knew what I was doing, my lips pressed into his. Our mouths softened into each other, fitting together like the last two satisfying pieces of a puzzle. His hands raised to cradle each side of my face, holding my head like he didn't want to let me go but gentle enough that it was up to me. My hands on top of his, assuring him I didn't want to be anywhere but here.

And we stayed there, hands layered, lips locked, as the sun set and the singer repeated his promise of safety.

*****

I didn't even need a doorbell. The minute someone walked through my front gate, Parker would bark her head off, keeping me safe. I was never a dog person, but the ex and I rescued Parker from a bad situation and when things didn't work out with him, I didn't give him a choice about her. She was mine. She needed someone she could rely on when things got rough. She needed someone to show her love, not just say it, and she needed someone who wouldn't lie or betray the trust we built together. He just wouldn't cut it.

Parker lost her mind at the door and I looked through the peephole, because that's what peepholes are for. I recognized the eye I saw looking back at me.

"How did you find me?" I said with a smile as I opened the door.

"Er. I'm sorry to show up like this."

I can tell he's not in the mood for jokes. And I wish it was as simple as one becoming a detective making one lose their sense of humor, but this felt much more personal. To be fair, we hadn't spoken in so long. Maybe I didn't know him anymore…

I ushered him inside and played a good host as I offered him something to drink, fully expecting him to decline. But he did not and there we were, sitting on my couch, sipping tequila in silence.

"I technically shouldn't be here."

He broke the silence with that and uttered it like it was one, long word.

"Yet, here you are."

He knew I hated that. I hate when someone tries to get you to ask a question instead of just sharing the information with you. Like when you're in a room with someone and they're reading something, audibly exclaiming along the lines of, "Oh wow. I can't believe it. Wow, that's really something." Just say it. Stop trying to get me to ask and just *spit it out.*

"Er, I have to tell you something. You'll be getting an official call but I wanted to tell you myself."

I stared into his eyes and felt like I was back in the treehouse. I wanted to be mad that he never followed up after I ignored his text. I wondered why he didn't fight for me when he saw I was engaged. But all of that melted away when I looked into his eyes. I just wanted to make him feel okay again. I wanted him to know he could tell me anything—anything. I wanted him to know that I was actually glad my engagement ended because my soul knew in that treehouse that he is the person for me and all I have been doing my entire life is trying to find people that fit the Alex shaped space in my heart—and none of them have. I wanted him to know that he could trust me. I'm reliable. He could depend on me when times got rough. I would protect him.

"Okay," I managed to get out. "Wait..."

I shot back the last gulp of tequila and it burned all the way down.

"Okay, now I'm ready"

*****

Mom, dad, and I watched Allie flip her tassel over her cap and smile her impossibly beautiful smile as she glided across the stage. Alex and his father came too. Ben didn't make it and, at that point, it would have been a bigger shock if he had.

After the ceremony, we all went back to the house and ate. Alex

Lucano Sr. insisted on grilling and mom was agreeable as long as "no one will be upset if there are vegetables on the plate!" That's the thing about mom, she would make herself the villain in everyone else's story so you feel sorry for her—and dad was no help. Maybe he used to reassure her, but by those days he seemed to openly agree that she was the bad guy.

The entire afternoon was a celebration of Allie's achievement. She graduated high school and was determined to jump into the Fall semester at NYU. But despite the happy occasion, it all just felt heavy; Ben's absence was palpable, mom and dad were barely pretending to like each other anymore, like they just had to get through this one last thing before they were free. The passive aggressive comments were becoming less passive, and I felt an unfortunate conversation with Alex was inevitable.

He and I had done this dance for years now; the kissing when no one was looking, the cuddles, the long talks about running away together and being the type of couple that we didn't see growing up. But I hadn't been back to Cortlandt Manor in nearly a year. Allie was coming to stay with me and Ben when she wanted to get away or she and I would escape into the Catskills when we needed to escape Ben too. Alex had enrolled in and graduated from the police academy, which he swore he would never do. I hated the thought of this being my fault while assigning myself the blame that no one asked me to do. Why had I abandoned him? Why couldn't I make it back here—for him? I think I answered that question when I pulled my hand away from his in the backseat of the car on the way to the house.

I agreed to stay a couple of days. The summer was slow at the studio so I managed to get a full week away from booking photoshoots for other people and classes wouldn't start again until August. The timing was perfect to spend a few days with Allie in our childhood home, reliving the neglect that made us who we are and commiserating at an elevated level of awareness that the years had afforded us.

We walked through the neighborhood, just the two of us. Allie and

I called it the Skinned-Knees tour; she fell off of her bike on this corner, I short-jumped the rocks in that part of the stream, we both toppled from the treehouse countless times. As we strolled down memory lane, I think we both longed for the simple pain of cuts and scrapes compared to the deeper kind that seemed to accompany adulthood. I looked into Allie's eyes and she was a little girl and a young woman and, at times, I saw the shadows cast her face in a way that showed me what she will look like at 40 or 50. I mean, what she would have looked like. Allie was my baby sister but there were times it felt like she had lived a hundred lives before I came to be.

"You know, they've been waiting for this so they can split up and feel less bad about it—the irony being, having happier parents would have been better for all of us." she said, cradling a tiny frog in her hands.

"Has it been bad? Are they fighting a lot?"

"No. That's the thing. Even fighting would be nice—at least there would be some expression of emotions in this house. If they're both home at the same time, it's just… quiet."

She held this little frog in her hand so gently, petting the top of its head, knowing it could leap back into the stream at any moment. She didn't mind, as she knew this frog wasn't hers to keep. We were in the frog's home, lucky to see it, even luckier to interact with it, to hold it, to visit for a few minutes before it was off on its next adventure. I realized how lucky I was to have that with Allie, especially with Ben's gradual departure from our lives becoming more and more apparent. I lived with him and I never knew where he was—even when we were in the same room. But there I was, in the quiet night of nearly summertime, sitting by the stream we knew so well, knowing that Allie was soon off on her next adventure, but she chose to sit with me, to let me visit. I reached my hand out and tucked her hair behind her ear like I did when we were little. She looked at me, the moon in her eyes, as the tiny frog leapt out of her hands, and she hugged me tighter than she had ever hugged me before.

We got home and I tucked her in like I had done so many times before. Neither of us made any smartass comments about being too grown up for this. It felt sacred and understood that this would be the last time I was going to do this, and neither of us would jeopardize that with a joke. I kissed her forehead and whispered, "don't let the bed bugs bite" as I made my way to the door. I clicked the light off and took one last look at her before I went to my room.

"Hey. Aren't you forgetting something?" she said, with her eyes still closed.

"I love you, Allie-gator."

"I love you bigger, Er-Bear."

As I walked through the quiet hallway to my childhood bedroom, tears ran down my face. I was consumed with gratitude for the friendship with my sister and excited for her to leap out of my hands into her next destination soon. These were tears of pure happiness and hope.

They found her body in the treehouse three days later.

*****

"Say it again."

"You heard me the first time, Er"

The tequila had warmed me up, as it so often had before. The words Alex just spoke to me bared repeating.

"But, Detective Lucano, sir, I didn't quite hear you," as I took a proper pose and raised his glass to my lips. Mine was already empty. With a pout, I begged him once more.

"Please, sir?"

His lips bent into a smile.

"I'm reopening Allie's case. I'm starting a new cold case unit and Allie is at the top of the list."

And just as his lips bent into a smile, my smile melted away. My blood ran cold as the misery of the mystery rushed back into my body.

"Er, this is a good thing." he assured me, like he was reading my mind and sensed the doubt, the panic, the trauma of living this hell all over again. His hand on mine.

"You can tell Ben, or I can if you'd like."

I took a deep breath and told him not to bother. A few months shy of his eight-year chip, Ben fell off the wagon—hard. Michelle didn't hang around long after that happened and I don't blame her. It had been months since Ben returned a phone call and it was only the inheritance from dad that was keeping the power on for my brother, in more ways than one.

"Shit. I had a feeling but I was just hoping he was busy with the program. I've tried him a few times."

"Well you can arrest him, or don't. I don't care. I can't anymore. He isn't my brother when he's on that shit and I'm done."

Alex's tequila must have been stronger than mine.

"You know Allie was killed when some of us were fully conscious. And dad died when life was happening to all of us. And some of us planned weddings while our fiances were fucking other people and some of us had to drop out of school to take care of our shitty addict brothers. Some of us deal with our problems like grown ups!"

The irony of this rant being fueled by tequila was not lost on me and I promptly shut up so I could wait for Alex to say something perfect and comforting.

"He didn't deserve to marry you, Er."

I collapsed into a pile of flesh and tears, sobbing, my bones feeling like they had shredded away from each other, drifting loose inside of me and disconnecting from my body. Immediately, Alex wrapped his arms around me on the floor, holding me in place and letting the guttural sounds wail from somewhere deep inside me, as his body became the fortress that prevented mine from breaking apart.

*****

The four of us had not been in the same room for a long time but there's nothing like the youngest child's murder and subsequent funeral to bring a family together.

We sat at the kitchen table staring into our coffees. Mom and dad kept sneaking looks at Ben far more than they would look at me or each other. I get it, he looked like hell. I was probably staring at him too. It was actually the first time he had admitted to being on heroin and he did that by telling us he was detoxing. He said "this whole Allie thing" had really scared him into getting sober. I think, back then, we even believed him. This whole "addict in the family thing" was still fresh. There's a lot of hope in the beginning.

He kept saying he wished he had been around more, like that would have stopped this from happening. He kept making it about himself and how bad he felt. How messed up he was. How sorry he was for putting the family through this, and the timing of it all. He didn't know why he was like this but he was determined to get better—for all of us and, especially, for Allie.

So we caught him all the way up. We talked about how normal everything was and how beautiful she looked at her graduation. We hadn't even gotten the pictures developed yet; she vanished the day after. I reminded him that I told him about the ceremony already when I came home the next day and, of course, he nodded as if he remembered.

I was the one to tell him we waited so long for the funeral because we wanted to know what happened first. We needed to wait for the full autopsy and coroner's reports. We needed to know the cause of death and the manner of death and that it was absolutely a homicide; determined by the clean toxicology report and, more importantly, by the ligature marks on her neck. I was the one to tell my big brother that some monster strangled our baby sister and tried to cover it up. They took her life away and left her dead body where we used to go to feel alive.

At the news, he went gray, and rushed to the restroom near the den to expel the coffee and whatever else was in his stomach. That's the thing about talking to someone who is detoxing—you never know when they won't be able to hold it in any more. And at that exact moment, he needed to get something out of him.

*****

It was rough not being in the same school as Allie, but Ben and I were getting reports from her as much as we could. When we came home that Friday, she was crying in her room and it didn't take long before we found out she got her period and some boys made fun of her for it.

"What are their names?" Ben asked. He emerged from his lair very rarely these days, but if we managed to confer before he got there, he was still lively.

"I'm not telling you that!" Allie shrieked. I wasn't the only one who protected those who hurt me.

Ben didn't press for their names, instead he softened into the brother I forgot I had. He put his arm around her and explained that boys can be total idiots, especially when it comes to things they don't understand. He told her she was perfect and, even if it's hard to believe, that pretty soon those same boys were going to start being really nice to her for their own reasons. He made her promise that she wouldn't give them the time of day when that day comes.

He was so good at knowing what you needed to hear. He was intuitive and clever. He could spin any situation to your liking and manipulate an awful reality into a promising fantasy that, more often than not, would come to fruition.

We left Allie alone for a while and fixed some snacks for a movie night. After going around in circles, we decided it was time to show her Carrie. He and I melted chocolate onto pretzels and laughed and teased in the kitchen until Allie came into the den, smiling with her blankie in her hands. The thing Ben didn't know about getting your first period is that you suddenly understand that you are going to be an adult someday, which makes you want to stay a child as long as you can.

That's why Allie had me, because what Ben could never understand, I always could.

*****

We all knew it was coming. Dad had put up a hell of a fight to live long enough to see justice for Allie, but on what would have been her twenty-seventh birthday, we all felt defeated.

It had been over ten years since she graduated, ten years since she was murdered, and there was no word from the department in the last few. Those first several years, every few months we would get a phone call or a visit. Something would seem promising, we would get our hopes up, and then—nothing. Mom went through the motions of the day. She lit the candles on the cake and we sang happy birthday to Allie's senior portrait—we were so accustomed to this, none of us even cried this time.

Dad was cleaning up before heading back to his place and I sat with mom at the table, looking at photos of Allie as a baby, as a toddler, as a teenager… in sync, our heads turned towards the door as it opened. For a moment I thought the wind had forced it, letting the flickering smell of autumn gust inside. The door swung wide open and there stood Alex with a bottle of wine in his right hand—and he wasn't alone.

"I'm so sorry we're just getting here. I didn't want to show up empty-handed."

He stepped into the light of the foyer and out of the doorway, followed by someone none of us recognized. The last time we had seen him, he was incoherent and gaunt. But here, chauffeured by Officer Lucano Jr. was a handsome, healthy, Mets-shirt wearing, clear-eyed Ben.

Mom sprinted to hug him in the doorway, practically knocking him over.

"Oh sweetie. Oh my goodness. Benny, you look so good, honey!" she cried through happy tears. Dad dried his hands off as he joined the embrace. Mom kept wiping her face as her gaze shifted to Alex.

"Oh, Alex, thank you. Tell us, do you have anything new?"

"I wish, Gayle. I'm sorry."

But we had already accepted this as much. And much like the relief my parents felt when they finally got divorced, this felt like maybe it was safe to stop trying to force it. Of course none of us wanted to give up, but all of us had grown comfortable with little-to-no news. We had mostly stopped even asking, accepted the possible theory that some dangerous drifter was in the treehouse and Allie scared him, he panicked and killed her and vanished. It wouldn't have been the first time someone was surprised by one of us in the treehouse and it wasn't far enough into the woods to go completely unseen by anyone taking a stroll through that meadow. Maybe it felt safer to think this was a one-off, freak occurrence. Maybe we could all just accept it and move on. Maybe we had to give ourselves that closure.

"Hey big bro."

Ben smiled at me and held his arms out, inviting me into them. I got up from the chair and made my way in. Ben wrapped me up into his chest, I took a deep inhale, and looked up at him. His eyes closed tightly as the tears bravely fought their way out.

That was the happiest birthday we had in ten years.

*****

Alex had done a good job of keeping me posted about everything but it had been a couple of weeks since he replied to my texts, which was wildly out of character. The only time he took more than a few hours to get back to me was when he was asleep, and even then it wasn't out of the question to get a reply from him at two or three in the morning. He had trouble sleeping through the night, from the job, mostly, and he also knew it was always okay to text me. I had trouble sleeping too—but I could never blame my work. Taking photos of people wasn't the kind of work that kept me awake; the guilt of being alive when Allie wasn't, the last time I had seen Ben, the sinking feeling that I knew more than I realized… those were the types of things that haunted me.

I sent Alex another message a few hours earlier but I still had no reply. I got myself fired up to go directly to the station and have a conversation with him. This wasn't just anyone looking for answers, this was me. This was for Allie. He couldn't just abandon us like Ben willfully had or like my father didn't want to. He could not reawaken hope for me and mom just to go cold on us. He made it his own business to come to my home that night to tell me, and since then he had involved me in anything he was allowed to, but now? Nothing? This was just disrespectful. This was the way you treat strangers. I wasn't going to let him get away with it.

I threw on a pair of jeans and slid into my boots as I snagged the keys from the kitchen counter. My bag was hanging on the doorknob and with one hand I unlocked it and slid the tote onto my wrist. With fury I swung the door open and was not even remotely prepared for what was standing on the other side -

Ben jolted back violently, almost falling backwards into the bushes that line the walkway to my door.

"What the fuck are you doing here?!"

Parker stood guard, ready to lunge at my command. To be fair, she never warmed up to him, but when we were staying at his place she didn't have a choice but to be nice.

He straightened himself out and asked if he could explain. The adrenaline was still coursing through my body, but I agreed to let him try, and we were back inside before I knew it.

He didn't look great, but I had certainly seen him in much worse shape. He was not the color of a healthy human but his eyes were clear and his clothes were clean.

"You have five minutes, Ben. I swear to god if you ask me for money—"

"No, Er, jeez. No. I'm not here for money. I'm clean."

The look I gave him spoke for itself and if that didn't, Parker's skeptical growls did.

"I'm on medical detox, okay? Today is day ten. So, yeah, I'm not technically clean but I'm good. I needed to be good before I came here."

I'm sure I was rolling my eyes and I'm sure any of his advocates would have told me I should have been receiving this with love, but after everything, that was the best I could do.

"Erin, I'm sorry."

He waited for me to say something. I gave him nothing.

"I'm sorry for everything. I, um. I'm sorry I haven't been here for you, with the whole Allie thing."

My blood was boiling.

"I don't mean that, like—I just—sorry, this is—hard for me-"

I was not going to let him go down the road he had gone down so many times before.

"It's *hard* for you? For *you?!* This has been hell for me, Ben. I'm so fucking sick of you always showing up, wanting forgiveness, launching into your bullshit. I don't care how hard it has been for you. I don't actually think it has been. How hard can it be when you're not even on the same planet as the rest of us?"

It was my turn to wait for him to say something. Surprisingly, he did not, he just waited for more.

"You can't do this anymore, Ben. Get clean, get loaded, rinse and repeat. Show up out of nowhere and expect me to act like mom, happy and hopeful. No. You cannot manipulate me like her. I am not her. I fucking know better. I know you. That's why you don't come around me—because I see you. I see all the way through you."

His eyes glued to his feet.

"You're right," he let out, "you do. You always have. And I'm sorry."

He braced his hands on his knees as he stood up. He was resigned, almost humble.

"I understand why you don't trust me. I wouldn't trust me either and I'm not going to try to convince you. At this point, you really shouldn't. I'd be worried about you if you did."

He made his way to the door.

"I won't come around here again. I don't have your new number so don't worry about me calling or texting. I just wanted to make sure I told you how sorry I am."

And with that, he left. I watched through the peephole as he moved toward the gate and noticed he checked my mailbox on his way out. Figures. Once a junkie always a junkie, looking for anything he can take.

I spent a few minutes digesting what just happened. I was tempted to open a bottle and forget, but determined to get the answers I needed, I reminded myself where I was going before being significantly interrupted by the past. I made sure to thank Parker for being a good girl and I headed back out the door—this time, with a little more caution.

On my way, I, too, checked the mailbox to see if there was anything besides junk mail or bills. To my surprise, there was. Ben wasn't looking to take anything, he was leaving something for me. Something I scared him from giving to me while I ripped him to shreds and dismantled his ego… I retrieved the small envelope and got into my car.

*****

I miss when there was no traffic in this town. But even an hour outside of New York City means the commuters have taken over. Whenever I come back here, I'm flooded with the nostalgia of how things used to be, how I used to be, how all of us used to be.

Sitting at a red light, if I don't get held up anymore I am maybe five minutes from the station. I'm anxious. Why haven't I heard from Alex? Is this even about the case? Is it possible I'm not as important to him as I believed myself to be? Maybe there really weren't any updates and he just felt more comfortable keeping a distance. It's possible he's seeing someone and it's getting serious. Is he delaying the inevitable conversation where he tells me he can't be friends with me anymore? That he's moved on, met someone who can give herself fully to him, like he deserves?

Why am I thinking about this?

I grab Ben's envelope from the passenger seat. I wanted so badly to be strong enough to ignore it, throw it away without even looking at it. I wanted to be big enough to not let him in anymore. But the way he looked when he left, the way it felt like things might really be different this time, like what I said mattered. Maybe he *can* change. He had a solid seven years at one point and it usually takes a few relapses to get it right. Maybe this time will stick.

The light is taking forever to turn green. I rip open the envelope and prepare to read whatever story he has to tell me, but with a more open mind than I had earlier today. I reach in for the letter, ready to read my way through this red light that is taking far longer than any red light should take.

But there was no letter. It was one of his tiny collages. The word "Sorry" consumed most of the background and a tiny frog-shaped bead was glued to a bottom corner. Wisps of blue and green leaves dart from the edges inward and delicate threads of stars dangle from the bottom. A bold, black frame outlines three tiny faces that appear to be cut from a photograph, compiled to create the shape of a heart. I stared at the childhood images of me, Ben, and Allie and traced my fingers against their depth, the raised paper of the photos in the center, and I felt dizzy… wrong… sick. I was seeing this collage for the first time, but I knew these faces. I knew this photo was taken during Allie's ninth birthday party and the last time I saw it, Ben and I had cut it up, carefully placing our own faces into the locket we got for her when she was turning ten.

I couldn't breathe.

*****

The car behind me is leaning on their horn and I look up. I've sat here so long, the light is turning yellow again and I press the gas pedal, speeding right by the turn I would make for the station and onto the freeway. If cops try to pull me over, they're in for a chase. I'm not stopping until I get there. It's three exits away, and a straight shot West on Adams with a right turn onto Greenfield Avenue, after I pass the old Conway's place. The new owners painted it blue but they kept the red door.

I'm home. The home I shared with Ben when I left Cortlandt Manor, the home where Allie would escape to when she needed us… when she needed me. The home that felt empty as Ben slipped further into addiction and full again when he came back to us, when he was nursing my heart back from being broken. Every terrible, wonderful, awful, beautiful memory comes flooding back in waves in the time it takes my body to get to the front step.

The screen door is shut but the other one is open. It makes sense, I realize, that he just got home. He didn't leave my place long before I did. He might even be in the bathroom, having just returned home and getting ready to relax into the night. I move through the living room and see the bathroom door, slightly ajar, and from his room I hear him.

"I didn't expect to see you again."

"Ben. That collage. Those photos of us… Allie's locket."

I step lightly toward his room, though I'm not sure why, he knows it's me and he knows why I'm here. I push open the door. He's sitting up in his bed. His phone and a gun rest on the pillow in front of him.

"What… why do you have that?" my voice shaking

"Er, I meant it when I said I'm sorry."

"Ben, you can't do this. It'll be okay. Please. Just… tell me what happened. Just explain to my why-"

"I can't explain it, Er! There's no good reason why. She caught me! She caught me up in the treehouse and she let me have it. A lot like you just did, but Allie did it 20 years ago."

I'm frozen at the foot of his bed, listening while watching how close his hand is to the gun. How can I get that away from him?

"It's okay, Ben. Just tell me what happened."

"She came up there and just started screaming at me for… everything. For missing her graduation, telling me what a piece of shit I am. How I was letting you down, letting her down, I just… I snapped. I was dopesick and she slapped the only shit I had into the weeds and I—I lost it."

Stoic and surreal, the tears are streaming down my face but I can't feel them. I can't feel anything. I know what's happening and I can't move.

"I fucked everything up. And I know that. I know that now. I can't fix this! I can't fix me! The only thing I can do is this." as he lifts up his phone.

"Let's just go see Alex. Let's get you a lawyer and they'll… they'll be lenient. You're telling the truth now, they'll go easy on you, Ben. Let's just go see Alex."

"Stop trying to protect me, Er. This is what you do—you need to stop."

He clicks a few things on his phone screen and tosses it on the floor. "There. Done."

His phone vibrates on the floor and I see Alex's name on the screen. It buzzes and buzzes as we both stay exactly where we are.

"Ben, just answer it. Talk to him. He'll tell you the best thing to do just talk to him."

My pocket starts to vibrate. I don't need to look, I know who it is.

"I'm sorry, Er. I love you so much. None of this is your responsibility. None of this is your fault."

His hand grips the gun and everything moves in slow motion. He raises it to his head, my feet made of cement as they shuffle forward. My arms lift from my body as I lunge—as I scream—as the bullet discharges into his brain and I leap, out of my own skin but entirely contained, I land on his lap. The gun, smoking in his hand.

*****

By the time I lift my head out of the toilet, I am sure there is nothing left in me. The water swirls with a kaleidoscopic reflection of orange and pink, a color combination that's always bothered me but, until now, I could never understand why. My throat hurts, my eyes are bloodshot, and there is no way I will forget how I got the bruises that decorate both of my knees.

I have no idea how long I have been in here; it could have been hours or it could have been minutes since my shoulder slammed hard enough into the bathroom door that it took off the top hinge. No sooner than the screws hit the floor did my legs buckle underneath me. I stare at the toilet. Or maybe I just know exactly what it looks like.

I have been in this bathroom so many times I could paint it from memory. I know the handle was installed backwards and, at one point, I had grown so used to it that every other toilet confused me. I know the rust stain on the base of the bowl that he never manages to scrub away. I know the sea-green and gray two-inch tile pattern on the floor and how it's chipped where his right foot stands when he takes a leak. And I know the bubbling of the paint where the hose enters the wall due to a leak that he has "fixed" at least four times. It's the bloated white wall behind the can that reminds my stomach to erupt again, but with nothing left in me, I just cramp from the heaving. With that, I'm snapped back into the reality of what had just happened.

As I attempt to swallow any moisture that could ease the burning in my throat, it occurs to me I can't stay here forever—after all, my brother is still out there.

I get up and slide out of the door, careful not to let it come entirely off the frame.

As I make my way back into his bedroom, my left hand slides against the wall to flick up the switch. It clicks on and I squint my eyes as they slowly adjust and the mattress comes into focus. I breathe a slight sigh of relief when I see Ben right where I left him. Still my brother. Still in his Mets t-shirt. Still dead.

Sirens boom onto the street. The front yard lights up in reds and blues as cops fill the house with their guns drawn. Again, I hear everything and I can't move. I'm staring at my brother with a hole in his head when I feel a hand on my shoulder.

"Er, are you okay?"

"No."

"Are you hurt? Do you need medical?"

"No."

Alex puts his jacket on me and walks me out the front door, ignoring the officers that pepper him with well-intentioned questions. He walks me to his car and guides my body against the hood. He, himself, is in shock.

"I don't really know what to say, Erin. I'm just… Are you sure you're okay? I need to know you're okay."

"Why haven't you gotten back to me?" I ask, as if nothing has happened.

A chuckle, which he quickly rectifies.

"I, well, we found something and I needed to wait for some results to come back. I didn't want to alarm you for no reason."

"Oh? What did you find?"

Alex tells me they found a syringe that was in the evidence box that was never looked into back when this happened. It tested positive for heroin, obviously, and for male DNA. They couldn't find a match in the system, so Alex had followed Ben around for a while until he could snag an empty bottle from the trash outside of the detox clinic. He says they got the confirmation this afternoon and they wanted to move quickly, but they didn't have the DA's green light.

"You didn't tell me because I would have argued with you. I would have protected Ben."

He doesn't say anything, but I'm right.

"What did Ben's text say?"

He pauses for a moment.

"He said you beat me to it. And he wanted to make sure you're going to be okay."

*****

We pull up to my place and see Parker's shadow through the glass in the door. I'm still wearing Alex's jacket and we sit for a moment before he speaks.

"Er, I will call you tomorrow… check in. If I can pick anything up for you or make any calls, you know I'll do it."

Ben's text echoes in my head. I don't know if I am going to be okay, but for the first time, handling this on my own doesn't seem like the answer.

"I can't… I don't want to be alone."

Without hesitating, he unbuckles his seatbelt and walks through the gate. Parker doesn't bark. A few minutes later, he returns and opens the back door behind me. Parker jumps in, followed by her travel bag and my backpack. She lies down in the backseat, more comfortable than she's ever been in a car.

The drive is silent, with the exception of Parker's breathing and the ambient noise of the freeway. We're heading right back to Cortlandt Manor, but it feels—okay. I'm not nostalgic for anything, I'm not sure what I am, but I don't hate it.

We pull up to Alex's house and he turns the key. Parker stands up, ready to get out. We sit for a moment before Alex gets out and brings Parker inside with our things.

And now, alone in his car, it's just now that everything is starting to hit me; I am an only child. My dad is gone. It's just me and mom now. I know the emotions will come, I know that this will not be linear or easy, but, in this moment, I feel a peace that I have not felt since childhood. The only memories flooding my head are the happy ones; being foolish in the kitchen with Ben, tucking Allie in at night, reading scary stories to both of them around a campfire in the backyard. They're gone now, and it does occur to me that if I don't have them to take care of, my life is going to look vastly different. I'm going to have time to feel all of this. I'm going to have the space to look after myself. I'm not going to have excuses anymore—and, for a moment, I'm terrified.

Just then, the car door opens and Alex is standing there with his hand out. I take a deep breath and place mine in his. He guides me out of the car and gently closes the door without letting go of me. We walk up to his door and my body stops. I want nothing more than to go inside, but I know what crossing this threshold means. It means I won't be an island anymore. It means I am allowing him to help me through this, and so much more. It means I have to shed the unhealthy lifestyle I have constructed that keeps me safe. I have to remove my armor, put down my weapons, and be a human being.

He squeezes my hand and I jolt back into my body. He's looking at me and my eyes meet his, searching them, swimming in them, waiting for him to say the perfect thing.

"Let's go inside, Erin. You will be safe in here."

Jukebox Memories
Carol Goodman Kaufman

The ride back from Northern Maine to Pittsfield was long, but Sally enjoyed the quiet in the car, especially after the raucous weekend surrounding her cousin Nigella's wedding. She drove across vast stretches of flat earth, farms popping up miles and miles apart from one another. How hard it must be to have no neighbors nearby. Yet so freeing. She could walk naked around the house and there'd be nobody to see her. To laugh at her.

And the trees! They never seemed to stop. Up hills and down into valleys they grew, their conical forms reaching into the robin's egg blue sky.

At noon, just as her stomach began to rumble, she saw a billboard for a diner in Biddeford. *One last chance to enjoy my little vacation before going back into my normal, everyday, boring world.* Sally steered her car off the highway and followed the signs into a jam-packed parking lot.

The heady aroma of marinara sauce hit her the moment she entered the diner, making her stomach grumble again. A waitress with the name Kim embroidered on the pocket of her pink uniform approached her.

"I'm sorry, but we're really busy today. Do you mind sitting at the counter? That way you won't have to wait."

"Not at all." Sally took a stool at the far end of the long formica island. Kim handed her a menu and offered coffee.

"New here?" Kim asked as she poured.

"Just passing through. This billboard on the highway claims you have four stars, so I thought I'd give it a try."

"We've got the best fries and the tastiest pies."

"Sounds like an advertising tagline to me," Sally said.

Kim laughed. "I just made it up, but I think we'll use it!"

Sally sipped from a crimson Fiestaware mug as she pored over the offerings on the menu. Once she'd ordered, she looked up to get a feel for the place. Women were dressed in their Sunday best. Suits, dresses, even some hats. Men wore jackets and ties. Good-natured banter flew across tables, with wry observations about the pastor's sermon. *So, people still go to church up here.*

This may have been 1969, but the diner itself was definitely 1950s and reminded her of the soda fountain her grandfather had operated in his Rexall store. The counter was a pristine laminate, along which stood ten bolted-down metal stools with padded red vinyl seats. Behind the counter Sally saw a three-spindled Waring milkshake machine and a Bunn coffeemaker. Every few feet sat napkin dispensers, salt and pepper shakers, ketchup bottles, and glass syrup dispensers.

On the counter and at every booth was a vintage Seeburg Wall-o-Matic jukebox. Sally flipped the pages with the little metal tabs. She had been a junior in high school when these tunes were popular, and virtually every one of them brought back memories.

Abruptly, she stopped flipping the pages. There, on the left side of the third title page was "Be My Baby" by one of her favorite girl groups. Sally pulled the wallet out of her bag and extracted a quarter from the zippered change pocket. She slid the coin into the slot at the top of the jukebox and punched the D and 3 keys. The machine whirred and clicked for a few seconds before the disk fell into place. But it wasn't the Ronettes whose voices Sally heard. Her heart seized and her throat constricted as the sounds of "Brown Eyed Girl" filled the air. The lyrics and lilting melody shoved her back into high school.

Hands shaking, she clawed at the jukebox, trying to find a way to cancel the song. *How could I have punched the wrong buttons?*

*****

Sally had recently moved to town, her father having been transferred yet again in his job as a chemical engineer for GE. She hated having to move every few years and leave friends behind. They always said they'd keep in touch, and they did for a few months, but then they'd drift apart. Making new friends was such an effort.

But that time was a little different. Luckily, the house her parents had bought was right next door to Annie Taylor's, and the two struck up a friendship immediately. Both girls were honor students, and both shared a love of chess, ice skating, and music. Annie brought her into her circle of friends, a group squarely on the B list in the 11th-grade popularity contest, but she was okay with that. At least she had a group.

Every Friday night Sally and her friends would head up to the Boys Club, where local bands played in a gym transformed by dim lights and colored spots into The Lighthouse. The girls walked around the perimeter of the room in groups, talking and sneaking peeks at the boys who hung out in the center of the room. Sally never danced. She knew that nobody would ever ask her to dance because she was too tall. But then again, nobody ever asked her friends to dance, either. So, now that she thought about it, why did they even go to those dances?

But one Friday night, somebody did ask her to dance. Her heart pounded in her chest as she followed Jimmy Dwyer into the middle of the floor, her friends' giggles echoing in her head. Jimmy was the most popular boy in school, quarterback of the football team and a top honors student. He sat behind her in calculus class, and she took every opportunity to gaze into his deep blue eyes whenever she had to pass a paper to him. But he never noticed her, or so she thought.

That night they danced to Van Morrison's "Brown Eyed Girl," one of her very favorite songs. And she fell in love.

When the song was over, Tammy Clark came over to talk, followed by the rest of the popular girls—the cheerleaders, the prom co-chairs. The very girls who had passed her in the hallway without a word were suddenly paying attention to her. The following Monday they even invited her to sit at their table in the cafeteria.

And she did. She began to hang out with that select little clique and leave her B-list friends behind.

Jimmy Dwyer called her every night. He brought her to all the places on the song. He called her his "brown-eyed girl" and said they made the perfect pair. They made out in the football stadium, at the waterfall, in the fog.

One night, he told her that he wanted to show her just how much he loved her. Taking her by the hand, he led her to a spot behind the bleachers. He turned on his transistor radio and placed it next to a blanket he spread on the ground. The song playing was "Brown Eyed Girl." Sally's heart raced as he peeled her clothes off, piece by piece. When he finished, he gazed at her naked body with a grin that she believed showed his love for her.

Just as she thought life couldn't get any better, Jimmy's friends jumped out from behind the equipment shed, laughing and pointing at her. Pete Jamison snapped pictures with his Instamatic camera. Sally crossed her arms in front of her body, dropped to the ground, and reached over to grab her clothes from the pile Jimmy had left under the bleachers. But Tammy got to them first and held them up. The only way to get them back was to get off the ground and expose her body.

Cheerleader Tammy led the jeering. "Who would ever go for you, you piglet? Did you actually think Jimmy Dwyer would like you? Want you as his girlfriend? You, who go all dopey-eyed every time you hand him his calculus paper?"

*****

The sound of their derisive laughter haunted her to this day. Thank God her father had been transferred again, this time to Schenectady, far enough away to start over. A new life. Nobody would ever know her humiliation. From then on, she would be very, very careful around people. And if another creep should try anything on her, or if some bitch should grab her clothes, she always carried protection in a little can of mace. Just in case.

Sally carried her hatred with her, often lulling herself to sleep at night thinking of ways to exact her revenge on that gang of bullies. On all of them, but on Jimmy Dwyer most of all. Even though it had been five years since her humiliation, and even though she'd probably never see any of them ever again, she found comfort in thinking up ways to hurt them the way they'd hurt her.

Kim appeared with her lunch and set it down on the counter. As she cleared the place next to Sally, she looked up and smiled.

"Hey, Coach!" she called.

Sally turned to look in the direction she was facing. Her heart skipped a beat and she blinked twice to be sure she wasn't hallucinating.

Because there stood Jimmy Dwyer.

Oh my God. What is he doing here in Maine?

Jimmy had aged well. Wearing jeans and a down vest over a plaid flannel shirt, he looked as if he had just walked out of an LL Bean catalogue. Patrons greeted him and he waved in return. Sally twisted away and began to examine the ketchup and mustard bottles as if they contained the wisdom of the ages.

While thoughts tumbled through her brain, she hadn't noticed Jimmy take the stool next to her.

"Hi. You're new here."

Sally froze, the color draining from her face.

"Chili, Coach?" Kim asked.

"Yeah, thanks Kimmy."

"They seem to know you here," Sally said.

"I come here a lot." With a smile, he extended his hand, exposing a tattoo of an eagle on his forearm. "I'm Bill. What's your name?"

Bill? Don't try fooling me, you bastard. I can see the damn tattoo. You were so proud of it.

"I'm Sally." She felt faint as his warm hand enveloped hers.

"I've never seen you in town before. Are you from around here?"

"No, I'm from Massachusetts."

"What a coincidence! So am I."

I know you are. But you don't recognize me, do you?

"What brought you here? It's so far away," she asked.

He paused. *For dramatic effect? Thinking up a good story? Or did he already have one in his pocket?*

"I had to get away. Big family. Not always such a great family."

Or did you get into some real trouble back home? Did somebody finally have the guts to press charges?

"Do you have family here?" Sally couldn't stop herself from probing.

"No. I'm on my own."

"What do you do?"

"I teach history at the local high school and coach basketball and baseball."

Of course you do.

"So that's why they call you Coach?"

Bill laughed. "Good deduction, detective. So, tell me about yourself."

Sally thought fast. "I'm looking for a change myself. It's so pretty here I might have found the right place."

"What do you do?"

"I'm a website designer."

"You can do that anywhere, can't you?" Bill smiled, his dimples deepening. "If you'd like, I can show you around town."

The dimples. I remember those deep dimples. I wanted to dive right into them.

"That would be really nice. A tour by an actual local would give me a good idea of the place."

"Then let's go as soon as we finish lunch. My truck is outside."

"No, I'll follow you in my car."

*****

Sally turned the key in the ignition and pulled out behind the green Ford F-150. She followed the truck through the streets of the little town until they pulled into the driveway of a large brick and gray building. A pole-mounted American flag flapped in the breeze on the front lawn.

Jimmy got out of his truck and led Sally to the playing fields.

"The school is closed today and there are no games scheduled, but I think you'll get a feel for how people feel about the community by seeing how well the school is kept."

"It's so clean and well-manicured, not like where I live."

"This is my favorite place. The baseball field."

"You played ball in school?"

"Sure. Baseball, basketball. I love sports."

What? You won't even admit to football? Sally bit her cheek to keep from saying anything.

Bill squinted and frowned at something over Sally's shoulder. "What's that?" he asked and started walking across the diamond. On the ground underneath the bleachers, lay a softball, scuffed and a bit frayed. He picked it up and looked carefully at it.

"It's one of ours. Our team manager must have missed this after practice."

"You'd better fire him," Sally said.

"Nah. He's a good kid. Not the brightest bulb in the chandelier, but a good kid." He squinted in the bright sun. "Look, there's a bat, too. Want to hit some?"

"Sure, why not?"

Bill sauntered to the pitcher's mound and lobbed the ball toward Sally. She whiffed it and groaned.

"No worries. Let's try again."

Again, she swung and missed several more times.

"I give up. That's enough for me," she said, laying the bat down. "I'll never make the big leagues."

"Most of us don't, Sally," he said, tossing the ball to her.

"Here you go, Jimmy," she said and threw it back.

"Jimmy? My name is Bill."

"No. I recognize your tattoo. Those cute dimples. I know who you are. And this is for you." She pulled a little can from her pocket and, holding her breath, sprayed mace directly into his face. He screamed and fell to his knees.

"What are you doing?" he cried, his voice croaking from the chemical.

Sally picked up the bat from the ground and clubbed him over the head. Jimmy dropped to the ground and folded himself into a fetal position, but it was no use. Over and over, she pounded him, until he lay dead.

"That's what you get for taking advantage of me, you bastard. Now who's laughing?"

Sally made her way to her car and drove straight back to Massachusetts, stopping for only one bathroom break.

The minute she walked in the door, she dropped her bags and headed toward her computer. She scanned the news to see if anybody had found

Jimmy Dwyer's body. Nothing yet. She set up a Google alert to be sure to get the story as soon as it came out.

The next day Sally's email showed an alert. She clicked on the message and found four stories listed. She took her laptop to the sofa and clicked on the first one.

"William John 'Bill' Dwyer, Jr. beloved teacher and coach, was found beaten to death behind the bleachers at the Biddeford high school. Police are asking people with any information to please call …"

Yada yada yada. Beloved, yeah. By whom?

She went to the next story, the obituary. It listed his educational achievements, his athletic prowess, and his beloved—again with the beloved—status in the Biddeford community. Following these plaudits was a humorous story about the four brothers going on a road trip to Florida, where they drank a little too much and got matching tattoos.

"Bill is survived by his parents, Janet and William Sr., and three brothers, Peter (Amy) of Phoenix, Andrew (Cynthia) of Chicago, and Matthew (Lauren) of Minneapolis. A fourth brother, James, died in 2000. Bill was predeceased by his wife, Phoebe, in 2009.

Sally felt her heart drop into her stomach. Died? Matching tattoos?

She began to search the net for more information about Jimmy Dwyer, and a lot came up. James Allen Dwyer, it turned out, had not turned out as well as his high school yearbook had predicted. Sure, he got into Dartmouth, but he was expelled after a classmate accused him of rape. As a registered sex offender, he had trouble finding work, but eventually got a job in his uncle's envelope factory. Apparently, Jimmy hadn't learned his lesson about how to treat women because three coworkers filed sexual harassment complaints with the company's human resources department. Fired, Jimmy went on a three-day-long bender, after which a bartender accused him of rape. He stood trial in Superior Court a year later and was convicted and sentenced to 20 years at MCI Concord. Less than a year in, he was murdered by a fellow inmate.

What had Bill said? He had to get away.

Just like me.

The Usual Unusual Suspects

Nina Mansford is a Connecticut based author and playwright. Her short mystery fiction has appeared in multiple anthologies and various publications including *Ellery Queen Mystery Magazine* and *Alfred Hitchcock's Mystery Magazine*. Her plays have had over 100 productions throughout the world. *Antigone: 3021,* her futuristic adaptation of the Ancient Greek classic, recently enjoyed productions in England, Australia and throughout the United States and is available through Stage Partners. Nina is a member of MWA, SCWBI, ITW, The Dramatists Guild and co-President of the NY/Tri-State Chapter of Sisters in Crime.

Vera Brook is a neuroscientist turned multi-genre fiction writer who gets way too attached to her characters (even the villains). She is fueled by coffee and forever torn between reading books and writing them. Learn more about her writing at www.verabrook.com.

donalee Moulson's first mystery book *Hung out to Die* was published in 2023. A historical mystery, *Conflagration!*, was published in 2024, and it won the 2024 Daphne du Maurier Award for Excellence in Mystery/Suspense (Historical Fiction).

A short story, *Swan Song,* was one of 21 selected for publication in *Cold Canadian Crime*, and was shortlisted for an Award of Excellence. Other works have been published in numerous magazines and anthologies. donalee's short story, *Troubled Water,* was shortlisted for a 2024 Derringer Award and a 2024 Award of Excellence from the Crime Writers of Canada.

As a freelance journalist, she has also won awards from print and online publications across North America including *The Globe and Mail, Chatelaine, Lawyer's Daily, National Post,* and *Canadian Business.*

Her non-fiction work includes *The Thong Principle: Saying What You Mean and Meaning What You Say*, and is co-author of *Celebrity Court Cases: Trials of the Rich and Famous*.

Jill Hand is a member of International Thriller Writers. Her work has appeared in many anthologies, including *Weird Fiction Quarterly*. She is the author of the Southern Gothic thrillers, *White Oaks, Black Willows,* and *Red Pines*.

Stormy White is a writer of mysteries and science fiction whose stories have appeared in *Low Down Dirty Vote, Volume 2*, edited by Mysti Berry, *Bold Awards, Volume 1*, and *Serial Magazine*. She is the author of *From Beneath,* a science fiction novel and won second place in a short story contest of the St. Louis Writers Guild. Her story, "Tell No Lies," appears in *Yeet Me in St. Louis,* crime fiction from under the Arch edited by Sandra Murphy. While working as a public defender, she began volunteering at the St. Louis Zoo and continues to regard it as her happy place.

N. M. Cedeño writes crime and mystery short stories and novels, ghost stories, and science fiction. She is a Plan II graduate of the University of Texas at Austin. As a member of Sisters in Crime: Heart of Texas Chapter, she served as chapter vice president and president. She is a member of the Short Mystery Fiction Society. Her short fiction has appeared in anthologies, including in the Crimeucopia series, and in magazines, including Analog: Science Fiction and Fact, After Dinner Conversation: Philosophy and Ethics, Black Cat Weekly, and Black Cat Mystery Magazine. Her short story entitled "A Reasonable Expectation of Privacy" placed third for Best Short Story in the 2013 Analog Readers Poll. Ms. Cedeño blogs with several other Heart of Texas mystery writers at InkStainedWretches.home.blog. For more information please visit nmcedeno.com.

Maroula Blades is a multifaceted artist living in Berlin. She won 2nd place in the German 2023 Amadeu Antonio Prize for her interdisciplinary project, "Stones in Symphony". In June 2023, the UK Society of Authors Foundation awarded her a novella-in-progress grant. And in April 2023, she received a project grant from the Swiss Jan Michalski Foundation for Writing and Literature for her multimedia project "Ominira". The Academy of Arts in Berlin selected her for the 2021 INITIAL Special Grant. In 2020, Chapeltown Books (UK) released her flash fiction collection "The World in an Eye". Her works appeared in The Caribbean Writer, Thrice Fiction, The Decolonial Passage, Ake Review, Abridged Magazine, The London Reader, and the Nonwhite and Woman anthology, as well as in the Crimeucopia series, among other publications. Ms. Blades gives bilingual (in English and German) creative writing workshops in Berlin schools and colleges. She presents her multimedia projects at many international literary festivals in Germany, such as the Berlin International Poetry Festival, Humboldt University, Brecht House, and Lit-Cologne.

Mary Jo Rabe grew up on a farm in eastern Iowa in the American Midwest, got degrees from Michigan State University (German and mathematics) and University of Wisconsin-Milwaukee (library science). She worked in the library of the chancery office of the Archdiocese of Freiburg, Germany, for 41 years, and live with her husband in Titisee-Neustadt, Germany.

Published work includes *Blue Sunset*, inspired by Spoon River Anthology and The Martian Chronicles, and has had poems and stories published in *Fiction River, Pulphouse, Mysterious Christmas, Mystery Tribune, The Dark City Crime* and *Mystery Magazine*, along with other magazines and anthologies.

Denise Johnson has written several mystery, horror, and science fiction short stories that have appeared in *Kings River Life* and *Blood Moon Rising* magazines as well as several anthologies, including *Determined Hearts: A Frankenstein Anthology; Black Buttons Vol. 3: A Family Affair; Buried; Murder of Crows; WhoDunit!; A Warm Mug of Cozy;*

and *Portal: The Inner Circle Writer's Group Children's Anthology 2019*; 518 Pub's anthology, *Cold and Crisp* and PulpCult's *It's All in My Mind* anthology.

Her debut novel, *Misconception*, written as Denise Forsythe is available everywhere books are sold.

Visit her website: https://deniseforsythe.com/ to keep up with her latest publications.

Christina Hoag is the author of novels *Girl on the Brink*, named Suspense magazine's Best of YA, and *Skin of Tattoos*, a Silver Falchion Award finalist, *Law of the Jungle* and *The Blood Room*, an Audible bestseller. Her short stories and essays have been published in numerous literary reviews, including *Black Cat Mystery Magazine, Mystery Tribune, Shooter, Other Side of Hope* and *Toasted Cheese*, and have won a number of awards. Christina is a former journalist for the *Miami Herald* and foreign correspondent in Latin America where she reported for *Time, Business Week, Sunday Times of London, Financial Times* and *The New York Times*, among others. Born in New Zealand, she grew up around the world and now lives in Los Angeles, USA.

Marie Anderson is a Chicago area married mother of three millennials. She is the author of two books available on Amazon, *What Good Moms Do and Other Stories* and *Sharp Curves Ahead, Stories*. Her work has appeared in over 70 publications, including *Calliope Interactive, Shotgun Honey, Roundtable Magazine, Mystery Magazine, Woman's World,* and *Thema*. She has been leading and learning from a writing critique group at a public library in IL since 2009.

Heather C. Morris writes across genres, for both kids and adults. Her debut picture book, *Trunk Goes Thunk! A Woodland Tale of Opposites* was released in October 2024. Her short stories have been published in multiple anthologies and arts journals, including *The Haunted States of America Anthology* (Godwin Books/Macmillan), *Hindsight: Untold Stories from 2020*, and the *Birmingham Arts Journal*. When she's not at her writing desk, you'll find her hiking the foothills of the

Appalachian Mountains with her husband, their three kids, and their rescued border collie mix. Find out more about her upcoming projects at www.heathercmorris.com.

Wendy Harrison is a retired prosecutor who turned to short mystery fiction during the pandemic. Her stories have been published in numerous anthologies including *Peace, Love & Crime, Autumn Noir, Crimeucopia (Tales from the Back Porch–and–One More Thing to worry About), The Big Fang, Gargoylicon,* and *Death of a Bad Neighbour* as well as in *Shotgun Honey*. When Hurricane Ian destroyed her home in Florida, she moved to Washington State, as far from Florida as she could get.

Ruth Morgan is an attorney living in California with his two unbelievably adorable dogs. His fiction has appeared in *Mystery Tribune, The Emerson Review, Riprap, Jokes Review, Corvus Review, The Penmen Review,* and *The Quotable.*

Diane Arrelle is the pen name of Southern New Jersey writer, Dina Leacock. She has sold more than 350 short stories and has three published books including *Seasons On The Dark Side,* her collection of horror stories and the rerelease of her updated and expanded short story collection, *Just A Drop In The Cup.* She is the editor of the anthology *Crypt Gnats: Horror You've Been Itching to Read,* the mystery anthology, *WhoDunit,* and Jersey Pines Ink's newest horror release, *Trees* (for which she painted the cover).

Retired from being director of a municipal senior citizen center, she is now co-owner of Jersey Pines Ink LLC. She resides with her sane husband and her insane cat on the edge of the New Jersey Pine Barrens (home of the Jersey Devil). Finder her at www.arrellewrites.com and FaceBook: www.jerseypinesink.com

Issy Jinarmo is the pen name of writing trio Jill Baggett, Narelle Noppert and Maureen Kelly OAM. Never having physically met each other—living thousands of miles apart in Australia—they first 'met'

through The Fellowship of Australian Writers NSW Inc.

From there they began their collaboration and started writing as a group by email in 2020 when Life as the world knew it took a sudden shift, and online pastimes became a way of keeping friends in touch. And from that collaboration, Issy Jinarmo was born.

Issy's successes have included Specul8's supernatural anthology, *Haunted*, (https://www.specul8.com.au), the Australian magazine *Mona* (https://www.monamagazine.com/), and is involved with the Fellowship of Australian Writers NSW

(https://fawnsw.org.au/membership/bulletin/back-issues/)

Lyn Fraser teaches a course in crime fiction for New Dimensions, the Lifelong Learning Program at Colorado Mesa University. Her publications include a mystery novel (Mainly Murder Press) and short fiction in the AMERICAN LITERARY REVIEW, the MID-AMERICAN REVIEW, MYSTERICAL-E, and COSY NOSTRA (Murderous Ink Press Crimeucopia). She lives in western Colorado and travels extensively across Native lands in New Mexico, Utah, and Colorado.

Kimberly Scott hails from New York and has been residing in Las Vegas, Nevada, long enough to be considered a local. She is a descendant of several authors and is happy that she will never have to do what her great aunt did; use a man's name to garner interest in her stories.

Carol Goodman Kaufman, in a prior life, was a psychologist and criminologist who reached her limit on writing about abuse and violent extremism. She now writes about happier subjects, from food history to children's picture books, but when she decided to take the plunge into fiction, she chose to write mysteries, quite often of the murder variety. Ironic, huh? But not totally out of character. Since her first encounters with *The Happy Hollisters* and *Nancy Drew*, her guilty pleasure has been curling up with a good whodunit.

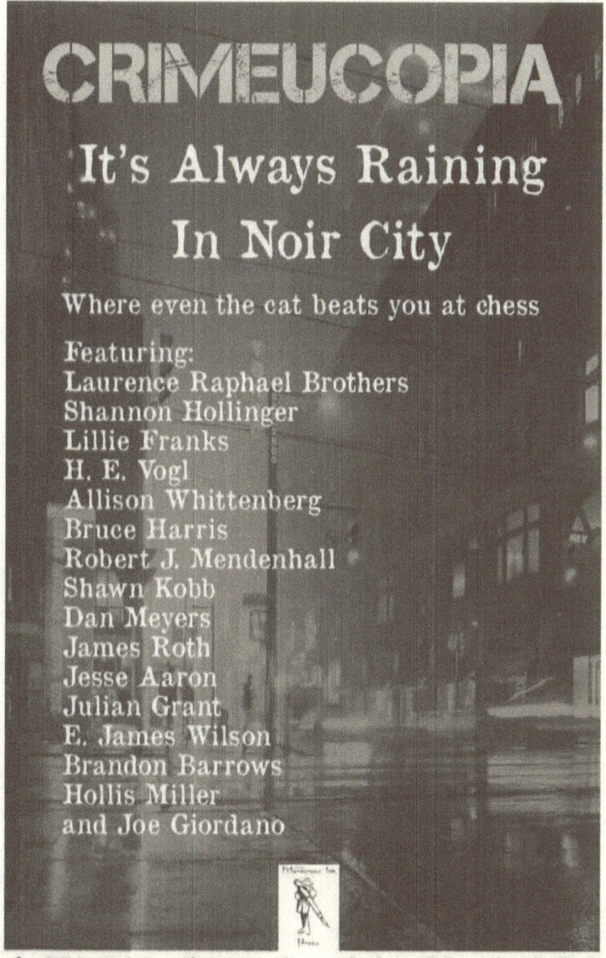

Is the Noir Crime sub-genre always dark and downbeat? Is there a time when Bad has a change of conscience, flips sides and takes on the Good role?

Noir is almost always a dish served up raw and bloody - Fiction bleu if you will. So maybe this is a chance to see if Noir can be served sunny side up - with the aid of these fifteen short order authors.

All fifteen give us dark tales from the stormy side of life - which is probably why it's *always* raining in Noir City….

Paperback Edition ISBN: 9781909498341
eBook Edition ISBN: 9781909498358

I Remember the Dame Well...

Mainly as she had a laugh that reminded me of two cheese graters energetically fornicating in an iron bathtub. I looked out the open window at the Johnson Memorial, standing upright and resolute in the persistent rain. The clock on it said it was 3:15 in the a.m. and I figured, what-the-Hell, it was time to review the 14 case files scattered across my desk.

I glanced back out across the skyline and wondered: *Why is it* always *raining in Noir City?* I got up and moved over to the chess board. I hadn't see the cat in several hours, so I rearranged the pieces a little to give myself a bit of an advantage...

As with all of these anthologies, we hope you'll detect something that you immediately like, as well as something that takes you out of your investigative comfort zone — and puts you into a completely new one.

Because, in the spirit of our Murderous Ink Press motto:

You never know what you like until you discover it.

Paperback ISBN: 9781909498624 eBook ISBN: 9781909498631

It Was In The Year Of….

Historical/Period Crime short fiction ranging from Cosy. Noir, PIs, Narrative Crime, and a whole spectrum of Crime sub-genres in between

21 authors — Gary Thomson, Edward St. Boniface, Terry Wijesuriya, Frances Stratford, Dennis E. Delaney, Joan Leotta, Hope Hodgkins, Karen Odden, J. F. Benedetto, S. B. Watson, Hal Dygert, Merrilee Robson, John G. Bluck, David Hagerty, Avi Sirlin, Karl El-Koura, Penny Hurrell, Kai Lovelace, Maddi Davidson, J. Aquino and Kirk Landers — take you from 420 BC through to AD 1969, and give you a criminal history, laid out in a case by case Crimeline.

Paperback 9781909498587   eBook 9781909498594

Alright My Son, Say No More, Leave It 'art!

As I best recall, it was one afternoon here at MIP Towers – must have been a touch after the start of tiffin, so around 4.35pm – when some smart young cove decided to politely call attention to himself by saying he had a proposal: 'Why can't we do an all-British Crimeucopia?'

And, bless my soul, after several pots of tea — Darjeeling (mid-season second flush, naturally) the general consensus was a resounding: 'Why not indeed?' From there was born this anthology, containing, we hope, stories that, were you to cut them in half with a knife, they would flash you their Union Jacks without a moment's hesitation.

Rule Britannia - Britannia Waves The Rules features fiction from
Daniel Marshall Wood, Gerald Elias, S. E. Bailey, Alexander Frew,
Kelly Lewis, Carew S. Bartley, Madeleine McDonald, Edward Lodi,
Michaele Jordan, J. Aquino, David Rich, Kelly Zimmer, Sharon Richards,
T. K. Howell, Maroula Blades, David William Johnson and Harris Coverley

The fiction ranges from general British cosy, through Harry Palmer and George Smiley territory, before going deep into very British Modern Noir. And as with all of these anthologies, we hope you'll find something that you immediately like, as well as something that takes you out of your comfort zone – and puts you into a completely new one. In other words, in the spirit of the Murderous Ink Press motto:

You never know what you like until you read it.

Paperback: 9781909498501 eBook: 9781909498518

With 16 vibrant authors, a wraparound paperback cover, and pages full of crime fiction in some of its many guises, what's not to like?

So if you enjoy tales spun by

Anthony Diesso, Brandon Barrows, E. James Wilson, James Roth, Jesse Aaron, Jim Guigli, John M. Floyd, Kevin R. Tipple, Maddi Davidson, Michael Grimala, Robert Petyo, Shannon Hollinger, Tom Sheehan, Wil A. Emerson, Peter Trelay, and Philip Pak

then you'd better get

CRIMEUCOPIA - Strictly Off The record

by the sound of it!

Karen Skinner - Hilary Davidson - Pauline Gostling - Linda Kerr - Kate Miller - Tiffany Lindfield - Lena Ng - Ginny Swart - Sandrine Bergèss – Michelle Ann King - Amanda Steel - Kelly Lewis - Paulene Turner- Claire Leng - Madeleine McDonald - Joan Hall Hovey

16 stories ranging from the 14th to the 21st Century, all from women authors whose forte is crime.
Paperback Edition 9781909498198
eBook Edition 9781909498204

Don't You Never Look Inside the Mojo Bag...

…'Cos it got the juju! An' that is hot stuff…

However, it's true to say that all the wordsmiths contained within the covers of this Crimeucopia, have been looking inside all sorts of Mojo bags, and are more than willing to recount what it is they've seen.

So sit back, relax, and let:

Anthony Kane Evans, Carlos Ramet, Tristan J. Deehan, Christopher Deliso,
Tucker Struyk, Ed Teja, Gene Kendall, Hal Dygert, Ian Blackwell, L.C. Adams,
Patrick Ambrose, Kamal Mouhoune, Rand Gaynor, Rob Loughran,
and *Edward St. Boniface*

take you on guided tours around their worlds—going from Cosy Country to Noir Central, and back again, provided you booked a return ticket that is.

Because we hope that, whenever and wherever these authors take you, you'll find something that you immediately like, as well as something that takes you out of your GPS and Timezone monitored comfort zones—and puts you into a completely new one.

Because, in the Random Shuffle spirit of our Murderous Ink Press motto:

You never know what you like until you read it.

Paperback ISBN: 9781909498648 — eBook ISBN: 9781909498655

CRIMEUCOPIA

Let Me Tell You About...

If Looks Could Kill, She Would Have Been An Uzi...

…Or more likely a shotgun. I mean, Lawd knows what those two ever saw in each other in the first place, and that's a fact. Don't believe me? Well, let me tell you about the time when…. But that's how it usually starts, doesn't it? Someone says something, which reminds someone else about…. And so the anecdotal avalanche begins.

This time there's 19 storytellers: **Vinnie Hansen, V.S. Kemanis, David Krugler, Robert Jeschonek, Beverle Graves Myers, Kirk Landers, James Lee Proctor, Victor Kreuiter, K. Arlington Andrews, Michael Bracken, Kevin R. Tipple, William Flores, Robert Sumner, Jim Guigli, James Roth, Michael Zimecki, Sebastian Corbascio, Martin Zeigler, and John Bertram Fawet III**

All gathered around the front counter of the Crimeucopia *Shots to Hell* Bar & Grill — and more than willing to tell you about how it is, or was, or even will be….

So, over the background sounds from an old jukebox loaded with worn out 45s (vinyl rather than the likes of a Px4 Storm), settle back and take in their individual stories – and we guarantee there's going to be Crimesapleanty indeed…

Paperback Edition ISBN: 9781909498600 — eBook Edition ISBN: 9781909498617
Amazon Paperback Edition ISBN: 9798337923338